The Wraith

David Lee Corley

Table of Contents

Quote

"Science without conscience is but the ruin of the soul."

- Francois Rabelais

Old Ways

The woman's name was Elena Kozlov. Frank knew because he'd studied her file for three weeks. Biochemist. Mother of two. Developing nerve agents for the Russian military in a laboratory that officially didn't exist.

She sat tied to a chair in the abandoned factory outside Volgograd. Winter wind howled through broken windows, carrying snow that settled on concrete floors like ash from cremated hopes.

Frank adjusted the small video camera sitting on a stack of cider blocks. Digital recording that would capture every word for analysts who never left air-conditioned offices in Virginia.

"Formula," Frank said in Russian.

Elena's lip was split, blood frozen on her chin. But her eyes held defiance that twenty years of Soviet discipline couldn't break. "I told you. I don't know what you're talking about."

Frank's orders were clear. Extract the information. Record everything. Eliminate the asset. No witnesses. No connection to American intelligence operations that couldn't be acknowledged.

He tried interrogation techniques learned in schools that trained men to break other people's minds. Pressure points. Stress positions.

The camera recorded it all with mechanical indifference.

Nothing worked. Elena Kozlov was stronger than her file suggested. Sometimes the threat of violence accomplished what violence itself couldn't achieve.

"Mikhail eight. Anya six," Frank said. "School Number Forty-Seven on Leninsky Prospekt."

Elena's defiance cracked. Not from fear for herself, but from understanding that her children had become tactical assets in a war she'd never chosen to fight.

"You wouldn't," she whispered.

Frank let the silence stretch while the camera captured her breaking point. Professional interrogators understood that imagination was more effective than actual violence. Let her mind create scenarios worse than anything he would actually do.

"Formula," Frank repeated.

Elena broke. Words spilled from her lips like blood from a severed artery. Chemical compounds, molecular structures, synthesis protocols that could kill thousands with microscopic amounts of invisible death.

The camera recorded every word. Every formula. Every secret that would be analyzed by people who had never looked into a mother's eyes while stealing her life's work.

Through the broken windows, Frank caught movement in the snow. White figures against a snow-covered landscape. Russian security forces surrounding the building with automatic weapons. A T-80 main battle tank along with three BTR-80 armored personnel carriers pulled up in front of the building.

His mission had been compromised.

Frank turned back to Elena. Her eyes held understanding. She knew what came next.

"Don't my children," she whispered. "You promise?"

Frank responded by shooting her twice in the chest. Quick, clean, professional. The mercy she deserved and the mission required.

He grabbed the digital recording card from the camera and sprinted toward the rear exit as automatic weapons fire erupted outside.

Muzzle flashes lit the winter darkness like deadly fireworks. The tank's main 120 mm gun roared. The security force didn't want Elena harmed, but letting the American intelligence operative escape would have far worse consequences. They opted to flatten the building.

The explosion came as Frank reached the doorway. RPG warhead punching through the factory's concrete wall in a cascade of flame and flying debris. The blast wave picked Frank up and hurled him backward into steel machinery that crushed ribs and snapped bones.

Frank lay pinned under twisted metal as the building collapsed around him. Steel beams crashed down like the sky falling. Concrete slabs sealed him in darkness where Elena's body lay somewhere in the rubble.

His legs were broken. His left arm bent at impossible angles. Blood filled his mouth with the taste of copper and failure.

The Russians would find him. Interrogate him. Resistance was futile, but he would resist anyway. It wouldn't matter. They would learn things that would compromise operations spanning three continents.

Frank closed his eyes and waited for capture that would make Elena's questioning look gentle.

Frank jerked awake with a strangled gasp, phantom pain shooting through legs that had healed years ago. Cold sweat soaked his shirt despite the lighthouse's chill air.

The nightmare again. Elena's face. The explosion. The weight of steel and concrete crushing bones that had been surgically repaired.

4:23 AM. The Atlantic stretched dark and endless beyond windows that framed his insomnia like prison bars made of salt-stained glass.

The feral cat hissed. Yellow eyes reflected the emergency lighting that cast red shadows.

Frank sat up on the military cot, testing limbs that still remembered being broken. The surgeons had done good work, but phantom pain was harder to repair than bone and sinew.

Some missions ended in extraction. Some ended in capture. Some ended in nightmares that followed you across oceans to lighthouses where you tried to build something instead of destroying it.

He reached for his boots.

Genetic Grail

The Daou Therapeutics building rose thirty stories above downtown Baltimore like a glass and steel monument to human ambition, its reflective facade catching the morning sun and throwing it back at the city in brilliant sheets of light. The architecture spoke of confidence and permanence—clean lines ascending toward sky, foundations sunk deep into bedrock, materials chosen to last generations.

The conference room's main video display showed two chimpanzees in split-screen format. On the left, Subject 12 appeared ancient - white fur, deep wrinkles around tired eyes, movements slow and arthritic. The timestamp showed the recording was six months old.

On the right, the same chimpanzee looked decades younger. Dark fur had returned to areas that had been gray. The animal moved with fluid grace, swinging from perch to perch with energy that belonged to a juvenile rather than a geriatric primate.

"Same subject," Dr. Sarah Foster explained to the assembled research team. "Before and after longevity therapy. Complete cellular regeneration in laboratory conditions."

The researchers leaned forward in their chairs, studying visual proof that their theoretical work had produced tangible results. Subject 12 on the right groomed itself with steady hands that showed no tremor, no arthritis, no signs of the advanced aging visible in the earlier footage.

"Telomere restoration exceeded projections," Dr. Mitchell added. "DNA repair mechanisms functioned perfectly. We're looking at biological age reversal of approximately fifteen years."

Dr. Martinez whistled through his teeth. "The muscle mass recovery alone defies every aging model we've studied."

On screen, the rejuvenated chimpanzee performed cognitive tests with responses that measured faster than baseline juvenile levels. Problem-solving abilities that had improved beyond the subject's original capabilities before aging had begun.

"Intelligence enhancement was unexpected," Foster said. "The therapy appears to optimize neurological function rather than simply restoring it."

The video evidence eliminated any remaining doubt about their breakthrough's effectiveness. What had seemed impossible six months earlier was now documented reality playing on high-definition monitors.

Foster clicked to the next slide showing champagne bottles arranged on the conference table. "Ladies and gentlemen, at eight-seventeen this morning, the FDA officially approved our longevity therapy for clinical trials."

Applause erupted from the dozen researchers gathered around the mahogany table, hands clapping with the enthusiasm of people who had just watched the future become the present through careful application of genetic science.

Foster stood before the assembled scientists, holding a crystal flute she hadn't touched. She studied the faces around the table—colleagues who had shared her vision when the rest of the scientific community called them delusional. Men and women who had sacrificed marriages, children, normal lives for the pursuit of knowledge that could reshape human existence.

At forty-two, Foster carried herself with the quiet confidence of someone who had spent twenty years pushing the boundaries of human genetics. Auburn hair pulled back in the practical style of a woman who lived in laboratories rather than boardrooms. Gray eyes held the intensity of someone who saw possibilities others missed, who looked at aging and death and refused to accept them as inevitable.

The champagne flute felt fragile in her hands. Crystal worth more than most people earned in a day, provided by executives who understood that presentation mattered as much as substance when courting investors. Foster preferred the honest weight of laboratory glassware—beakers and flasks designed for function rather than elegance.

"Ladies and gentlemen," Foster began, setting down her untouched glass on the polished table. "At eight-seventeen this morning, the FDA officially approved our longevity therapy for clinical trials."

Applause erupted from the dozen researchers gathered around the mahogany table, hands clapping with the enthusiasm of people who had waited years for this moment. The sound echoed off glass walls and polished surfaces, creating a symphony of validation that made even the most cynical scientists smile.

Dr. James Mitchell, Foster's closest collaborator and the man who had shared her vision since graduate school, whistled through his teeth—a sound that carried two decades of shared failures and small victories that had led to this breakthrough. His hair had gone gray during their research, his marriage had ended during the lean years when grants were scarce, but his faith in Foster's work had never wavered.

"Twenty years of work, Sarah," Mitchell said, his voice carrying wonder at the magnitude of what they had accomplished. "Twenty years of eighteen-hour days and failed experiments and grant applications that went nowhere. Colleagues who said we were chasing fantasies. And now..."

Foster nodded, but her expression remained serious despite the celebration around her. Success brought new responsibilities, new dangers, new enemies who would see their breakthrough as a threat to the natural order they preferred to maintain. The pharmaceutical industry was built on treating diseases, not eliminating them. The insurance sector calculated premiums based on actuarial tables that assumed death in the seventh or eighth decade.

What happened to those industries when death became optional?

"This is just the beginning. There is no telling how far we can go or how long humans can live," Foster said, her voice cutting through the champagne-fueled chatter. "Phase one trials start next month. If the results match our laboratory work, we're looking at extending human lifespan by decades, and eventually... maybe centuries."

The room fell quiet as the implications sank in. They had been so focused on the science, the technical challenges of modifying cellular repair mechanisms, that some had never fully considered the societal consequences of their success. A world where people lived for one hundred and fifty years would bear no resemblance to current civilization.

Social Security systems would collapse overnight. The concept of retirement would become meaningless. Generational wealth transfer would stop, creating permanent dynasties. Political leaders could rule for a century or more. Religious concepts of mortality and afterlife would require fundamental revision.

Dr. Lisa Chen, the team's youngest member at twenty-eight, leaned forward across the table with excitement evident in her voice. "The Nobel committee is going to love this. You're going to Stockholm, Dr. Foster."

Foster's expression softened slightly. "We're all going. This was never about individual recognition. This is about changing what it means to be human. About giving people time to become everything they're capable of becoming."

Chen had joined the team three years earlier, fresh from MIT with a doctorate in biological engineering and the enthusiasm of someone who believed science could solve every human problem. Foster envied that optimism even as she understood its limitations. Young scientists saw possibilities. Experienced researchers understood obstacles.

"Think about it," Mitchell added, warming to the theme. "Leonardo da Vinci lived sixty-seven years and revolutionized art, engineering, anatomy, and physics. Imagine what he could have accomplished with one hundred and fifty years of active life."

"Or Einstein," Chen continued. "Mozart. Marie Curie. All the brilliant minds who died before completing their life's work."

Foster watched the city below through the conference room windows. Baltimore sprawled beneath them in all its urban complexity—row houses and office buildings, highways carrying commuters to jobs they might hold for the next forty years if they were lucky, if their bodies didn't betray them first. Three million people living their brief lives, accepting death as inevitable because no one had ever given them another choice.

Soon, that acceptance would become optional. Death would transform from fate to decision, from certainty to choice. The implications stretched beyond medicine into philosophy, economics, religion, the very structure of human civilization.

"There will be opposition," Foster said quietly, her words cutting through the celebration like a scalpel through healthy tissue. "Religious groups who believe we're playing God. Politicians who worry about social implications. Foreign governments who want to steal or destroy what we've created."

The champagne glasses paused halfway to lips as the researchers absorbed this reality. Science operated in laboratories under controlled conditions. The real world was messier, more dangerous, driven by emotions and interests that didn't respond to peer review.

"Let them come," Mitchell replied, emboldened by champagne and the magnitude of their achievement. "We have the science. We have the data. We have twenty years of research that proves this works."

Foster studied the faces around the table—brilliant minds who had dedicated their lives to extending human life, who had sacrificed normal existence for this moment. They believed in the purity of their mission, the righteousness of their cause. They hadn't yet learned that good intentions offered no protection against those who profited from human mortality.

Dr. Robert Martinez, the team's expert in cellular biology, raised his glass toward Foster. "To the woman who made death optional."

"Death isn't optional yet," Foster corrected. "We've only proven the concept works in laboratory conditions."

"But the breakthrough is real," Chen insisted. "The cellular repair mechanisms respond exactly as predicted. Telomere restoration exceeds our most optimistic projections. DNA damage reversal is practically complete."

Foster had spent the previous night reviewing their latest test results. Laboratory chimpanzees treated with the longevity therapy showed complete reversal of aging markers within six months. Organ function returned to juvenile levels. Cognitive performance improved beyond baseline measurements. The animals were literally growing younger.

But laboratory animals weren't humans. Controlled environments weren't the real world. What worked in sterile conditions might fail when exposed to the chaos of human biology and environmental variables.

"The therapy will change everything," Foster continued, her voice carrying a weight that sobered the room. "Population dynamics, economic systems, social structures. When people stop dying on schedule, the world as we know it ceases to exist."

"And we help create something better," Chen added. "A world where people have time to solve problems, to create art, to become wise instead of just old."

Foster nodded, but her mind was already racing ahead to the obstacles they would face. Governments whose entire economic structure depended on people dying before they could collect too much in social benefits.

Foster had created something that could save humanity or destroy civilization, depending on how it was implemented and controlled.

"We'll need security," Foster said finally. "Enhanced protocols for data protection. Background checks on anyone with access to our research. This therapy represents the greatest breakthrough in human history, which means it also represents the greatest threat to those who control human suffering."

Mitchell's expression grew more serious as he considered the implications. "Industrial espionage?"

"…or worse." Foster walked to the windows and looked down at the protesters who had already begun gathering outside the building.

The celebration continued around her, but Foster's attention had already moved beyond champagne and congratulations to the war that was coming.

Dr. Martinez stood and moved to the windows beside Foster. "You're worried about something specific."

Foster watched the protesters below, their signs demanding that science respect God's plan for human mortality. "I'm worried about everything. We've just announced that we can eliminate humanity's oldest enemy. Every institution built around death and aging will resist us."

"The medical community will support us."

"Some will. Others won't. Oncologists make fortunes treating cancer that our therapy will prevent. Geriatricians would lose most of their patients. Entire medical specialties would become obsolete overnight."

Through the windows, Foster could see news vans arriving at the building's perimeter. Reporters who would frame their breakthrough as either humanity's salvation or its damnation, depending on their editorial preferences. The story would dominate news cycles for weeks, creating pressure from stakeholders who had never considered the implications of defeating death.

"What about the government?" Chen asked from across the room.

"Complicated," Foster replied. "The military applications are obvious—soldiers who could fight for a century, never weakening with age. But Social Security would collapse if people stopped dying. Medicare would bankrupt the country. Every government program assumes people die on schedule."

Foster had run the numbers during sleepless nights over the past month. If even ten percent of the population chose longevity therapy, the federal budget would become unsustainable within decades. If everyone chose it, civilization would require complete restructuring.

The financial implications alone were staggering. Pension funds that expected to pay benefits for twenty years would face centuries of obligations. Life insurance companies would either go bankrupt or stop writing policies. Investment strategies based on generational wealth transfer would become meaningless.

"We'll figure it out," Mitchell said with the confidence of someone who had spent his career solving impossible problems. "Humanity adapts. We always have."

Foster hoped he was right, but adaptation required time, and their breakthrough was about to compress centuries of social evolution into decades. The changes would be too rapid for institutions to accommodate, too fundamental for gradual implementation.

She returned to the conference table where her research team waited for guidance. These were the people who had made immortality possible. Their names would be remembered for as long as humans existed— which might now be forever.

"Phase one trials start in six weeks," Foster announced. "Volunteer patients with terminal diagnoses who have nothing to lose. If the therapy works in humans as well as it works in laboratory animals, phase two will involve healthy subjects."

"Timeline for general availability?" Martinez asked.

"Hard to say. The FDA approval process is designed for conventional treatments, not therapies that redefine human existence."

Foster had already begun preliminary discussions with regulatory officials who seemed as confused as everyone else about how to evaluate a treatment that could make death optional. The existing approval framework assumed that medicines treated diseases. What regulatory pathway applied to treatments that eliminated fundamental aspects of human biology?

The champagne had grown warm while they talked, bubbles dissipating into flat liquid that nobody wanted to drink. The celebration was ending, replaced by the sobering reality of what came next.

Outside the conference room windows, Baltimore continued its ancient rhythm, unaware that a small group of scientists had just changed the fundamental equation of human existence. In laboratories around the world, other researchers would read their published papers and understand what had been accomplished. Some would try to replicate their work. Others would try to improve it.

The war for control of human mortality had begun with champagne and congratulations. It would continue in boardrooms and laboratories, government offices and foreign capitals, wherever power was concentrated enough to matter.

Target Practice

The lighthouse beam swept across black water before dawn, its ancient Fresnel lens catching the last starlight and hurling it against the granite cliffs below. Frank Kane opened his eyes in the darkness. No alarm clock. No need. His body knew the hour the way predators know the hunt.

He sat up on the narrow military cot, hair matted with sleep and old sweat. The iron bed frame groaned under his weight—four hundred pounds of muscle and bone that had been forged in places where weakness meant death. Scars crisscrossed his massive chest and arms like a roadmap drawn in violence. Puckered bullet wounds. The ropey tissue of knife cuts. Shrapnel scars that looked like someone had pressed hot coins into his flesh. Each mark told a story he preferred not to remember. But such was Frank's life.

He stretched, feeling the familiar burning as damaged nerves woke with him. His left shoulder carried fragments from an IED in Helmand Province. His right knee held pins from a Mogadishu rooftop that had given way under mortar fire. The scar tissue pulled tight each morning, reminding him that survival came with a price.

Pain was information. Nothing more.

The lighthouse walls curved around him, gray stone blocks fitted together by craftsmen who understood that some things needed to last beyond their makers. Salt stains streaked the windows where decades of storms had left their mark. The floor beneath his feet was worn smooth by the passage of lighthouse keepers who had tended this beacon when ships still needed such guidance.

Frank reached for his boots—scarred leather that had walked through blood and sand and places that didn't appear on any map. The double shoulder holster came next, settling against his ribs like old friends returning home. The twin Ruger Super Redhawk revolvers hung heavy, their grips modified for his enormous hands. Six rounds each of devastating .44 magnum power. Enough to stop charging bears or heavily armed humans with equal efficiency.

The Colt Cobra went into his jacket pocket along with two speed loaders, their brass cartridges heavy. Even carrying multiple weapons, Frank planned for redundancy. In his world, there was no such thing as too much firepower.

The lighthouse stairs spiraled upward through scaffolding Frank had erected to keep the staircase from falling from its own weight until he had time to retore it. Steel poles and crossbeams reached up toward the lamp cupola in patterns that would support his weight while he cleaned the interior walls of mold and dust.

Frank moved through the maze of iron supports with practiced ease, weaving between vertical posts and ducking under horizontal braces that would have clotheslined a smaller man. The scaffolding had become a steel forest that only he knew how to navigate, each pole and platform memorized through daily passage.

In the corner, the feral cat stretched on a pile of paint-stained tarps. One and a half ears, the left one torn away in some long-ago violence that had left only a ragged stub. Piss-yellow eyes reflected what little light filtered through the salt-stained windows, studying Frank with the suspicious attention of something that had learned not to trust easily.

The tom was battle-scarred and mean, gray fur matted despite Frank's consistent feeding. It had claimed the lighthouse the same way Frank had—by surviving everything that tried to kill it. Neither had asked permission of the other. Both understood the terms of their coexistence.

Frank examined his restoration work in the dim light. Stone that needed repointing where winter freeze had cracked mortar joints. Steel that required welding where salt air had eaten through protective coatings. Glass that needed replacing where time and weather had introduced flaws that scattered light instead of focusing it.

Each task required patience, exactness, and tools that felt comfortable in his scarred hands. Work that created rather than destroyed. Projects that built rather than demolished.

The lighthouse had guided ships for over a century, weathering storms and wars and the constant assault of salt air. Previous keepers had maintained it through two world wars, the Great Depression, countless hurricanes that had tried to tear it from its granite foundation.

Frank intended to ensure it lasted another century.

He ran his fingers along the curved wall, feeling hairline cracks where decades of thermal expansion had stressed the mortar. Tomorrow he would mix a new batch, match the original formula as closely as possible.

Traditional lime mortar that would flex with the building's movement rather than fighting it.

Modern Portland cement was stronger but less forgiving. It cracked under stress instead of yielding. Frank preferred materials that bent without breaking, systems that adapted to pressure rather than shattering under load.

"You coming?" Frank rasped, his voice barely more than gravel scraped across concrete.

The cat hissed, showing fangs yellowed with age and poor nutrition. Then it followed anyway, padding silently with the fluid grace of something that moved through the world like smoke.

Neither spoke during the descent. Neither needed to. The hunt was older than words, more honest than civilization, more necessary than the laws that tried to contain it.

Outside, the lighthouse stood seventy feet above the rocky shoreline, its white tower streaked with rust and decades of bird droppings that painted abstract patterns across the weathered surface. It served as Frank's watchtower over a world that had no more use for either lighthouses or the men who tended them.

The pre-dawn air carried the scent of sea spray and wet stone, overlaid with the smell of seaweed rotting in tidal pools. Waves crashed against the granite below with the endless rhythm of something that would outlast every human ambition.

Frank walked the gravel path to his battered pickup truck, boots crunching on crushed stone that had been white once, before years of weather turned it gray. The cat trotted beside him with its tail switching in irritation at being dragged away from warm tarps for whatever madness Frank had planned. Next to the truck sat Frank's war machine – the fully-restored 1965 Chrysler

Imperial covered with a heavy canvas tarp that couldn't disguise eighteen feet of Detroit steel underneath.

The truck started on the third try, its engine coughing like an old man with too many cigarettes in his past. Frank let it warm while he loaded his net, a metal bucket, and the plastic container that held his morning's ammunition. Bait for the hunt ahead.

He studied the horizon while the engine warmed. Weather coming in from the northeast, low clouds that might bring rain by afternoon. The restoration work would have to wait if the storm arrived early. Exterior painting required dry conditions, proper temperature, time for the coatings to cure before moisture arrived.

Frank had learned patience through years of restoration projects that couldn't be rushed. Stonework progressed at its own pace. Steel welding required precise heat and timing. Glass cutting demanded steady hands and measured pressure.

The lighthouse restoration had become his meditation on permanence in a world where everything else decayed toward inevitable failure. Each stone properly set, each joint carefully pointed, each piece of metal cleaned and protected would last decades beyond his own life.

Some things deserved to endure regardless of whether anyone appreciated the effort involved.

Twenty minutes down the coast road brought them to Granite Lake, the asphalt giving way to gravel and then to dirt as civilization thinned toward the margins where Frank preferred to live. The boat rental shack squatted at the water's edge like a wooden toad that had been left too long in the sun, its weathered siding gray with age and neglect.

A hand-painted sign advertised BOATS - BAIT - BEER in letters that had faded until they looked like old scars. Light already glowed through windows clouded with years of fish scales and cigarette smoke, promising that someone inside was awake enough to take money.

Frank parked beside two other vehicles—a rusted Chevy with local plates and a newer Ford that probably belonged to weekend fishermen from the city. Early morning was prime time for serious anglers who understood that fish fed at dawn and dusk, when light levels triggered feeding instincts.

The owner looked up from his coffee as Frank approached, belly straining against flannel that had seen better decades, beard yellowed with tobacco stains and whatever else a man accumulated when he stopped caring what the world thought of him. His eyes took in Frank's massive frame and the predatory stillness that surrounded him like an aura.

"Morning," the man said, sizing up Frank's potential as customer versus threat. "Need a boat?"

Frank grunted.

"Fishing?" The owner's eyes moved to Frank's net, bucket, and container, then back to his scarred face. "Need a pole? Tackle box? I got some nice setups, top quality gear that'll—"

Frank shook his head once.

The owner studied Frank's equipment again, noting the absence of conventional fishing gear. Rod holders empty. No tackle box. No cooler for keeping the catch fresh. Just a net, bucket, and a plastic container.

"Twelve-foot aluminum johnboat. Twenty bucks for four hours. Gas extra if you want the motor."

Frank paid cash from a roll of bills that looked like it had been through a washing machine. No motor needed. He preferred things that didn't make noise, didn't require fuel.

The johnboat sat low in the dark water, aluminum scarred by years of rental abuse but sound enough. Aluminum benches, no frills, no comfort. Frank dragged it to deeper water and climbed in with movements that barely disturbed the surface.

The cat leaped into the bow without invitation, then hissed when water from an oar splashed its paws. It settled on the forward bench and began the process of ignoring Frank while maintaining constant surveillance.

Frank rowed toward the center of the lake with smooth, powerful strokes. The ancient oars creaked in rusted oarlocks that had guided fishermen across these waters since before Frank learned to kill. Mist hung low over the surface like smoke from a dying fire, and other boats already scattered across the expanse.

Weekend fishermen with their expensive rods and electronic fish finders and thermoses full of coffee, waiting for luck to substitute for skill. Men who worked office jobs during the week and came to the water seeking something they couldn't find in cubicles and conference rooms.

Frank understood the appeal. Water had its own logic, different from the urban rhythms that governed most lives. Fish moved according to weather patterns, water temperature, seasonal cycles that operated outside human schedules.

But Frank hadn't come for the meditation of angling. He opened the plastic container and scattered flies across the glass-still water. The insects spread like black pepper across a white plate, their movements sending ripples that would carry the scent of food to predators lurking in the depths. Chemistry and biology combining to trigger feeding responses honed by millions of years of evolution.

A bass broke the surface fifty yards away, mouth wide for breakfast, water cascading from its flanks as it cleared the lake in a perfect arc of hunger and opportunity. The fish hung suspended for a moment, silver scales catching early sunlight, before gravity began its inevitable pull.

One of the Redhawks cleared leather with the smoothness of countless repetitions. Frank's draw was economy of motion refined through years of practice, muscle memory that bypassed conscious thought. The massive revolver bucked in his scarred hands, the .44 magnum round traveling at over twelve hundred feet per second.

The fish disintegrated in a pink mist of scales and flesh that painted the water in expanding circles. Hydrostatic shock from the heavy bullet turned living tissue into spray, the bass turned to goo in the time it took the round's thunderous crack to bounce off the stone walls surrounding the lake. He wasn't just fishing… it was target practice.

Frank rowed over and netted the largest chunks of what remained, dropping the pieces into the bucket with the methodical efficiency of someone who understood that waste was a luxury he couldn't afford. Protein was protein, regardless of how it was acquired.

The cat whined—a sound like rusty hinges—then hissed when Frank didn't immediately share the bounty.

"Jesus Christ!" A voice carried across the water from one of the other boats, the words echoing off distant hills. "What the hell was that?"

Frank ignored the shouts and scattered more flies. The explosion of violence had scattered the surface fish, but deeper dwellers would rise to investigate the disturbance. Blood in the water triggered feeding responses in species that had learned to associate trauma with opportunity.

Another fish jumped for the bait, silver flanks flashing in the early light. The Redhawk spoke again with the same devastating result. Fish transformed into soup.

The cat's whine became more insistent, backed by a low growl that promised violence if breakfast didn't arrive soon.

"That bastard's shooting fish!" Another fisherman, his voice carrying the outrage of someone whose peaceful morning had been shattered by the intrusion of reality. "Someone call the game warden!"

Frank holstered the massive revolver and drew the Colt Cobra from his jacket pocket. The .38 spoke sharper, cleaner, with less flash and thunder but equal lethality. The next fish exploded in a smaller shower of scales and blood, leaving more substantial pieces for collection.

The Cobra was Frank's backup weapon, lighter and more maneuverable than the Redhawks but still capable of stopping threats that required immediate termination. He'd carried it through three war zones and countless covert operations, trusting its reliability when stealth mattered more than raw stopping power.

Frank netted the remains and tossed a chunk to the cat, who stopped complaining and began eating with the focused attention of something that had learned not to take meals for granted. Between bites, it shot Frank accusatory glares that suggested this was too much noise for breakfast.

The sound of gunfire carried differently over water. The lake acted as a natural amplifier, bouncing echoes off surrounding hills and trees. What seemed like reasonable noise levels to Frank registered as warfare to civilians who expected their recreation to proceed without ballistic interruptions.

Outboard motors started across the lake as other fishermen decided that sharing water with an armed madman wasn't worth whatever fish they might catch. Boats moved away in expanding wakes, their occupants' voices fading with distance as they carried news of the lunatic with the cannon who was turning fish into chum.

"Crazy son of a bitch!"

"Should be locked up!"

"Probably escaped from somewhere!"

Frank scattered more flies with deliberate patience. The Cobra spoke again and again, each shot precisely placed, each fish transformed from predator to prey in the time it took to squeeze a trigger. He filled his net with what the bullets left behind, sharing the best pieces with the cat while keeping enough for his own purposes.

The morning's work proceeded with mechanical efficiency. Flies scattered to attract surface feeders. Fish responding to stimuli. Bullets delivering terminal ballistics. Net collecting protein. Each step in the process serving the larger goal of acquiring food through the application of superior firepower.

Neither Frank nor the cat spoke during the harvest. Neither needed to. The hunt was older than words, more honest than civilization, more necessary than the laws that tried to contain it. Survival earned through the willingness to take what was needed from a world that gave nothing freely.

When the ammunition was spent and the bucket was full, Frank rowed back toward shore through water that had turned red with fish blood. The cat dozed in the bow, belly full and conscience clear. The lake belonged to them now, quiet and empty except for the ripples their passage left behind.

By the time they reached the rental dock, the other fishermen had already spread the story. The owner watched Frank tie up the johnboat without comment, recognizing the type of man who paid his bills and that was enough.

Money changed hands. Equipment was unloaded. The transaction completed without discussion because both parties understood the terms. Frank provided payment, the owner provided service, and what happened on the water stayed on the water.

Frank loaded his catch into the pickup truck while the cat supervised from the passenger seat. Then they drove back toward the lighthouse.

The lighthouse beam had stopped its nightly sweep by the time they returned, the sun climbing high enough to make such guidance unnecessary. Frank parked beside the building and climbed the steel stairs to the lamp room, the cat following with fish-scented breath and the satisfied expression of something that had been fed properly.

The world was full of people who preferred their violence sanitized, packaged, hidden behind clean walls and polite words. Frank understood that such people needed protecting from the truth about what kept them safe.

But sometimes the truth came looking for them anyway.

Unity

The crowd had been gathering since dawn, assembling in the pre-morning darkness with the dedication of true believers. By ten in the morning, nearly three hundred protesters pressed against the police barriers outside Daou Therapeutics, their voices rising in hymns and chants that echoed off the surrounding buildings like prayers hurled at an indifferent heaven.

Signs bobbed above their heads like religious banners: "LIFE HAS MEANING BECAUSE IT ENDS" and "GOD DECIDES, NOT SCIENCE" and "DEATH IS NOT A DISEASE." Hand-lettered cardboard mounted on wooden stakes, carried by people who had driven from across Maryland, Virginia, and Pennsylvania to make their opposition known.

The protesters represented a cross-section of religious America. Baptist ministers from rural Virginia stood beside Catholic priests from Baltimore's inner city. Jewish rabbis shared space with Methodist pastors, Islamic clerics, and Hindu spiritual leaders. The longevity therapy had accomplished something remarkable—uniting every major faith in opposition to scientific progress.

Sister Margaret O'Brien stepped forward from the crowd, her nun's habit marking her as someone who had dedicated her life to serving others in preparation for eternal reward. At seventy-three, she moved slowly, her voice carrying the authority of someone who had spent fifty years caring for the dying.

"I've held the hands of thousands as they passed from this world to the next," she said, taking the microphone. "Each death taught me something about the preciousness of life. When we know our time is limited, every moment becomes sacred."

The crowd hung on her words. Here was someone who had witnessed the reality of human mortality, who understood death not as abstract concept but as daily experience. Her opposition to the longevity therapy carried weight that academic arguments couldn't match.

Reverend Thomas Walsh stood on the makeshift platform constructed from milk crates and plywood, his silver hair catching the sunlight as he gestured toward the glass tower that housed humanity's latest attempt to improve on divine design. At sixty-eight, he commanded attention through presence rather than volume, his weathered face carrying the authority of someone who had spent decades interpreting God's will for those too confused to understand it themselves.

"They want to play God," Walsh declared, his voice carrying over the crowd through a bullhorn that squealed with feedback. "They want to decide who lives and who dies, who gets to be young forever and who ages into dust according to their bank account."

The crowd responded with murmurs of agreement, heads nodding in unison as they absorbed wisdom that confirmed what they already believed. Faith required no peer review, no double-blind studies, no replication of results. Truth was revealed through scripture and tradition, not through laboratory experiments.

Behind the police barriers, officers in riot gear stood ready with hands resting on batons, watching for signs that peaceful protest might transform into something requiring more direct intervention. Baltimore PD had experience with religious demonstrations, but nothing quite like this. The longevity therapy had tapped into fears that ran deeper than politics or economics.

The protesters weren't just opposing a medical treatment. They were defending the fundamental structure of human existence against scientists who claimed they could improve on God's creation.

A reporter from Channel 11 pushed through the crowd, her cameraman following with equipment that recorded everything for the evening news. She thrust a microphone toward Walsh as he stepped down from the platform, her professional smile barely concealing the predatory hunger that drove all successful journalists.

"Reverend Walsh," she began, "Daou Therapeutics says their therapy could end human suffering from aging. Isn't preventing suffering a good thing?"

Walsh fixed her with steady brown eyes that had witnessed six decades of human folly. "Suffering teaches us compassion, young lady. Death gives life meaning. When we remove these things, we remove our humanity. We become something else entirely."

"But if science can prevent death—"

"Science can do many things," Walsh interrupted, his voice carrying the weight of absolute certainty. "The atomic bomb proved that. Chemical weapons proved that. Genetic engineering proves it every day. Just because man thinks he can improve on God's design doesn't mean he should."

Behind him, the crowd surged against the police barriers as their voices rose in unison, chanting prayers and singing hymns that had comforted believers for centuries. "Amazing Grace" echoed off glass and steel buildings, its familiar melody transforming the urban landscape into something that felt like church.

The sound carried up the walls of the Daou building, where scientists worked to defeat death itself while protesters below demanded they accept it as God's will. Two worldviews in fundamental conflict, neither capable of understanding the other's perspective.

"What about the argument that this therapy could help millions of people?" the reporter pressed, following Walsh as he moved through the crowd like a shepherd among his flock.

Walsh looked up at the Daou building, its glass walls reflecting the crowd below in fractured images that multiplied their numbers into an army of believers. "Millions of people die every day, miss. That's not a tragedy. That's the natural order. When we try to change that order, we become something less than human."

A young protester, barely twenty, stepped forward with his own sign reading "MY GRANDMOTHER DESERVES TO LIVE." He shouted over the crowd noise, his voice cracking with emotion. "What if this could save your family? What if this could save everyone you love?"

Walsh placed a gentle hand on the young man's shoulder, his touch carrying the comfort of someone who had counseled the grieving through decades of loss. "Son, saving everyone means condemning everyone. Death isn't the enemy. Forgetting how to live is the enemy."

The exchange captured the fundamental divide that the longevity therapy had created. Young people who couldn't imagine accepting death as inevitable faced older believers who had spent their lives preparing for it. Science offered hope for unlimited time, while faith promised meaning in limited existence.

Dr. Michael Santos, CEO of Daou Therapeutics, watched the protest from his office window thirty floors above the street. The demonstrators looked like ants from his perspective, their signs reduced to colorful dots moving in patterns that seemed almost choreographed.

"How many today?" he asked his assistant.

"Three hundred and counting. Police estimate it could reach five hundred by this afternoon."

Santos had expected opposition, but not at this scale or with this level of organization. The protesters had arrived with professional-quality signs, sound equipment, and media coordination that suggested significant backing from religious organizations.

"Any violence?"

"None reported. They're being very peaceful. Singing hymns, reciting prayers, holding signs. Model citizens exercising their First Amendment rights."

Santos appreciated the irony. The same constitutional protections that allowed scientists to pursue their research also protected those who opposed it. Democracy in action, even when it slowed progress that could benefit humanity.

The protesters had begun singing "How Great Thou Art," their voices carrying enough power to be heard even through soundproof glass. Whatever else could be said about their position, they sang beautifully.

Down on the street, Reverend Walsh was explaining his opposition to another reporter, this one from CNN. "This isn't about denying medical progress. This is about preserving what makes us human. When death becomes optional, life becomes meaningless."

"But surely you support medical treatments that extend healthy lifespan?"

"Of course. We should treat disease, heal injury, ease suffering. But there's a difference between medicine and longevity. This therapy doesn't treat illness—it attempts to eliminate mortality itself."

Walsh had been preparing for this moment since reading about Foster's research months earlier. As senior pastor of Baltimore's largest evangelical church, he understood that the longevity therapy represented the ultimate test of faith. Would humanity trust in God's plan, or would they attempt to write their own?

"Reverend," the CNN reporter continued, "what if this therapy could eliminate cancer, heart disease, all the conditions that cause premature death?"

"Death is never premature in God's eyes. We're given the time we need to fulfill our purpose. When that purpose is complete, we're called home. This therapy would trap souls in bodies that should be returning to their Creator."

The theological implications had been debated in seminary circles since Foster's breakthrough was announced. Traditional concepts of afterlife assumed that souls departed physical existence at death. What happened to spiritual progression if bodies never died? Did souls become trapped in eternal physical form, unable to advance to whatever came next?

Catholic doctrine struggled with questions about the soul's journey through purgatory toward Heaven. Protestant theology wrestled with concepts of resurrection and eternal life that might conflict with immortal physical bodies. Eastern religions faced contradictions between cycles of reincarnation and permanent physical existence.

Sister Margaret took the microphone again, her voice steady despite the emotional weight of her words. "I've worked in hospice care for fifty years. I've seen what happens when people can't accept death as natural. They suffer more, not less. They fight the inevitable instead of finding peace in it."

Her experience gave weight to arguments that mere philosophy couldn't provide. She had witnessed thousands of deaths, good and bad, peaceful and painful. She understood that acceptance of mortality often brought comfort that medical intervention couldn't match.

"When people know they're dying, they often experience profound spiritual growth. They reconcile with family members, they express love they'd held back, they find meaning in their suffering. This therapy would rob them of that opportunity."

Dr. Abraham Goldstein, a rabbi from Baltimore's Orthodox community, stepped forward to add his perspective. "Our tradition teaches that every moment of life is precious precisely because it's limited. The knowledge of mortality gives urgency to our choices, meaning to our relationships, purpose to our actions."

"Without death," he continued, his voice carrying the weight of centuries of Jewish thought, "what incentive would people have to grow spiritually? Why would they seek forgiveness, practice charity, pursue wisdom? Immortality might preserve the body, but it could damn the soul."

The reporters scribbled notes furiously, recognizing that they had stumbled onto a story that went far beyond medical science into the deepest questions of human existence. The longevity therapy wasn't just about biology—it was about philosophy, theology, the very meaning of consciousness itself.

As the afternoon wore on, more protesters arrived. Buses from churches across the mid-Atlantic region discharged passengers who carried signs in multiple languages. Spanish-speaking Catholics from Baltimore's Latino community joined forces with Korean Presbyterians from the suburbs. African Methodist Episcopal congregations stood with white evangelical churches that rarely agreed on anything else.

The longevity therapy had accomplished something that decades of interfaith dialogue had failed to achieve—complete unity among religious communities in opposition to scientific progress.

Dr. Foster watched the growing crowd from her laboratory window, recognizing that the protest represented more than religious opposition. It was a manifestation of humanity's deepest fears about change, progress, and the unknown consequences of scientific advancement.

She understood their concerns even as she disagreed with their conclusions. Death did give life meaning, urgency, poignancy that immortality might diminish. Relationships were precious partly because they wouldn't last forever. Achievements mattered because time was limited.

But Foster had also seen too many brilliant minds cut short by aging, too many loving relationships ended by premature death, too many contributions to human knowledge lost because bodies failed before their work was complete. The protesters saw death as natural. Foster saw it as humanity's greatest enemy.

The demonstration continued into the evening, voices growing hoarse but spirits remaining strong. Candles appeared as darkness fell, creating a sea of flickering lights that transformed the protest into something resembling a prayer vigil.

Police maintained their perimeter without incident. The protesters remained peaceful, committed to making their point through moral suasion rather than force. They believed they were defending God's plan against scientific arrogance. Foster believed she was defending human potential against unnecessary suffering.

Both sides were convinced they were saving humanity from the other's mistakes.

As midnight approached, many protesters began departing, but core groups remained to maintain the vigil through the night. They would return tomorrow with fresh voices and renewed determination, continuing their opposition until either the research stopped or their faith was vindicated.

Inside the building, Foster worked late in her laboratory, reviewing cellular regeneration data while protesters sang hymns forty floors below. The distance between them was measured in more than vertical feet— it was the gap between faith and reason, tradition and progress, acceptance and rebellion against the limitations of human existence.

Tomorrow would bring new demonstrations, new arguments, new pressures from forces that wanted to control or destroy her life's work. But tonight, Foster focused on the science that had brought them to this moment, the careful manipulation of genetic codes that could give humanity time to become everything it was capable of becoming.

The protesters sang "Nearer My God to Thee" as midnight chimed from church bells across Baltimore. Above them, Foster worked by artificial light to make death further away than it had ever been before.

Frank sat at a small table in the lighthouse, sipping a coffee-like sludge and studying building schematics spread across the weathered wood. Original blueprints from 1847 showed the lighthouse's internal structure in faded ink and careful measurements.

The cat jumped onto the table and stepped directly across the schematics, leaving paw prints on century-old paper. Frank looked at the cat with annoyance.

The cat scratched behind its half ear with frantic intensity, claws raking against matted fur that hadn't known peace in weeks.

A flea jumped from the cat onto Frank's neck. Frank felt the tiny bite, reached up, and pinched the insect between his fingers. He examined it for a moment, then squished it.

Frank looked at the cat accusingly. The cat hissed and scratched harder.

Frank reached for his boots.

The IGA stayed open until midnight in the small coastal town near Frank's lighthouse. He walked through fluorescent-lit aisles at 11:43 PM, heading to the pet section.

Frank selected flea powder from the shelf, then headed for the register. Simple errand. In and out.

The store was nearly empty. Night clerk reading a magazine behind the counter. Elderly janitor mopping floors that would be dirty again by dawn.

"Nobody fucking move!"

Three teenagers burst through the glass doors. Ski masks. Baggy clothes. Cheap pistols that looked like they'd been stolen from bedroom drawers. Saturday night specials. The youngest couldn't have been sixteen.

Frank stood in the soup aisle. The leader waved a rusty .38 at the night clerk while his partners spread out. Textbook robbery formation learned from movies rather than experience.

"Open the register! Now!"

The clerk's hands shook as he tried to work the cash drawer. Fear made simple tasks impossible. Small-town stores didn't have bulletproof glass or armed security.

Frank had the Colt Cobra in his jacket pocket. Three shots. Three dead teenagers. Problem solved.

But these weren't enemy combatants. Just kids making stupid choices. Frank looked at the shelf beside him. Campbell's tomato soup. Sixteen ounces each. He picked up a can.

The first can caught the nearest robber in the side of the head. The boy dropped like a stone.

The second robber turned toward the sound. Frank's next throw hit him center mass, doubling him over. The cheap pistol clattered across linoleum toward the dairy section.

The leader spun toward Frank, rusty .38 rising. Frank threw two cans simultaneously. One caught the boy's wrist, snapping bone. The other opened his forehead. Blood streamed down his face as he fell backward into a potato chip display.

Frank walked toward the robbers while they groaned on the floor. Collected the three pistols. The boys would live, but they'd hurt for weeks.

The leader looked up through blood and confusion. "Who the fuck are you?"

Frank pulled off their ski masks. Local faces. Kids he had seen around town. Send them to jail and they'd learn from career criminals how to steal better, fight harder, kill easier. He considered for a moment, then…

"Go home."

"What?"

"Leave. Now."

The teenagers struggled to their feet, holding broken ribs and bleeding heads. They stumbled toward the door without looking back. Lessons learned through pain lasted longer than jail time.

The night clerk stared as Frank walked to the register. "Why'd you let them go? They were robbing me."

Frank set down the flea powder and pulled a slab of beef jerky from a jar on the counter. "Kids."

"Kids with guns."

Frank looked at the clerk. Middle-aged man who probably had children of his own. "Still kids."

The clerk rang up Frank's purchases, hands still shaking from adrenaline. "What if they come back?"

"They won't."

"How do you know?"

Frank thought about Grace. His niece. Smart teenager who'd made stupid choices until someone showed her there were consequences.

"Consequences," Frank said.

Frank paid exact change and walked outside. He threw the three pistols into the harbor. They sank without a trace, joining whatever other secrets the dark water held.

Frank drove back to the lighthouse carrying flea powder and chewing on beef jerky. Even his attempts at normal errands ended with broken bones and hard lessons. But sometimes mercy worked better than justice.

Marcus Whitfield's corner office occupied the top floor of the Whitfield Capital building, forty stories above downtown Manhattan where lesser mortals conducted their business in the shadows of true power. Floor-to-ceiling windows offered a commanding view of Central Park, but Whitfield's attention was focused on the financial documents spread across his glass desk like battle plans for an economic war.

The desk itself was a statement—a single piece of tempered glass supported by chrome pillars, transparent except for the documents that covered its surface. Financial projections, market analyses, regulatory timelines, competitor assessments. Paper that represented billions of dollars in potential profit or catastrophic loss, depending on decisions made in rooms like this one.

At fifty-five, Whitfield had the lean build of a marathon runner and the calculating eyes of a man who had turned money into more money for three decades. His Italian suit was perfectly tailored to conceal the slight bulge of the .380 pistol he carried in a shoulder holster— a precaution that had saved his life twice in thirty years of making enemies through success.

Silver hair was precisely cut, every detail suggesting control and the ruthless efficiency of someone who treated human lives as line items in a profit-and-loss statement. His office reflected the same aesthetic— minimalist furniture, abstract art that cost more than most houses, technology that connected him instantly to markets around the world.

The morning's financial reports painted a picture of unprecedented opportunity. Biotech stocks had surged following Daou Therapeutics' FDA announcement. Competitors scrambled to develop similar treatments. Pharmaceutical giants prepared acquisition offers for any company with relevant research.

But Whitfield understood what the market hadn't yet grasped. The longevity therapy wouldn't just create a new industry—it would destroy existing ones. Insurance companies, pension funds, healthcare systems, entire sectors of the economy built on the assumption of human mortality.

The smart money wasn't betting on who would profit from longevity therapy. The smart money was positioning to control it.

The elevator chimed with the soft whisper of expensive machinery, and Michael Santos, CEO of Daou Therapeutics, entered the office with the nervous energy of a man who understood that his company's survival depended on the goodwill of predators like Whitfield.

Santos was younger, softer, still believing that good intentions could coexist with big money, that scientific breakthroughs automatically benefited humanity rather than whoever controlled access to them. His suit was expensive but not perfectly fitted, his handshake firm but slightly damp with perspiration.

"Marcus," Santos said, settling into the leather chair across from Whitfield's desk. The furniture cost more than most people earned in a year, hand-crafted by artisans who understood that true luxury lay in details invisible to casual observation. "I got your message. You sounded concerned."

Whitfield didn't look up from his papers immediately, letting Santos wait while he finished reviewing quarterly projections that showed Daou Therapeutics poised to become the most valuable company in human history—or completely worthless, depending on political decisions being made by people who had never risked their own capital on scientific advancement.

The delay was calculated. In negotiations, whoever spoke first usually lost. Whitfield had learned to use silence as a weapon, discomfort as leverage, the natural human need to fill conversational voids as a tool for extracting information.

"Seven hundred million dollars, Michael," Whitfield said finally, his voice carrying the weight of numbers that could build hospitals or buy governments. "That's our current investment in your company."

"I'm aware of the numbers," Santos replied, though his tone suggested he still couldn't quite comprehend the magnitude of money involved. Seven hundred million was abstract wealth, difficult for normal minds to process in concrete terms.

Whitfield stood and walked to a wall-mounted display that showed real-time market data from exchanges around the world. Green numbers indicated gains, red showed losses, but the colors changed so rapidly that patterns were visible only to trained observers.

"Are you aware of the UN ethics committee vote scheduled for next week?" Whitfield asked without turning from the displays.

Santos shifted in his chair, leather creaking under the pressure of his discomfort. "It's preliminary. Non-binding. The international community is just exploring the implications of longevity research, considering guidelines and restrictions that might—"

"The international community is exploring ways to ban your research," Whitfield interrupted, his gray eyes flat and cold as winter sky. "Permanently. Completely. Without regard for the seven hundred million dollars we've invested in making their constituents immortal."

Whitfield's intelligence network had provided detailed briefings on the UN committee's private discussions. Religious groups were pressuring their governments to ban longevity research as blasphemous. Environmental organizations opposed it as a threat to global population stability. Economic advisors warned that immortal populations would bankrupt social welfare systems.

The vote would be close, but current projections favored restrictions that could shut down longevity research worldwide. Seven hundred million dollars would become worthless overnight if the committee voted to ban therapeutic life extension.

"Even if they vote for restrictions, it would take years to implement," Santos argued. "Multiple countries would have to agree, pass legislation, coordinate enforcement across international boundaries. The bureaucratic process alone would—"

"Your naivety is charming," Whitfield said, moving to the windows where Central Park spread below him like a green carpet reserved for his personal use. "But charm doesn't protect seven hundred million dollars from political stupidity."

From forty stories up, Manhattan looked manageable. Cars moved along predictable routes. People followed sidewalks toward destinations that served economic purposes. Order imposed on chaos through systems that Whitfield helped design and control.

But the longevity therapy threatened that order. Immortal populations would consume resources indefinitely. Economic models based on generational turnover would collapse. Political systems designed for finite lifespans would require complete restructuring.

Santos leaned forward in his chair, hands clasped as if in prayer to the god of venture capital. "The FDA just approved our therapy for clinical trials. We're moving to phase one testing next month. The science works, Marcus. Once people see the results, once they understand what we've accomplished—"

"People are afraid." Whitfield turned back from the windows, hands clasped behind his back in the posture of a general addressing troops before a battle they might not survive. "They're afraid of change, afraid of inequality, afraid of playing God. Fear makes them do stupid things like ban medical breakthroughs that could save their children's lives."

Whitfield had spent the morning reviewing polling data from twelve countries represented on the UN ethics committee. Public opinion ranged from cautious optimism to outright hostility, depending on religious affiliation and cultural background. Western Europeans showed more acceptance than Americans. Secular populations were more supportive than religious ones.

But fear was winning. Fear of overpopulation, fear of social disruption, fear of technologies that seemed to challenge divine authority. Politicians responded to fear more quickly than they responded to opportunity.

"Then we educate them," Santos said with the confidence of someone who had spent his career believing that rational arguments could overcome emotional resistance. "We show them the benefits, demonstrate the applications, prove that longevity therapy represents progress rather than—"

"We protect our investment." Whitfield's voice cut through Santos's optimism like a blade through silk. "I didn't build this company to watch politicians destroy it because they're afraid of living too long."

Santos was quiet for a long moment, studying Whitfield's expression with the growing understanding that he was dealing with someone who viewed human mortality as a market inefficiency to be corrected through appropriate application of capital and violence.

The office's silence was broken only by the soft hum of climate control systems and the distant sound of traffic forty floors below. Whitfield's desk displays continued their endless dance of numbers, tracking wealth that flowed between accounts like digital blood through electronic arteries.

"What are you suggesting?" Santos asked finally, his voice carrying the wariness of someone who suspected the answer would change everything.

"I'm suggesting that vote needs to go our way. Whatever it takes. However much it costs."

"Marcus, the ethics committee is made up of respected diplomats from twelve countries. You can't just lobby them or buy them off like some city councilman in a zoning dispute."

Whitfield smiled, but the expression didn't reach his eyes, didn't soften the predatory calculation that drove every decision he made. His wealth had been built on understanding that everything had a price—elections, legislation, human lives. The only question was whether someone was willing to pay it.

"Michael, you focus on the science. Let me worry about the politics."

Santos stood to leave, recognizing that the conversation had moved beyond his comfort zone. At the door, he paused with the expression of someone who had just realized he was swimming with sharks.

"The therapy could help billions of people, Marcus. Isn't that worth some political uncertainty?"

"Helping people is excellent public relations," Whitfield replied, returning to his desk and the financial documents that reduced human suffering to profit margins. "But seven hundred million dollars is excellent motivation for ensuring that help reaches the people who can afford it."

After Santos left, Whitfield returned to his market analysis. The longevity therapy represented more than medical breakthrough—it was a tool for reshaping civilization according to his preferences. Control the therapy, control who lived forever. Control who lived forever, control the future of human development.

Whitfield pulled up intelligence files on the UN ethics committee members. Twelve diplomats from twelve countries, each representing different cultural, religious, and economic perspectives on longevity research.

Whitfield studied photographs of the committee members—men and women who believed they were serving their countries' interests in routine diplomatic consultation.

Dr. Elena Vasquez of Spain, age fifty-seven, grandmother of four. Ambassador Klaus Weber of Germany, age sixty-two, widowed, devoted to international humanitarian law. Dr. Amara Okafor of Nigeria, age forty-nine, first woman from her region to represent her country at the UN.

But Whitfield had learned long ago that sentiment was a luxury he couldn't afford. Business required hard choices, calculated risks, acceptance that some people's lives mattered less than others.

Market forces at work. Supply, demand, and the ultimate arbitrage of death.

Outside his windows, Central Park spread green and peaceful in the afternoon sun. Families played on lawns that Whitfield's contributions had helped maintain. Children ran along paths that his tax dollars had paved. Citizens enjoying freedoms that his investments in American prosperity had helped preserve.

Soon, those same people would have the opportunity to live forever—if they could afford it. The longevity therapy would create the ultimate luxury market, where death became optional for those with sufficient resources. Natural selection mediated by economic selection, ensuring that only the most successful genetic lines continued indefinitely.

He opened a secure drawer that contained items not found in ordinary business offices. Inside was a single business card with no name, no company, just a phone number that connected to services most people preferred not to think about. Professional solutions to political problems.

Next to the card was a stack of cellphones still in their plastic retail casings. This was the type of business transaction that needed plausible deniability. He picked up one of the phones, opened the package, inserted the SIM, and dialed the number with steady fingers. Someone answered on the first ring without speaking.

"It's Whitfield," he said. "We need to talk."

Cocktails

The reception hall on the thirty-eighth floor of the United Nations building hummed with conversations in a dozen languages, the sound rising and falling like ocean waves against diplomatic shores. Crystal chandeliers cast prismatic light across assembled delegates while Manhattan spread below them through floor-to-ceiling windows, eight million lives continuing their brief existence unaware that their mortality was being debated four hundred feet above the street.

The evening's gathering served multiple purposes beyond social networking. Diplomats used such events to conduct informal negotiations away from recording devices and official transcripts. Cultural attachés arranged trade discussions over champagne and canapés. Intelligence operatives gathered information while maintaining cover as economic advisors or language interpreters.

Tonight, however, the conversation centered on a single topic that had consumed diplomatic circles for weeks. Daou Therapeutics' longevity therapy had forced the international community to confront questions that had never required answers. What happened to civilization when death became optional? How did governments maintain social stability when populations could live for centuries? It wasn't a reality yet, but it soon could be unless it was stopped.

Ambassador Elena Vasquez of Spain stood near the windows overlooking the East River, speaking quietly with Dr. Klaus Weber, Germany's representative on the ethics committee. Weber's weathered face showed the strain of a man carrying an impossible decision, his wire-rimmed glasses reflecting the city lights as he struggled with questions that had no clear answers.

At sixty-two, Weber had spent his career mediating international disputes through careful application of law and precedent. But the longevity therapy challenged every assumption that underpinned modern civilization. Legal frameworks designed for finite lifespans would require complete revision. Economic theories based on generational turnover would become meaningless.

"The science is undeniable," Weber said, adjusting his glasses with the nervous gesture of someone who spent more time in libraries than diplomatic receptions. "Dr. Foster's research could eliminate aging entirely. Every person born after implementation could live decades longer, possibly centuries. But the implications..."

Weber had spent the previous night reviewing Foster's published research, trying to understand the technical mechanisms that made cellular immortality possible. The genetic modifications were elegant in their simplicity, brutal in their effectiveness. Telomere restoration, DNA repair enhancement, mitochondrial regeneration—the therapy attacked aging at every level simultaneously.

"Overpopulation," Vasquez replied immediately, her accent adding music to words of mathematical certainty. "If people stop dying on schedule, where do we put them all? How do we feed them? The planet already struggles with seven billion humans consuming resources faster than they can be replaced."

Vasquez had commissioned studies from Spain's leading demographers, economists, and environmental scientists. Their conclusions were unanimous—immortal populations would strip the earth bare within decades. Agricultural systems couldn't support indefinite population growth. Energy resources couldn't sustain consumption patterns that never ended with death.

The math was simple and terrifying. Current birth rates minus current death rates equaled population growth that would overwhelm planetary resources in less than fifty years. If death became optional, growth would accelerate beyond any possibility of sustainable management.

"That assumes everyone gets access to the therapy," Weber pointed out, swirling his wine glass with the automatic motion of someone who had attended too many such gatherings. "More likely, it becomes another tool for the wealthy to separate themselves from the poor. Imagine a world where the rich live forever and the poor die on schedule according to their bank account."

The economic implications had kept Weber awake for weeks. Immortal wealthy classes would accumulate resources indefinitely, creating permanent dynasties that could never be challenged by generational change. Political power would become hereditary in fact rather than law, as immortal leaders ruled over mortal populations who aged and died while their rulers remained young.

Property ownership would become permanent, with immortal landlords controlling real estate that could never be inherited or transferred. Capital would accumulate in immortal hands, creating wealth disparities that made current inequality look trivial.

Across the room, Ambassador Chen Wei of China was engaged in heated discussion with his Russian counterpart, Dmitri Volkov. Their voices carried despite their efforts to keep the conversation private, diplomatic training unable to completely contain the magnitude of what they were discussing.

Chen represented a nation of 1.4 billion people who already struggled with resource allocation and environmental degradation. China's one-child policy had been abandoned, but population pressures remained enormous. The longevity therapy could transform demographic challenges into existential threats.

"Space colonization becomes mandatory, not optional," Chen was saying, his English precise despite the passion underlying his words. "If we perfect longevity therapy, we must also perfect interplanetary travel within decades. Otherwise, we create a prison planet where immortal populations consume finite resources until civilization collapses under its own weight."

Chen had been briefed by China's leading space scientists, who explained that current technology could support small research stations on Mars and the Moon, but nothing approaching the scale required for mass emigration. Developing space colonization infrastructure would require decades of investment and technological advancement.

Meanwhile, Earth's immortal populations would grow exponentially, consuming resources and producing waste at rates that would overwhelm every ecological system. The planet would become uninhabitable long before space colonies could accommodate meaningful population transfers.

Volkov shook his head, gray hair catching the light from crystal chandeliers. "Assuming we survive the transition period. Every major religion condemns this research as blasphemy. We're talking about civil unrest, possibly war, between those who accept the therapy and those who reject it as an offense against God."

Russia's intelligence services had been monitoring religious extremist groups across multiple continents. The longevity therapy had unified previously fractured movements in opposition to scientific progress. Orthodox Christians, fundamentalist Muslims, traditional Jews, conservative Hindus—all saw immortality as humanity's attempt to usurp divine authority.

Preliminary assessments suggested that religious conflicts triggered by the therapy could destabilize governments from Nigeria to Indonesia, from Brazil to Pakistan. Nations with strong religious traditions would face internal warfare between secular populations who wanted the therapy and faithful populations who saw it as satanic.

Dr. Amara Okafor, Nigeria's representative, joined their conversation with the graceful stride of someone accustomed to being the only woman and the only African in rooms full of powerful men. At forty-nine, she had earned her position through demonstrated expertise in international law and bioethics, but her presence still drew attention in diplomatic circles dominated by aging white males.

"My government's position is clear," Okafor said, her voice carrying the authority of someone who spoke for 200 million people. "We cannot support research that fundamentally alters human nature. Death gives life meaning, urgency, purpose. Without it, we become something else entirely."

Nigeria's religious communities were among the most conservative in Africa, viewing scientific attempts to extend life as challenges to Allah's or Christ's authority over mortality. Okafor's government faced enormous pressure from both Christian and Muslim populations to oppose the therapy as blasphemous.

But Nigeria also struggled with public health challenges that the therapy could address. HIV/AIDS, malaria, tuberculosis—diseases that killed millions of Africans annually. The longevity therapy offered hope for populations ravaged by preventable illnesses, even as it threatened traditional beliefs about divine will.

"Something better," Chen countered, his tone carrying the conviction of someone who had studied his nation's five thousand years of history. "Imagine the knowledge one person could accumulate over centuries. The problems they could solve. The art they could create. The wisdom they could share with generations not yet born."

Chen had been raised in a culture that revered elderly wisdom and generational continuity. Chinese philosophy emphasized learning from ancestors and preserving knowledge across centuries. The longevity therapy offered the possibility of individual minds accumulating wisdom across multiple centuries, creating unprecedented reservoirs of human experience.

Traditional Chinese medicine already focused on longevity and life extension through natural means. Acupuncture, herbal treatments, qi gong—all aimed at extending healthy lifespan through harmony with natural forces. The therapy represented scientific achievement of goals that Chinese culture had pursued for millennia.

"Imagine the power they could accumulate," Okafor replied, her voice carrying the weight of a continent that had suffered under immortal-seeming dictators. "The control they could exercise over mortal populations.

You're talking about creating gods among mortals, permanent castes that could never be overthrown."

Okafor's concerns reflected Africa's experience with leaders who seemed to rule forever, passing power between generations of the same families while populations remained trapped in poverty. Immortal rulers would eliminate even the possibility of generational change, creating permanent oppression that could never be ended by natural death.

The longevity therapy would entrench existing power structures indefinitely. Dictators who lived for centuries. Corrupt officials who never retired. Wealthy families that accumulated resources across multiple lifetimes while poor populations aged and died.

Near the bar, Ambassador Sarah Thompson of the United Kingdom was explaining her country's position to a group of younger diplomats whose futures would be determined by decisions made in this room. Thompson's crisp accent reflected the precision that had made British diplomacy influential for centuries.

"The economic implications alone are staggering," Thompson said, her voice cutting through the ambient noise. "Social Security, pensions, healthcare systems—all built on the assumption that people die in their seventies or eighties. What happens to those systems when death becomes optional?"

Britain's actuarial experts had calculated the financial impact of immortal populations on government budgets. Pension obligations that currently lasted twenty years would extend indefinitely. Healthcare costs would compound across centuries rather than decades. Social welfare systems would require complete restructuring or complete elimination.

The British government faced a choice between supporting scientific progress and maintaining fiscal stability. Thompson's briefing materials suggested the therapy would bankrupt Western economies within decades unless fundamental changes were made to every social support system.

"We adapt," said Ambassador François Dubois of France, his continental sophistication barely concealing deep uncertainty about the forces they were attempting to control. "Humans always adapt to new circumstances. This could be the greatest advancement in our species' history."

France had historically embraced scientific progress and secular governance. The longevity therapy aligned with Enlightenment values that emphasized reason over tradition, progress over stability. French intellectuals saw immortality as humanity's next evolutionary step.

But French economists warned that adaptation might require abandoning social democratic principles that defined European civilization. Welfare states couldn't support immortal populations. Progressive taxation couldn't fund indefinite government obligations. The therapy might save individual lives while destroying the societies that made those lives worth living.

"Or our greatest mistake," Thompson replied, setting down her wine glass. "Some doors, once opened, cannot be closed. Some knowledge, once gained, cannot be forgotten."

Thompson spoke from experience managing international crises where good intentions had produced catastrophic consequences. British intelligence had identified multiple scenarios where the longevity therapy could trigger global conflicts, economic collapse, or civilizational breakdown.

The conversations continued late into the evening, each diplomat wrestling with questions that had no precedent in human history. Representatives from nations that had fought wars over territory and resources now faced decisions about the fundamental nature of human existence, about whether death itself should remain mandatory or become a choice for those who could afford alternatives.

Ambassador Yuki Tanaka of Japan discussed his country's aging population crisis with Dr. Sarah Mills of Australia. Japan faced demographic collapse as birth rates declined and elderly populations grew. The longevity therapy could solve Japan's labor shortage by keeping workers productive indefinitely, but it could also prevent necessary generational renewal.

Ambassador Carlos Rodriguez of Brazil explained his nation's environmental concerns to Dr. Erik Larsson of Sweden. The Amazon rainforest was already under pressure from current populations. Immortal Brazilians would accelerate deforestation and species extinction beyond any possibility of environmental recovery.

Ambassador Rajesh Patel of India outlined his government's concerns about religious violence to Ambassador David Kim of South Korea. Both nations had experienced sectarian conflicts that could be inflamed by debates over scientific challenges to divine authority.

Each conversation revealed how completely unprepared humanity was for the choice between mortality and immortality. Religious representatives quoted scripture about the sanctity of God's design. Scientists presented data about cellular regeneration and genetic modification. Economists calculated the cost of supporting populations that never died. Military advisors discussed the security implications of nations whose leaders could rule for centuries.

But no one could answer the fundamental question that haunted every conversation: What did it mean to be human if humans stopped dying?

The reception ended without resolution, delegates departing with the weight of impossible decisions ahead of them. In five days, they would vote on restrictions that could ban longevity research worldwide, condemning future generations to the same mortality their ancestors had endured.

Or they would choose to step through the door into a future where death became optional, forever changing what it meant to be alive.

Outside the windows, Manhattan's lights glittered like a circuit board made of stars. Millions of people lived and worked and loved in the city below, unaware that twelve diplomats were deciding whether future generations would face the same limitations that had defined human existence since consciousness began.

The city continued its rhythm as delegates departed for hotels where they would spend sleepless nights weighing the fate of human mortality. Some would pray for guidance. Others would consult with their governments. All would struggle with questions that had no right answers, only consequences that would echo across centuries.

Tomorrow would bring more meetings, more debates, more pressure from constituencies who demanded answers to questions that couldn't be answered. The longevity therapy had forced humanity to confront its own nature and choose its future evolution.

The choice would be made by twelve people in a room overlooking a city where millions lived and died according to schedules that might soon become obsolete.

Idealism

Dr. Foster found Dr. Mitchell in his laboratory at eleven PM, hunched over a computer screen displaying genetic sequences that spiraled across the monitor like DNA ladders climbing toward immortality. The building was nearly empty except for security guards and the occasional researcher too obsessed with their work to remember normal human existence.

Mitchell worked with the focused intensity of someone who had found his life's purpose and intended to pursue it until either success or death intervened. Test results covered his desk in organized stacks, each pile representing months of experimentation with cellular regeneration protocols. The laboratory around them hummed with the quiet efficiency of expensive equipment—centrifuges and spectrophotometers and gene sequencers that cost more than most people's houses.

At thirty-eight, Mitchell had devoted fifteen years to longevity research, following Foster through academic positions and research grants with the loyalty of someone who believed completely in their shared vision. His marriage had ended during the lean years when funding was scarce and success seemed impossible. His social life had withered as eighteen-hour days became routine.

But tonight, success felt real. The FDA approval had validated decades of work that critics had dismissed as science fiction. Pharmaceutical companies were calling with acquisition offers. Venture capitalists wanted meetings to discuss investment opportunities. The financial rewards that had seemed impossible were suddenly inevitable.

"James, you should go home," Foster said, settling into the chair beside his workstation. "Lisa and David left hours ago."

Mitchell looked up from his screen, blinking to refocus eyes that had been staring at molecular diagrams for the past six hours. Dark circles under his eyes told the story of too many late nights spent chasing the impossible dream that had finally become reality.

The laboratory's climate control system maintained perfect conditions for sensitive equipment, but the air felt sterile compared to the world outside. Foster preferred windows that opened, natural light that changed with weather patterns, reminders that their work served living creatures rather than abstract scientific principles.

"Just running final calculations on the cellular regeneration rates," Mitchell said, gesturing at columns of numbers that reduced human immortality to mathematical equations. "If our models are correct, a single treatment could reverse twenty years of aging within six months. Twenty years, Sarah. Multiple treatments will give them even more. We're talking about giving people back decades of their lives."

The data supported Mitchell's enthusiasm. Laboratory animals treated with their therapy showed complete reversal of aging markers within three months. Organ function returned to juvenile levels. Cognitive performance improved beyond baseline measurements. Physical appearance regressed to young adult characteristics.

But mice and chimpanzees weren't humans. Laboratory conditions weren't real-world environments. What worked in sterile cages might fail when exposed to the complexity of human biology and social behavior.

"The models are correct, James. We've tested them a hundred times with laboratory animals and human tissue samples."

Foster had spent the previous evening reviewing their latest results, confirming that the therapy worked exactly as designed. Telomere restoration exceeded expectations. DNA repair mechanisms functioned perfectly. Mitochondrial regeneration proceeded on schedule.

The science was sound. The applications were revolutionary. The implications were terrifying.

"But imagine the IPO valuation," Mitchell continued, his excitement building like a man who had just realized he was sitting on the greatest fortune in human history. "Conservative estimates put us at fifty billion dollars market capitalization. That's billion with a B, Sarah. With our stock options we're all going to be wealthy beyond imagination."

Foster was quiet for a moment, studying her colleague's face with the expression of someone who had just discovered that a trusted friend spoke a different language than she had assumed. Money had never motivated her research. Financial gain was a byproduct of scientific achievement, not its primary purpose.

The laboratory equipment around them represented millions of dollars in investment, but Foster valued it for its capabilities rather than its cost. Each machine served specific functions in their research protocols. Success was measured in cellular regeneration rates, not stock prices.

"Is that what this is about for you, James? Money?"

Mitchell blinked, surprised by the question and the cool tone in which she asked it. "Well, no, of course not. But we've worked for twenty years to get here. Don't we deserve some reward for what we've accomplished?"

Foster stood and walked to the window, looking out over Baltimore's skyline. The city stretched toward the harbor, where ships carried cargo that would outlast their crews, buildings that would survive their architects, institutions that would endure beyond their founders.

Some things lasted longer than the people who created them. Foster wanted her research to be one of those things.

"James, when I started this research, my father was dying of cancer." Foster pressed her palm against the cool glass, leaving a handprint that would fade like everything else mortal. "He was sixty-two, still had so much life ahead of him, so many things he wanted to see and do. I watched him waste away, watched him lose everything that made him who he was, one cell at a time."

The memory remained vivid despite the years that had passed. Her father had been a high school biology teacher who inspired students to pursue scientific careers. He'd encouraged Foster's interest in genetics, supported her through graduate school, celebrated every small breakthrough in her research.

Cancer had stolen him slowly, methodically destroying the body that housed a mind still eager to learn and contribute. Foster had watched helplessly as chemotherapy and radiation failed to stop the cellular rebellion that consumed him from within.

His death had transformed Foster's academic interest in genetics into personal crusade against mortality itself. Every experiment since then had been motivated by the memory of his unnecessary suffering, his premature death, the knowledge lost when his mind stopped functioning.

"I didn't start this research to get rich, James. I started it because death is the ultimate injustice. It takes people before they're ready, before they've finished their work, before they've said goodbye to the people they love."

Foster's reflection in the window showed a woman who had devoted her life to impossible goals, who had sacrificed normal relationships and conventional success for the possibility of eliminating humanity's oldest enemy. Gray eyes held the intensity of someone who saw beyond immediate concerns to ultimate consequences.

"But the money will help us continue the research," Mitchell pointed out, his voice carrying the reasonable tone of someone who believed that good intentions and profit margins could coexist peacefully. "Fund new laboratories, hire more scientists, develop additional therapies for other diseases."

"The money will also make us targets," Foster replied, turning back to face him with eyes that held twenty years of watching people die unnecessarily. "When seven billion people realize that death is now optional, what do you think happens to the people who made that choice possible?"

Mitchell was quiet, considering her words while the laboratory equipment continued its quiet humming around them. Machines that had helped unlock the greatest secret in human history operated without understanding the magnitude of their contribution to human knowledge.

The fluorescent lights cast harsh shadows that made the laboratory feel like an operating room where they were performing surgery on human nature itself. Their research would transform civilization as fundamentally as agriculture, writing, or industrial technology had changed previous eras.

"This isn't about profit, James. This is about fundamentally changing what it means to be human. Every person who takes our therapy will live to see things we can't imagine. They'll solve problems that haven't been invented yet. They'll create art that won't be conceived for centuries. They'll accumulate knowledge that could transform human civilization into something we can't even comprehend."

Foster moved closer to his workstation, her voice carrying the intensity that had driven her through two decades of failed experiments. The genetic sequences on his screen represented more than scientific data—they were blueprints for human transcendence, maps to territories that no species had ever explored.

"That's our legacy. Not money. Not Nobel prizes. Not IPO valuations. The knowledge that we gave humanity time to become something better than what mortality allowed."

Mitchell nodded slowly, the excitement fading from his face as he began to understand the magnitude of what they had accomplished beyond its financial and fame implications. The therapy would enable humans to develop wisdom that transcended individual lifespans, to pursue projects that required longer perspectives than mortal minds could sustain.

Artists could refine their craft for hundreds of years. Scientists could pursue research programs that spanned centuries. Philosophers could develop understanding that deepened across multiple lifetimes. The therapy wouldn't just extend life—it would expand human potential beyond anything that had previously been possible.

"You're right," Mitchell said quietly. "I got caught up in the numbers, in the idea of never having to worry about funding again. But this is bigger."

"The numbers matter," Foster admitted, returning to her chair. "But only as a means to an end. Our end is saving lives. Everything else is just paperwork."

Foster had spent countless nights calculating the economics of immortality, understanding that financial considerations would ultimately determine who received the therapy and how it was distributed. Insurance companies would resist covering treatments that eliminated their business models. Governments would struggle to fund therapies that bankrupted social programs.

But financial obstacles could be overcome if the therapy proved its value. Once people understood that death was optional, they would find ways to afford the treatments that preserved their lives indefinitely.

Foster gathered her research files and prepared to leave the laboratory. Outside the windows, Baltimore slept beneath a sky that held more stars than mortal eyes would ever count.

"Get some sleep, James," Foster said, turning off the laboratory lights. "Tomorrow we start changing the world, and the world is going to fight back harder than you can imagine."

After she left, Mitchell sat alone in the darkened laboratory, surrounded by machines that had helped unlock immortality while the city continued its ancient rhythm outside his windows. For the first time since the FDA approval, he began to understand that they had created something that would threaten every person and institution that profited from human mortality.

The war was coming, and they had just painted targets on their backs.

Special Agent David Park adjusted the telephoto lens on his camera and captured another image of the Daou Therapeutics building, the powerful optics bringing the executive floors into sharp focus despite the distance. From his position in the unmarked van parked across the street, he had a clear view of the main entrance and the windows where the world's most important genetic research was being conducted behind glass that reflected nothing but sky.

The van had been equipped with surveillance equipment—digital cameras with stabilized telephoto lenses, directional microphones that could capture conversations through windows, electronic monitoring systems that intercepted cellular communications within a three-block radius. Technology that transformed the vehicle into a mobile intelligence collection platform.

"Anything interesting?" asked his partner, Agent Lisa Rodriguez, who was monitoring electronic surveillance equipment that could intercept phone calls, emails, and text messages from three blocks away. Banks of computer screens displayed real-time data streams from multiple sources, creating a digital web that captured every electronic communication in the target area.

Rodriguez had been assigned to the operation based on her expertise in technical surveillance and signals intelligence. She understood the complex systems that modern corporations used to protect proprietary information, and more importantly, she knew how to penetrate those systems without leaving traces.

"Santos just arrived," Park replied, checking his watch like someone who had been documenting the same routine for weeks. "Nine-fifteen AM, same as yesterday, same as every day since we started this operation. Man's consistent in his habits."

Park lowered his camera and made notes in a logbook that documented every movement, every visitor, every deviation from established patterns. Two weeks of surveillance had revealed that Daou Therapeutics operated like clockwork—employees arrived at predictable times, meetings followed scheduled patterns, security protocols were implemented consistently.

The predictability made surveillance easier but also more boring. Most corporate targets eventually varied their routines enough to maintain operational security. Daou's consistency suggested either complete confidence in their security or complete ignorance of potential threats.

Rodriguez studied the readouts on her screen, green lines dancing across black backgrounds as computers analyzed digital communications flowing through the building's network. "Phone traffic is normal. Mostly scientific discussions about cellular regeneration and gene therapy protocols. Some investor calls about funding and clinical trial timelines. Nothing that screams federal crimes."

The electronic surveillance had produced thousands of hours of recorded conversations, emails, and text messages. Most involved routine business communications, research discussions, and administrative coordination. The FBI's artificial intelligence systems had flagged suspicious patterns, but human analysis had revealed nothing more threatening than scientific enthusiasm.

Park had been conducting surveillance operations for twelve years, working cases that ranged from domestic terrorism to corporate espionage. His experience had taught him to recognize the difference between legitimate business activity and criminal conspiracy. Daou Therapeutics exhibited none of the operational security patterns that characterized illegal enterprises.

"Remind me why we're surveilling a medical research company?" Park asked, voicing the question that had been bothering him since the operation began.

"Director's orders," Rodriguez replied with the automatic response of someone who had learned not to question assignments that came from above her pay grade. "Potential violations of federal bioethics laws, possible foreign intelligence connections, concerns about national security implications of longevity research and potential insider trading around an FDA announcement."

Rodriguez had been briefed on the operation's objectives, but the briefing had raised more questions than it answered. Bioethics violations typically involved improper research protocols or regulatory noncompliance, not the kind of criminal activity that justified weeks of intensive surveillance.

The national security concerns were even more vague. How did medical research that could benefit millions of Americans threaten national security? What foreign intelligence connections could exist in publicly funded research conducted by American scientists?

"Concerns from whom?" Park pressed.

Rodriguez shrugged, her attention focused on intercepted communications that revealed nothing more suspicious than scientists discussing the molecular mechanisms of cellular aging. "Above our pay grade, partner. We watch, we document, we report. Someone else decides what it means."

The operation had been authorized at the highest levels of the Justice Department, with funding that suggested serious concerns about Daou's activities. But two weeks of surveillance had produced no evidence of criminal behavior, foreign influence, or national security threats.

Instead, Park and Rodriguez had documented the daily routines of scientists who worked eighteen-hour days to develop medical treatments that could revolutionize human health. Their conversations revealed dedication to scientific progress, not conspiracy against American interests.

A Baltimore City Police patrol car pulled up beside their van with the slow, deliberate movement of officers who had spotted something that didn't belong in their territory. Officer Mark Thompson approached the back doors of the van and gave one a tap with his baton.

Thompson was a twenty-year veteran of Baltimore PD who knew his beat better than any federal agency. His experience had taught him to recognize surveillance operations, and his territorial instincts made him suspicious of outside agencies working without local coordination.

The back door opened revealing the agents and equipment.

"Morning," Thompson said, his tone polite but carrying the unmistakable authority. "We've been getting reports about suspicious activity in this area. Mind if I ask what you're doing?"

Park showed his FBI credentials, the gold badge catching sunlight as he held it steady for inspection. "Federal surveillance operation. Authorized by the Justice Department under Section 215 of the Patriot Act."

Thompson examined the badge carefully, comparing the photograph to Park's face. He recognized the credentials as genuine, but federal authority didn't automatically grant permission to operate in his jurisdiction without notification.

Baltimore PD maintained cooperative relationships with federal agencies, but those relationships required communication and coordination. Surprise discovery of surveillance operations created diplomatic problems that could affect future cooperation between local and federal law enforcement.

"FBI? What's the Bureau's interest in a medical building?"

"Classified," Rodriguez said from the passenger seat, her voice carrying the flat tone that federal agents used when they wanted local law enforcement to stop asking questions. "But we're conducting lawful surveillance in accordance with federal regulations and constitutional protections."

Thompson looked between the two agents, then at their sophisticated surveillance equipment, processing the implications of federal resources being directed at a building full of medical researchers. His expression suggested skepticism about the operation's necessity and legality.

The surveillance van's equipment was obviously expensive and sophisticated, designed for operations against serious criminal or terrorist targets. Thompson's experience suggested that such resources weren't typically deployed against medical research companies unless significant crimes were suspected.

"How long have you been here?" Thompson asked.

"Two weeks," Park admitted, recognizing that denying the obvious would only create more problems with local law enforcement.

"And you're watching the genetics company that just got approval for the longevity therapy?"

Park nodded, wondering how much the local officer knew about Daou Therapeutics and their research into extending human life. The FDA approval had generated significant media coverage, making the company's work public knowledge.

Thompson was quiet for a moment, his expression suggesting that he was calculating political ramifications that extended beyond his jurisdiction. "You know Senator Bradley represents this district? He's not going to be happy about federal agents spying on his constituents without local notification or coordination."

"The operation was authorized through proper channels," Rodriguez said, her voice carrying less conviction than her words suggested.

"Maybe so, but Baltimore PD should have been notified about federal operations in our jurisdiction." Thompson stepped back from the van, his hand moving instinctively toward his radio.

Thompson understood that federal agencies often operated with minimal local coordination, but surveillance operations in his jurisdiction required at least courtesy notification. Discovering federal agents through routine patrol created problems that could escalate into jurisdictional disputes.

After the patrol car left, Park and Rodriguez looked at each other with the shared understanding that their surveillance operation had just been compromised by the very people they were supposed to be protecting.

"Think this becomes a problem?" Park asked, already knowing the answer.

"Everything becomes a problem eventually," Rodriguez replied, returning her attention to the surveillance equipment that had detected nothing criminal in two weeks of monitoring. "Question is how big and how fast."

Park picked up his camera and continued photographing the Daou building, but he had the sinking feeling that their careful surveillance had just been transformed into a political incident that would reach levels of government far above his clearance level.

Inside the building, scientists continued their work on extending human life, unaware that federal agents were documenting their every move for reasons that remained classified even from the agents conducting the surveillance.

Oversight

Senator William Bradley was reviewing Medicare funding proposals in his Capitol Hill office when his chief of staff, Samantha Tillman, knocked on the mahogany door with the urgent rhythm that indicated crisis management rather than routine business. The sound echoed through his office like distant artillery, announcing the arrival of problems that would require immediate attention and careful political maneuvering.

Bradley looked up from paperwork that reduced human suffering to budget line items, noting the concern in Tillman's expression. At thirty-four, she had managed his political career for eight years, guiding him through congressional battles and constituent crises with the skill of someone who understood that politics was warfare conducted through legislation rather than violence.

Her expression carried the particular tension that accompanied news capable of destroying political careers. Bradley had seen that look before—during the healthcare reform debates, the defense spending controversies, the immigration battles that had defined his senate tenure.

"Senator, I just got a call from Baltimore PD," Tillman said, entering with a folder. "There's been a situation with federal surveillance against one of the genetic start-ups in your district."

Bradley removed his reading glasses and leaned back in his leather chair, studying his chief of staff's face with the practiced attention of someone who had spent two decades in Washington learning to read the political weather. At sixty-one, he had the gray-haired gravitas of a man who had survived multiple election cycles, but his blue eyes still held the sharpness of someone who paid attention to details that could make or break legislation.

The office around them reflected his political philosophy—government portraits celebrating public service, bookshelves filled with policy studies and legislative histories, constituent awards recognizing his commitment to Maryland's interests. Everything carefully arranged to project competence and dedication to democratic principles.

"What kind of surveillance?" he asked, though his tone suggested he already suspected the answer wouldn't improve his day.

"FBI agents have been watching Daou Therapeutics for two weeks. No notification to local law enforcement, no apparent warrant that anyone in the Baltimore police department knows about, no coordination with state or local authorities."

Tillman opened her folder to reveal documents that painted a picture of federal overreach disguised as national security. Surveillance reports, technical specifications for monitoring equipment, operational authorizations that bypassed normal oversight mechanisms.

Bradley was quiet for a moment, processing the implications of federal agents conducting unauthorized surveillance on a company that represented everything his constituents valued about American scientific leadership. "Daou Therapeutics. That's the longevity research company."

"The same one that just received FDA approval for clinical trials," Tillman confirmed, opening her folder to reveal documents that transformed routine surveillance into potential constitutional violations. "Baltimore police discovered the surveillance accidentally during routine patrol."

Bradley stood and walked to his window, looking out over the Capitol grounds where the business of democracy continued its ancient rhythm while federal agencies operated in shadows that Congress was supposed to illuminate. The view encompassed monuments to democratic principles—the Washington Monument, the Lincoln Memorial, the Jefferson Memorial—all dedicated to leaders who had fought to constrain government power through constitutional limitations.

"Samantha, pull the Senate Intelligence Committee files on bioethics investigations. Also get me the budget reports for Social Security and Medicare."

Tillman made notes on her tablet, recognizing the strategic thinking that had made Bradley effective in twenty years of congressional combat. He understood that successful politics required connecting immediate crises to broader policy implications.

"You think this surveillance is connected to the longevity therapy?"

"If people stop dying on schedule, the entire federal retirement system collapses overnight," Bradley said, his voice carrying the weight of someone who understood that scientific breakthroughs could bankrupt governments. "Social Security alone pays out nine hundred billion dollars annually, based on actuarial tables that assume people die in their seventies and eighties."

Bradley had spent his congressional career managing the mathematics of social welfare programs that depended on predictable mortality rates. Social Security worked because workers paid into the system for forty years and collected benefits for twenty years before dying. Medicare functioned because elderly patients required expensive care for limited periods before natural death ended their need for services.

The longevity therapy threatened to destroy that equilibrium by creating beneficiaries who collected payments for centuries instead of decades. Government programs designed for finite lifespans would become unsustainable if applied to immortal populations. Those that couldn't afford the longevity treatments would suffer the most if those social programs collapsed.

He turned back to his chief of staff, hands clasped behind his back in the posture of someone preparing for political war. "What happens to those programs if people start living to be three hundred years old? What happens to Medicare when people need medical care for centuries instead of decades?"

Tillman had never considered the question from that perspective, had never calculated the economic implications of defeating death itself. Her political experience focused on traditional issues—taxation, regulation, defense spending—not the fundamental restructuring of civilization that immortality would require.

"I suppose we'd have to restructure everything. Social programs, taxation, economic planning."

"Restructure, hell," Bradley replied, returning to his desk with the decisive movement of someone who had identified the enemy. "We'd have to eliminate everything.

Social Security, Medicare, Medicaid, federal pensions—the entire safety net disappears when people stop dying and start collecting benefits for centuries."

Bradley's calculator sat on his desk like a weapon waiting to be deployed. He began entering numbers that transformed abstract policy into concrete mathematics. Nine hundred billion dollars in Social Security payments annually, multiplied by centuries instead of decades. Medicare costs that compounded across lifetimes instead of aging into terminal care.

The calculations produced numbers that exceeded the federal budget, the gross domestic product, the total wealth of the United States. Immortal populations would consume resources that no economy could provide, creating fiscal catastrophe that would destroy the government before the therapy could benefit anyone.

Bradley picked up his secure phone and began dialing numbers that connected directly to the most powerful offices in Washington. "Get me Senator Walsh from the Intelligence Committee. Also arrange a meeting with FBI Director Harrison. I want to know why federal agents are investigating a company in my district without congressional oversight or constitutional authority."

As Tillman left to make the calls, Bradley opened his laptop and began researching Daou Therapeutics with the thoroughness of someone who understood that information was power in political warfare. If the federal government was worried enough to conduct unauthorized surveillance, he needed to understand what they were afraid of.

The longevity therapy's technical specifications were beyond his scientific expertise, but the implications were clear enough for political analysis. The therapy could save millions of lives and establish American leadership in genetic research for generations. It could also bankrupt the United States government by creating populations that lived for centuries while collecting social benefits.

Bradley studied financial projections that showed Daou Therapeutics poised to become either the most valuable company in human history or completely worthless, depending on government policies that his committee would help shape. The therapy represented the intersection of scientific progress and political power, where breakthrough discoveries met regulatory authority.

His desk phone rang with the tone reserved for calls from other senators. Walsh's voice carried the weariness of someone who had spent too many years managing classified information that couldn't be shared with the people who needed to know it.

"Bill, I can't discuss ongoing intelligence operations over unsecured lines. But I can tell you that certain agencies are concerned about national security implications of genetic research."

"What kind of national security implications?"

"The kind that require closed-door briefings with appropriate security clearances."

Bradley understood the language of classified information, the bureaucratic codes that indicated sensitive operations beyond normal oversight. But national security concerns about medical research suggested threat assessments that extended beyond routine regulatory compliance.

"Jim, I need to know if federal agencies are investigating companies in my district without proper authorization."

"I'll look into it. But Bill—be careful about pushing too hard on this one. There are interests involved that extend beyond your jurisdiction."

The line went dead, leaving Bradley with more questions than answers. Walsh's warning suggested political forces that operated outside normal congressional oversight, agencies that answered to authorities beyond legislative control.

Bradley's experience had taught him to recognize when federal operations crossed constitutional boundaries. Surveillance without warrants, investigations without oversight, activities that violated the separation of powers that defined American democracy.

His intercom buzzed with Tillman's voice. "Senator, Director Harrison can meet with you tomorrow morning. But his office wants to know the purpose of the meeting."

"Tell them it's about constitutional authority and congressional oversight of federal law enforcement activities."

Bradley returned to his research, studying Daou Therapeutics from every angle he could access through public records and committee databases. The company's breakthrough represented American scientific achievement at its finest—public and private funded research that could benefit humanity while establishing economic advantages for the United States.

But the therapy also threatened government programs that formed the foundation of American social policy. Bradley faced a choice between supporting scientific progress and protecting federal fiscal stability, between defending constitutional rights and accepting bureaucratic necessity.

His evening was consumed by financial calculations that transformed the longevity therapy from a medical breakthrough into an economic weapon.

The FBI surveillance suggested that someone in the executive branch understood these implications and was taking action to protect government interests. But such action without congressional authorization violated the constitutional principles that Bradley had sworn to defend.

Bradley worked past midnight, preparing for meetings that would determine whether American scientific achievement would be supported or suppressed by the government that had funded its development. The longevity therapy represented everything he valued about American innovation and everything he feared about government power.

Tomorrow would bring confrontations with federal agencies that operated in shadows, decisions about surveillance that violated constitutional protections, choices between scientific progress and political survival.

Bradley gathered his files and prepared to leave the office, knowing that tomorrow would bring the most important legislative battle of his career. The war between scientific progress and government control had found its first battlefield in a medical building in Baltimore where researchers worked to defeat death while federal agents watched for threats that might destroy democracy itself.

Bradley intended to ensure that choice was made openly, with congressional oversight and constitutional protection, rather than in shadows where accountability disappeared and democracy died of bureaucratic necessity.

Lighthouse Restoration

Frank stood in the lamp room at the top of the lighthouse, examining the massive Fresnel lens that had guided ships through dangerous waters for over a century. The morning sun streamed through the prismatic glass, casting rainbow patterns across the circular chamber while the ocean stretched endlessly beyond windows that had witnessed storms and calms and the passage of vessels carrying their human cargo toward destinations they might never reach.

The restoration work consumed his days now like a meditation on permanence in a world where everything else decayed toward inevitable failure. Stone that needed repointing where winter freeze had cracked mortar joints. Steel that needed welding where salt air had eaten through protective coatings. Glass that needed replacing where time and weather had introduced flaws that scattered light instead of focusing it.

He ran his fingers along a crack in one of the lens sections, feeling the flaw that would scatter light instead of focusing it into the beam that had once saved lives. Like everything else in the lighthouse, it could be repaired if you understood the principles involved and possessed the patience to do the work properly.

The cat appeared at the top of the spiral stairs, having climbed seventy feet through scaffolding and past restoration equipment to reach the lamp room. It surveyed the space with suspicious yellow eyes that had learned to distrust anything that disrupted the established order, then settled near the eastern window where morning sun created a warm patch on the metal floor.

Frank opened his toolbox and selected a channel lock, measuring tape, glass cutter, and putty knife—tools that had served craftsmen for generations before power equipment made such skills obsolete. The cracked lens section would need to be removed carefully, templates made, new glass cut to exact specifications. Work that could take days to complete properly, but Frank had days. Weeks if necessary. Time was the one resource he possessed in abundance.

He preferred it this way. Methodical progress toward clearly defined objectives. Quiet work that required skill rather than violence. Each step leading logically to the next without surprises or split-second decisions that left bodies cooling in dark places while politicians debated the moral implications of necessary action.

The scaffolding around the staircase was his work too, steel poles and platforms that would support his weight while he cleaned the interior walls and repaired the staircase. He had calculated load capacities and stress points and safety margins with the same detail he brought to mission planning, because engineering problems had solutions that didn't depend on killing people.

Frank removed the damaged lens section and carried it to his workbench near the windows, handling the century-old glass with the respect due to craftsmanship that had outlasted the men who created it. The cat watched without interest, then began grooming itself with the focused attention of someone who understood the importance of maintaining equipment.

Outside, the ocean stretched endlessly eastward where ships moved along shipping lanes that had guided commerce for centuries. The lighthouse had once been essential to their navigation, its beam cutting through fog and darkness to warn of rocks that could tear hulls apart and send crews to the bottom.

Now GPS satellites did the work and old towers like this one became curiosities, maintained by enthusiasts and historians who remembered when analog systems provided backup for digital failure.

But Frank understood the value of redundancy, the importance of systems that worked without electricity or computers or government authorization. When satellites failed or signals jammed or foreign governments decided to eliminate American navigation capabilities, ships would need lights again.

Frank measured the damaged section against templates he'd cut from cardboard, adjusting dimensions to account for thermal expansion and structural stress. Glass work required measurements within fractions of inches. Too large and the section wouldn't fit properly. Too small and the lens would leak light through gaps that weakened the beam.

The cat stretched and moved to watch gulls circling in the updrafts created by the lighthouse's thermal mass. Predators studying other predators with the interest of creatures that understood the hunt continued regardless of who watched.

Frank scored the glass with the cutter, applying steady pressure along lines marked with pencil and straightedge. The tool made a distinctive sound as it carved through the material—part scratch, part whisper—that indicated proper technique. Too much pressure would shatter the glass. Too little would leave incomplete cuts that cracked under stress.

He placed the scored section over a wooden dowel and applied gentle pressure until the glass separated along the intended line. Clean break, smooth edges, no chips or cracks that would weaken the finished piece. The work proceeded, each step building toward restoration of the lens's original function.

The lighthouse required constant maintenance to fulfill its purpose. Salt air corroded metal fittings. Rain found gaps in weatherstripping and mortar joints. Wind stressed structural connections until they loosened and failed. Without regular attention, the building would decay into ruins within a generation.

Frank understood the parallel to his own life. The missions took their toll in accumulated damage that required repair. Bullet wounds that healed wrong. Broken bones that set improperly. Scar tissue that limited mobility and caused pain. Each job added wear that time couldn't completely undo.

But the lighthouse offered different work. Building rather than breaking. Creating rather than destroying. Projects that lasted beyond the people who completed them.

Frank fitted the new glass section into place, checking alignment against adjacent pieces. The fit was precise, gaps minimal, the repair nearly invisible when viewed from appropriate distance. Light would flow through the restored lens without scattering or distortion.

He mixed putty to seal the joints, working the compound until it reached proper consistency for application. Traditional materials, proven over decades of use. Modern alternatives might be stronger or longer-lasting, but Frank preferred systems that had demonstrated reliability through actual performance rather than laboratory testing.

The cat had found a shaft of sunlight and settled into position for an extended nap. Its purr provided background noise that complemented the sound of tools and Frank's breathing and the distant rhythm of waves against rock. Simple acoustics that required no translation or interpretation.

By noon Frank had completed the lens repair and moved on to metalwork. Steel brackets needed cleaning before they could be properly painted. Rust removal required patience and elbow grease rather than power tools that might damage surrounding materials.

Wire brushes scraped away oxidation with metallic sounds that echoed off the curved walls. Frank worked methodically, exposing clean metal beneath decades of corrosion. Each bracket would be primed and painted to protect against future rust, extending its service life another generation.

The work satisfied something in Frank that missions couldn't address. Violence solved immediate problems but created new ones. Each death generated consequences that rippled outward in unpredictable patterns. Bodies led to investigations. Investigations led to complications. Complications led to more bodies.

But restoration work built on itself. Each repair improved the building's condition. Each improvement extended its useful life. Every hour invested returned dividends in functionality and durability that would benefit future users.

Frank's phone remained silent in his pocket. No messages from Culper. No emergency calls requiring immediate response. The world continued its violent rhythm while Frank worked to preserve something that had guided travelers safely through dangerous waters for over a century.

The lighthouse stood as testament to human dedication to preservation rather than destruction. Previous keepers had maintained it through wars and economic collapse and technological change. Their work enabled Frank's work, just as his work would enable the efforts of whoever came next.

He finished cleaning the metal brackets and began applying primer. Careful brushstrokes that covered every surface exposed to salt air. Foundation work that would support the final paint coats and protect the underlying steel for decades.

The cat opened one yellow eye to confirm Frank remained within acceptable proximity, then returned to sleep.

Some things endured through patient maintenance rather than dramatic intervention. Some problems were solved by steady application of skill rather than sudden violence. Some victories were measured in years rather than minutes.

Frank worked until sunset painted the ocean red and gold, then climbed to the lamp room where the beacon waited to begin its nightly guidance of ships he couldn't see toward destinations he would never visit.

The light reached across dark water toward vessels that might need help finding their way home. Simple purpose, essential function, honest work that served others without recognition or reward.

Frank activated the beacon and watched its beam sweep across the horizon. Somewhere in the darkness, captains would see the light and know their position. Ships would avoid rocks that could destroy them. Lives would be saved by the cumulative efforts of everyone who had ever maintained this tower.

Tomorrow would bring more restoration work. Stone to be pointed. Steel to be painted. Glass to be cleaned. Endless tasks that preserved something worth preserving.

FBI Director Robert Harrison sat across from Senator Bradley in the senator's private office, his expression carefully neutral as he calculated the political risks of this conversation. Harrison was a career law enforcement officer who had learned to navigate Washington's treacherous currents, but this meeting was testing his diplomatic skills against forces that could end careers with a phone call. Bradley had powerful friends and Harrison knew it.

The office's atmosphere reflected Bradley's twenty years of congressional experience—American flags positioned for optimal camera angles, constituent awards arranged to suggest popular support, bookshelves filled with legislation he had sponsored or influenced. Everything designed to project authority and democratic legitimacy.

"Senator, I understand your concerns about federal operations in your district," Harrison began, his voice carrying the measured tone of someone who had spent thirty years avoiding political landmines.

Bradley didn't waste time on pleasantries that would only delay the confrontation both men knew was inevitable. "Bob, my office received reports that FBI agents have been conducting unauthorized surveillance of a medical research company for two weeks. I want to know why."

"The surveillance operation was properly authorized through Justice Department channels in accordance with federal law and constitutional—"

"Authorized by whom?" Bradley interrupted, leaning forward across his desk with the intensity of someone who had identified government overreach disguised as national security. "For what purpose? Under what legal authority? With what congressional oversight?"

Harrison shifted uncomfortably in his chair, recognizing the signs of a senator who had done his homework and intended to use it as a weapon. Bradley's reputation for thorough preparation and aggressive questioning had made him effective in committee hearings and dangerous in private meetings.

"Senator, I'm not at liberty to discuss the details of ongoing investigations without proper authorization from—"

"This isn't an ongoing investigation, Bob. This is a fishing expedition that's about to become a political nightmare." Bradley's voice carried the steel that had made him effective in twenty years of congressional combat. "The company you're watching just received FDA approval for longevity therapy. Every news organization in the country is covering that story."

Harrison understood the political implications even as he struggled to defend the operation. FBI surveillance of a company receiving positive media coverage for medical breakthroughs would generate negative publicity that could damage the Bureau's reputation and congressional funding.

"I understand the sensitivity of the situation—"

"Do you?" Bradley interrupted again, standing to pace behind his desk like a caged predator who had identified prey. "Because when the Washington Post finds out that the FBI is secretly investigating the scientists who just figured out how to extend human life, what do you think that story looks like to the American people?"

Harrison was quiet for a long moment, understanding that the senator had identified the precise vulnerability that kept federal administrators awake at night. "Senator, there are legitimate national security concerns related to genetic research that could affect—"

"Name one."

"I can't discuss classified information in this setting without proper security clearances and—"

"Cut the bullshit, Bob." Bradley stopped pacing and fixed the FBI director with the stare that had intimidated witnesses in congressional hearings. "I've been in Congress for twenty years. I know the difference between national security and political paranoia."

He moved closer to Harrison's chair, using physical proximity to emphasize the power imbalance between them. "The longevity therapy threatens federal entitlement programs, doesn't it? Social Security, Medicare, federal pensions—all based on assumptions about life expectancy that are about to become obsolete."

Harrison's expression hardened as he recognized the accusation being leveled against his agency. "The FBI doesn't conduct political operations, Senator. We investigate legitimate threats to national security in accordance with—"

"Then explain the surveillance."

"I can't provide details about classified operations."

Bradley returned to his desk and picked up his phone. "Samantha, get me the chairman of the Senate Judiciary Committee. Also schedule a press conference for this afternoon. I want to discuss federal surveillance of American scientists."

Harrison stood quickly, recognizing the threat of public exposure that could destroy careers and agency budgets. "Senator, I think we can resolve this without involving the media or creating unnecessary public concern."

"How?"

"Give me twenty-four hours to review the operation and provide you with appropriate briefings through proper channels."

Bradley considered the request while Harrison calculated how much information he could reveal without compromising ongoing operations or admitting that the surveillance had been conducted for political rather than security reasons.

"Twenty-four hours," Bradley said finally. "Then I want answers, or I start asking questions publicly about why the FBI is afraid of medical researchers."

After Harrison left, Bradley called his chief of staff back into the office with the satisfied expression of someone who had just won the opening engagement of a larger war.

The FBI would either provide answers or face congressional scrutiny that could expose surveillance operations conducted without proper oversight. Either outcome would advance Bradley's goal of protecting scientific research from government interference.

But Harrison's nervous demeanor suggested something deeper than routine bureaucratic overreach. The FBI director had seemed genuinely worried about threats that extended beyond normal law enforcement concerns.

Bradley opened his secure computer and began researching federal surveillance authorities, looking for legal justifications that might explain why the Bureau was watching a genetics company. The Patriot Act provided broad surveillance powers, but those were designed for terrorism investigations, not medical research oversight.

His phone buzzed with a call from Walsh at the Intelligence Committee. The senator's voice carried unusual strain.

"Bill, I've looked into your surveillance concerns. There are national security implications that go beyond normal committee oversight."

"What kind of implications?"

"Foreign intelligence services are extremely interested in American longevity research. We've detected multiple attempts to infiltrate biotech companies working on life extension technologies."

Bradley made notes on his secure tablet. "Attempts by which foreign services?"

"Chinese MSS, Russian SVR, even allied services like French DGSE. Everyone wants to steal or sabotage research that could give America strategic advantages in genetic technology."

The information cast the FBI surveillance in a different light. If foreign intelligence agencies were targeting American biotech companies, protective surveillance might be justified even without direct evidence of infiltration.

"Has Daou Therapeutics been specifically targeted?"

"That's classified beyond my clearance level. But Bill—be careful about pushing too hard on this. Some operations require plausible deniability even from congressional oversight."

Walsh's warning revealed someone who had learned that national security sometimes required activities that couldn't be publicly acknowledged. But Bradley's oath was to the Constitution, not to agencies that operated beyond democratic oversight.

He spent the afternoon reviewing classified briefings about foreign intelligence activities in American biotechnology sectors. The scope of foreign interest was staggering—dozens of companies under surveillance, hundreds of researchers being recruited or targeted, billions of dollars in stolen intellectual property.

But Bradley also found evidence of domestic surveillance that went far beyond foreign counterintelligence. American citizens were being monitored for political activities, scientific research, and economic activities that posed no threat to national security.

The Daou Therapeutics surveillance appeared to fall into the latter category. No evidence of foreign contact, no suspicious financial transactions, no security violations or regulatory noncompliance. Just scientists working to extend human life being watched by federal agents who seemed more concerned about economic implications than security threats.

Bradley's evening was interrupted by a call from his wife, reminding him about their anniversary dinner reservation. He had forgotten completely, consumed by the implications of federal overreach disguised as national security.

"I'm sorry, honey. This surveillance issue is bigger than I thought. Can we reschedule?"

"You've been working eighteen-hour days for two weeks. When does it end?"

Bradley looked out his office window toward the Capitol dome illuminated against the night sky. "When I'm sure we're still living in a democracy."

Bradley was beginning to suspect that federal agencies had expanded their authorities beyond constitutional limits, creating shadow government operations that answered to no elected officials.

The longevity therapy represented a test case. If the government could suppress medical research because it threatened entitlement programs, what other scientific advances might be sacrificed to bureaucratic convenience?

Bradley worked past midnight, preparing for tomorrow's confrontation with Harrison. The FBI director would either provide convincing evidence of legitimate security concerns, or Bradley would begin the process of congressional oversight that could expose unconstitutional surveillance operations.

Outside his window, Washington slept while federal agents continued their watch on scientists who worked to defeat humanity's oldest enemy. The balance between security and freedom hung in the hands of elected officials who might lack the courage to defend constitutional principles against bureaucratic power.

Bradley intended to be different. Tomorrow would determine whether congressional oversight still had meaning, or whether federal agencies had achieved the independence from democratic control that their founders had feared.

Blind Date

The hostess at Marcello's led Dr. Foster through dim lighting past tables where couples leaned toward each other over wine. Red checkered tablecloths. Candles in Chianti bottles. The kind of place where first dates went to pretend they weren't nervous about impressing strangers with carefully constructed personas.

David Carpenter stood as she approached, displaying the practiced charm of someone who had learned to navigate professional social situations. Tall, good shoulders, expensive watch catching candlelight. The kind of surgeon who drove Italian cars and owned boats with names like "Cardiac Arrest."

"Sarah?"

"Dr. Foster. But Sarah's fine."

He pulled out her chair with movements that suggested familiarity with upscale dining rituals. Smiled like he'd practiced in mirrors. "Lisa said you were brilliant. She didn't mention beautiful."

Foster settled into her seat and studied the wine list with the attention of someone who preferred laboratory protocols to social protocols. "Lisa exaggerates about everything."

"Including the brilliant part?"

"Especially that."

The waiter appeared with practiced silence, recognizing regular customers and first-time visitors with equal professional courtesy. David ordered wine without asking her preference—a presumption that Foster noted but didn't challenge. First date protocols required patience with social mistakes that might become relationship problems later.

"So," David said, settling back in his chair with the confidence of someone who expected the evening to proceed according to his expectations. "Longevity research. Must be exciting work."

"It is."

"I read about the FDA approval. Historic breakthrough. Your whole team must be thrilled."

Foster nodded, but her attention drifted to the couple at the next table. The woman kept checking her phone. The man's hands moved when he talked. Normal people living normal lives, unaware that everything might change soon.

The restaurant's atmosphere felt artificial compared to the honest environment of her laboratory, where equipment served functional purposes and conversations focused on empirical evidence rather than social pleasantries.

"The biotech stocks went crazy after your announcement," David continued, warming to a topic that revealed his priorities. "My broker's been calling all week about investment opportunities."

"Is that why you wanted to have dinner? Investment advice?"

David's smile faltered slightly. "Of course not. I'm just interested in your work."

Foster's phone buzzed against the table, displaying the caller ID: Daou Therapeutics Security. The timing felt wrong—security personnel rarely called researchers directly unless something required immediate attention.

"Excuse me," she said, answering with professional courtesy. "Dr. Foster."

"Dr. Foster, this is Kevin Mitchell, night security supervisor. Sorry to bother you, but we've got a situation here."

Foster frowned. Kevin's voice carried an edge she'd never heard before—tension that suggested problems beyond routine security concerns. "What kind of situation?"

"Delivery attempt. Courier showed up twenty minutes ago with genetic lab equipment. Says it's for your department. High-priority stuff that can't wait until morning."

The wine arrived while Foster processed this information. David tasted it with ceremonial attention, nodded approval, watched the sommelier pour with obvious impatience. Foster waved away her glass, focusing on the phone call that felt increasingly suspicious.

"What kind of equipment?" she asked.

"He won't say exactly. Just keeps insisting it's for Dr. Foster's special project. Emergency delivery that has to happen tonight."

Foster's frown deepened.

"Kevin, I didn't authorize any equipment delivery. We're not expecting anything."

Silence on the line, then Kevin's voice with increased tension. "That's what I figured. Guy's getting pretty agitated though. Says he's been driving all day to get here before the weekend."

"Tell him there's been a mistake. We don't accept deliveries after hours without proper authorization."

"Already did. He wants to know where he should redirect the shipment. Says his company will charge massive fees if he has to return it to the warehouse."

Foster looked across the table at David, who was pretending not to listen while obviously hanging on every word. "That's not my problem. Turn them away."

"Will do. Sorry to interrupt your evening, Dr. Foster."

Foster ended the call and found David watching her with interest that seemed more than casual curiosity.

"Work emergency?" he asked.

"Someone trying to deliver equipment we didn't order. Happens sometimes with all the suppliers wanting our business after the FDA announcement."

David nodded and raised his wine glass with flourish. "To scientific breakthroughs and the brilliant women who make them."

Foster reluctantly picked up her glass, but her attention remained focused on the phone call.

Her phone buzzed with a text message: "Call me ASAP - urgent. Kevin."

Foster excused herself and tried calling Kevin's number. It went straight to voicemail. She tried again with the same result.

A cold sensation began forming in her stomach. Kevin always answered his phone during shifts. Security protocol required constant communication, especially during unusual incidents.

She tried the main security desk. No answer.

David was studying his phone with unusual intensity when she returned to the table. He looked up as she approached, expression shifting from concentration to casual interest too quickly.

"Everything alright?" he asked.

"I need to go. Something's wrong at the lab."

David signaled for the check without argument—itself suspicious behavior for someone who had planned an expensive dinner date.

The check arrived with unusual speed. David paid cash, leaving a generous tip that suggested either wealth or urgency. They walked toward the exit while Foster's unease continued growing.

"I really did have a nice time," David said as they reached the street corner where Foster's BMW waited under a streetlight. "I hope everything works out at your lab."

Foster unlocked her car while scanning the surrounding area. The brick-lined intersection felt intimate after the restaurant's warmth, shadows pooling between historic buildings that had witnessed two centuries of Baltimore's evolution from port city to medical research center. She dropped into the driver's seat.

"Thanks for understanding about dinner."

"No problem at all. Medicine never sleeps, right?"

She was about to respond when she heard footsteps approaching rapidly from behind. Heavy boots on brick pavement. Multiple sets. Moving with purpose rather than casual Friday night wandering.

Foster turned to see two men in dark clothing advancing toward them. Both wore black jackets despite the mild evening temperature. Their hands were empty but their movements suggested weapons nearby, that particular alertness that marked professional violence.

"Dr. Foster," the taller man called, his voice carrying authority that expected compliance. "We need you to come with us."

Foster's grip tightened on her car keys as recognition flooded through her system. "I'm sorry, do I know you?"

The shorter man reached inside his jacket with movement that confirmed her fears. David stepped forward, placing himself between Foster and the approaching figures with decision that seemed reflexive rather than calculated.

"Hey, what's this about?" David asked, his voice carrying confusion that sounded genuine. "Who are you guys?"

"Step away from the vehicle, sir," the tall man ordered, his tone suggesting that compliance was expected and resistance would be addressed through escalating force. "This doesn't concern you."

"Like hell it doesn't." David moved closer to Foster's car, positioning himself to block access to her door. "Sarah, do you know these men?"

The shorter man drew a taser with practiced efficiency—black plastic and steel designed to deliver fifty thousand volts of incapacitating electricity. He aimed it at David's center mass with the steady hands of someone who had used such weapons before.

"Final warning. Step back."

David raised his hands but didn't retreat, his body language suggesting someone who had never faced serious violence but was willing to learn quickly. "Whatever this is about, we can work it out. No need for violence."

The taser fired with a sharp crack that echoed off brick walls. David convulsed as electricity coursed through his nervous system, his body going rigid before collapsing onto the brick pavement. His head struck the street with a sound like a dropped melon.

Foster screamed and tried to slam her car door, but the tall man was already there. His hand caught the door's edge, preventing her from closing it while she fumbled for the gear shift. She managed to shift into drive and pressed the accelerator.

The car lurched forward, but the man held on, running alongside while trying to maintain his grip.

Foster swerved toward parked cars, trying to knock him away, but he released the door and dove clear as the BMW scraped against a delivery truck.

Foster gunned the engine toward High Street, hoping to reach the busier area where more people might help or at least witness what was happening. Behind her, she heard shouting and car doors slamming as her attackers regrouped.

The white van pulled out of its parking space and accelerated after her with the purposeful urgency of professional pursuit. In her rearview mirror, Foster could see David lying motionless on the brick street while people began gathering around him.

She reached for her phone and dialed 911, but the van rammed her rear bumper. The impact threw her forward against the steering wheel, sending her phone flying into the passenger footwell.

The van struck again, harder this time. Foster's BMW skidded sideways, tires screaming against brick as the heavier vehicle pushed her toward the narrow alley between two historic buildings.

Her car clipped a wrought-iron fence and came to rest against a brick wall with a grinding impact that crushed the hood and killed the engine. Steam rose from the damaged radiator while Foster struggled with her seatbelt.

The van's doors slammed open, disgorging the same two men plus three additional figures in similar dark clothing. All moving toward her disabled vehicle.

Foster managed to free herself and stumble from the BMW, but her legs felt weak from adrenaline shock and the impact that had rattled her brain against her skull.

The men approached from different directions, cutting off escape routes with tactical awareness that confirmed this was a professional operation rather than opportunistic crime.

"Dr. Sarah Foster," the tall man said, not asking but confirming identity. "You're coming with us."

"I don't know what you want," Foster said, backing against the brick wall that blocked further retreat. "If it's money, I can—"

"Get her in the van."

Foster broke left, hoping to reach the mouth of the alley before they could react. She made it six steps before strong hands grabbed her arms. She twisted and kicked, landing a solid blow on someone's shin that produced a grunt but didn't break his grip.

"Help!" she shouted toward the street where a small crowd was gathering around David's unconscious form. "Someone help me! I'm Dr. Sarah Foster! I work at Daou Therapeutics!"

They wrestled her toward the van despite her struggles. She managed to grab a fire escape ladder, wrapping her arms around the metal rungs while two men tried to pry her loose.

"Remember my name!" she screamed toward the street where bystanders were beginning to notice the commotion. "Dr. Sarah Foster! Daou Therapeutics! Tell the police!"

Her fingers slipped from the ladder as they applied leverage and superior numbers. They carried her to the van and forced her inside, where the vehicle's interior revealed equipment designed for detention rather than transportation.

As the van pulled away from the alley, Foster caught a glimpse of David through the rear window. He was sitting up now, holding his head while people knelt beside him offering assistance. Blood trickled from where he'd struck the pavement, but he was conscious and moving.

The van turned onto Pratt Street and joined normal traffic flow, becoming invisible among the other vehicles carrying people to Friday night destinations. Around them, Baltimore continued its evening rhythm while one of the world's leading geneticists disappeared into captivity.

Witness

Detective Maria Bianchi found David Carpenter in the emergency room at Johns Hopkins Hospital, sitting on the edge of a gurney with a bandage covering the taser burn on his neck. The cardiac surgeon held an ice pack against a swollen lump where his head had struck the pavement, his expensive suit torn at the knee and stained with blood.

The emergency room bustled with Friday night chaos—drunk drivers, domestic violence victims, overdoses from the harbor district. But Bianchi had seen enough crime scenes to recognize when someone's story didn't match their injuries.

"Mr. Carpenter, I'm Detective Bianchi with Baltimore PD. I understand you witnessed an abduction tonight."

David looked up from the ice pack, pupils dilated but tracking normally. "Is she alright? Did you find Dr. Foster?"

"We're working on it. I need you to tell me exactly what happened, starting with the restaurant."

"Maybe I should call my attorney."

"I would highly recommend that if you've done something wrong."

"No. I haven't. I'm just being cautious."

"I understand. Shall we begin?"

David considered for a moment, then nodded.

Bianchi pulled out a digital recorder and set it on the bedside table. The red light blinked steadily in the harsh fluorescent lighting. Around them, medical staff moved with practiced efficiency between treatment bays.

"We had dinner at Marcello's," David began, wincing as he shifted position. "It was a blind date. Our mutual friend Lisa Chen set us up."

Bianchi made notes in shorthand that meant something to her and nothing to anyone else. "How long had you known Dr. Foster?"

"We'd never met before tonight. Lisa said we'd have a lot in common. Both doctors, both workaholics." David attempted a smile that didn't reach his eyes. "She was right about the workaholic part."

The detective studied David's body language, noting micro-expressions and stress indicators that suggested emotional trauma consistent with witnessing violence. "Tell me about the phone calls."

"Sarah got a call during dinner. Someone from building security about a delivery at her lab. She seemed suspicious about it."

"Suspicious how?"

David closed his eyes, remembering details that felt increasingly ominous in retrospect. "She kept frowning, asking questions. Said she hadn't ordered any equipment. The whole thing seemed to bother her."

"Did she mention what kind of equipment?"

"Genetic lab gear. The security guard said it was high-priority, couldn't wait until Monday. But Sarah was adamant she hadn't authorized anything."

Bianchi looked up from her notes. The timing felt wrong—Friday night delivery attempts for research equipment that most facilities wouldn't accept without advance authorization.

"What happened after the first call?"

"She got a text message. Same security guard, asking her to call back urgently. She tried but couldn't reach him. That's when she decided to leave."

"How did she seem at that point?"

"Worried. Maybe a little scared. She kept looking around the restaurant like she was expecting trouble."

A nurse wheeled past pushing a crash cart, the smell of antiseptic and blood hanging in the air like medical incense. Bianchi waited for the noise to fade before continuing.

"Tell me about the men who approached you."

David opened his eyes, focus sharpening as he recalled details that would haunt his sleep. "Two of them initially. Maybe six feet tall, the other shorter. Both wearing dark jackets and gloves. They knew her name."

"They called her by name specifically?"

"Dr. Foster. Not Sarah, not ma'am. They knew exactly who she was."

Bianchi felt pieces clicking into place. Random street crime didn't involve victims being addressed by professional titles. "What did they say?"

"The tall one said they needed her to come with them. When I tried to intervene, they tasered me." David touched the bandage on his neck. "Fifty thousand volts. Felt like being struck by lightning."

"Then what happened?"

"I went down hard. Couldn't move for maybe thirty seconds. But I could see and hear everything. Sarah tried to drive away, but they had a van waiting."

"Describe the van."

"White panel van, maybe a Ford Transit. No windows in the back. They used it to ram her car."

Bianchi made more notes. Professional operation—multiple vehicles, coordination, specific target identification. "How many total suspects?"

"At least five. Two who approached us initially, plus three more who came out of the van. All dressed similarly, all moving like they'd done this before."

"Military training?"

David considered this while a doctor in scrubs approached to check his pupils with a penlight. "Maybe. Or police. They communicated without talking, knew exactly what each person was supposed to do."

After the doctor left, Bianchi resumed her questioning. "Did the attackers make any demands? Ask for money, credentials, anything?"

"Nothing. They just wanted Dr. Foster." David's voice carried the confusion of someone who had witnessed something beyond his experience. "No ransom demands, no threats, no explanation."

"Any idea why someone would target her specifically?"

David was quiet for a moment, processing implications he had avoided considering. "Her research. She just received FDA approval for a longevity therapy. Revolutionary stuff that could extend human life by decades."

"Worth kidnapping someone over?"

"Worth killing for, probably. We're talking about the biggest medical breakthrough in human history."

Bianchi closed her notebook and prepared to leave. "Mr. Carpenter, I need to ask—how well do you know Lisa Chen, the woman that set you up?"

"We went to medical school together. She's been trying to set me up with someone for months. Why?"

"Just trying to understand all the connections." Bianchi stood to leave and handed him her card. "If you remember anything else, anything at all, please call me immediately."

"Detective," David called as she reached the curtain. "The way they operated tonight. This wasn't random. They came specifically for Sarah."

Bianchi nodded grimly. She'd already reached the same conclusion. Dr. Foster hadn't been the victim of random street crime—she'd been targeted by professionals who knew her schedule and habits.

The question was whether they wanted her research or wanted to prevent her from continuing it.

The hospital's main corridor buzzed with activity as Bianchi walked toward the exit. Families waited for news about loved ones. Medical staff rushed between emergencies. The ordinary drama of a Friday night in Baltimore.

The Chief of Staff's office in the West Wing maintained the understated elegance of institutional power. Dark wood paneling reflected soft light from banker's lamps while oil portraits of former presidents watched silently from gilded frames. The room carried the weight of decisions that had shaped nations and toppled governments.

Culper sat across from James Wilson, the President's chief of staff.

"The President is deeply concerned about Dr. Foster's disappearance," Wilson began, sliding a classified folder across the mahogany desk. "This represents a direct attack on American scientific leadership."

Culper opened the folder and reviewed intelligence briefings that most senators would never see. Photographs of Foster, detailed analysis of her research, FBI surveillance reports, Baltimore PD incident files.

"The longevity therapy," Culper said.

"Exactly. If foreign adversaries can steal or destroy our genetics research, America loses strategic advantages that could determine the future of human civilization."

Wilson stood and walked to the windows overlooking the Rose Garden, where autumn leaves drifted past bulletproof glass. The peaceful scene belied the urgency that had brought them together on a Saturday morning.

"Why save research that bankrupts Social Security and Medicare?" Culper asked.

Wilson turned back from the windows. "Because whoever controls longevity technology controls everything else. Economic systems, political structures, the basic hierarchy of human civilization."

"Meaning?"

"Meaning that if China develops this technology first, they can force every nation to give them anything they want. Trade deals, military bases, natural resources, territorial concessions." Wilson returned to his desk. "What government refuses Chinese demands when the alternative is watching their population age and die while Chinese citizens live for centuries?"

Culper studied Foster's photograph. Intelligent eyes, determined expression, someone who had dedicated her life to pushing the boundaries of human possibility.

"Ultimate bargaining chip."

"Exactly. China tells Germany: give us your manufacturing technology or your citizens die at eighty while ours live to three hundred. They tell Japan: hand over your semiconductor industry or watch your economy collapse under demographic pressure." Wilson's voice revealed someone who understood power at its most fundamental level. "Every nation becomes a client state begging for access to immortality."

"And if America controls it?"

"We decide the terms. We choose our allies. We determine which governments survive and which ones face extinction through natural mortality."

"Another weapon of mass destruction?"

"Would you rather China or Russia controlled it?"

"No."

"Neither would the President."

"FBI declined the case," Culper noted.

Wilson's expression hardened. "Political complications with Senator Bradley. Director Harrison doesn't want congressional hearings about surveillance overreach."

"So federal law enforcement abandons a kidnapped scientist because of political pressure."

"Which is why you're here. When legal channels fail, we need operational alternatives."

Culper closed the folder. "Time constraints?"

"Unknown. If foreign agents have extracted what they need from Dr. Foster, they'll eliminate evidence and disappear."

"Resources?"

"Black budget, completely deniable funding. Presidential authorization for any measures necessary within reason."

"Oversight?"

"None. This conversation never happened."

Culper stood, preparing to leave. "And if the rescue fails?"

Wilson met his gaze. "Then China gains the power to extort any concession from any nation. They become the brokers of human mortality."

Culper moved toward the door. "Understood."

Some wars were fought by soldiers who couldn't be acknowledged by the governments they served. Some victories required methods that democracy couldn't officially sanction.

The longevity therapy represented more than scientific breakthrough. It was leverage over every government and every population on earth.

That leverage was worth any price to obtain. And any price to prevent others from obtaining it first.

The lighthouse stood above the rocky shoreline like a tower reaching toward Heaven, its ancient stone walls bearing witness to more than a century of storms and calms. Frank Kane worked at its base, welding support brackets to the iron framework that would eventually hold new stairs. The acetylene torch cast harsh shadows against curved stone walls as orange sparks fell like dying stars.

The sound of rotor blades made him shut off the torch and listen. The rhythmic thumping grew louder as it approached from the south. Frank set down his equipment and walked to the doorway.

A black military helicopter descended toward the cleared area beside his pickup truck, rotors whipping the autumn air into miniature cyclones that scattered leaves and dust. The aircraft settled onto the gravel.

The feral cat appeared from wherever it had been hiding, took one look at the machine, and hissed before retreating to higher ground on the scaffolding. Smart animal. Knew trouble when it saw it.

Culper emerged from the helicopter's passenger compartment as the rotors wound down. The pilot remained at the controls, engine idling.

"Frank."

Frank grunted acknowledgment and returned to organizing his welding tools. The conversation could wait. Metal needed cooling before it could be safely handled, and hasty decisions led to burned fingers or worse mistakes.

"I have a mission for you."

Frank shook his head without looking up. The torch needed cleaning, gas connections required checking, everything had its proper sequence. Order imposed on chaos through attention to detail.

Culper ignored the negative response.

"Dr. Sarah Foster was abducted yesterday in Baltimore. She's a geneticist working on longevity therapy at Daou Therapeutics. We think foreign agents may have taken her for her research."

Frank continued his equipment maintenance, checking gas connections and cleaning torch tips. The ritual of tool care gave his hands something to do while his mind processed unwanted information.

"Professional operation," Culper continued. "Multiple personnel, advance intelligence about her schedule and habits. This wasn't random street crime."

Frank hung his welding helmet on a scaffold pole and began coiling air hoses. Each movement precise, economical, the kind of efficiency learned through years of practice in situations where mistakes meant death.

"FBI won't take the case. Political pressure from Senator Bradley about federal harassment of medical researchers."

"No," Frank said, the word coming out like gravel scraped across concrete.

Culper ignored the negative response once again.

"Dr. Foster's research could extend human life by centuries. Foreign adversaries want to steal it or destroy it."

Frank moved to his toolbox and began organizing wrenches by size. Chrome steel in perfect rows, each tool in its designated place.

"Forty-eight hours maximum before they extract the information they seek and kill her. Local police don't have the resources or expertise to find her in time."

Frank looked up, meeting Culper's gaze with eyes that had seen too much death in too many places. "No."

"Frank, this woman—"

"No." Frank returned to his tools, methodically cleaning the torch tip with wire brush strokes that rang like small bells against metal.

"She's a scientist. Civilian. Kidnapped by professionals who will torture her for information before they kill her."

Frank tested the gas connections. Each fitting checked twice, safety protocols that had kept him alive through decades of dangerous work.

"The longevity research could save millions of lives," Culper pressed. "Or it could be used by foreign governments against American interests."

Frank coiled the acetylene hose in perfect spirals. Order imposed through repetition and focus. The lighthouse restoration needed finishing. Stone required repointing where winter had cracked mortar joints.

"Forty-eight hours, Frank. After that, she's dead and the research disappears into Chinese laboratories."

Frank secured his equipment and walked toward the lighthouse entrance. The cat followed, understanding that conversations were ending and decisions had been made.

"Find someone else," Frank said without turning around.

Culper's voice carried across the gravel. "There is no one else."

Frank paused at the lighthouse door. The helicopter's rotors continued their idle rhythm, waiting for orders to depart or remain.

"Every agency that should protect American scientists has been neutralized by political pressure. FBI won't investigate. Local police lack resources. She's alone except for what we can provide."

Frank's hand rested on the lighthouse door handle. Inside, restoration work waited. Honest labor that created rather than destroyed. Projects that built rather than demolished.

"Alright," Frank said finally, the words carried away by salt wind.

"Then you'll take the mission?"

Frank turned and nodded once. A simple gesture that transferred responsibility for Dr. Foster's life from the government agencies that couldn't act to the man who would act regardless of official sanction or personal cost.

Culper handed him a thick manila envelope. "Everything we know. Foster's background, abduction details, witness statements. Baltimore PD is cooperating unofficially."

Frank opened the envelope and reviewed photographs and documents with methodical attention. Foster's face stared back at him from official portraits—serious expression, intelligent eyes, someone who believed science could save the world and was learning that some people preferred the world unsaved.

"Grab your gear and I'll give you a lift."

"No. I'll drive."

"Frank, we don't have time for—"

"I'll drive."

"Okay. Fine. I'll meet you in Baltimore. But hurry, Frank. Foster doesn't have much time."

The helicopter's rotors began spinning up, preparing for departure. Culper walked backward toward the aircraft.

Frank headed toward the lighthouse door. The cat followed at a distance, keeping well clear of the aircraft.

The helicopter lifted off, carrying Culper back toward whatever crisis required his attention next. Frank watched it disappear over the treeline.

The cat trailed behind with suspicious yellow eyes. Both of them understood that their quiet life was ending again, interrupted by the demands of a world that preferred to solve its problems through violence rather than patience.

War never stayed away long. It just waited for the next excuse to return, dressed in the language of national security and strategic necessity.

Frank found David Carpenter in the hospital parking garage after his discharge. The cardiac surgeon walked carefully toward his BMW, favoring his left side where he'd hit the pavement. His expensive suit had been replaced by hospital scrubs and a visitor's windbreaker that hung loose on his frame.

Frank approached slowly, hands visible, trying not to appear threatening. His massive frame and scarred face made that difficult under normal circumstances. In a dimly lit parking garage, it was nearly impossible.

"David Carpenter."

David turned, startled by the gravelly voice emerging from the shadows between concrete pillars. He took an involuntary step backward, hand reaching toward his car keys with the instinctive movement of someone who had learned to fear unexpected encounters.

"Investigating Foster's abduction."

"I already talked to the police. Detective Bianchi has my complete statement."

"Need clarification."

David unlocked his car but remained standing beside it.

"What kind of clarification?"

"Phone call. Equipment delivery."

"What about it?"

Frank studied David's face carefully, noting micro-expressions and involuntary muscle tension. Signs of deception learned through years of interrogating people who lied for a living. Small tells that separated truth from fiction.

David's pupils dilated slightly when Frank mentioned the phone call. Classic stress response that indicated the subject was uncomfortable with the topic. Not necessarily lying, but definitely holding something back.

"Time?"

"Around nine PM. We were just beginning our dinner at Marcello's."

"Duration?"

"Maybe two minutes. Sarah talked to their security guard about some delivery she hadn't authorized."

Frank nodded, watching David's eyes for the telltale movements that indicated deception. Truth so far, but something underneath. Like sediment in still water that became visible when disturbed.

"Security guard's name?"

"Kevin something. Kevin Mitchell, I think."

"Response?"

"She told them to refuse the delivery. Said she hadn't ordered anything and they should turn away whoever was trying to make the delivery."

Frank was quiet for a moment, processing information while maintaining eye contact. The silence stretched until David felt compelled to fill it with additional details—a common interrogation technique that often produced more honest responses than direct questions.

"Then she got a text message from the same guard, asking her to call back urgently."

"Call back?"

David hesitated slightly—a pause that lasted half a second too long but felt like minutes under Frank's unwavering stare. "She tried, but got voicemail. That's when she decided to leave the restaurant."

Frank noticed the hesitation, the minor change in breathing pattern. Classic indicators that someone was editing their story, leaving out details or changing timelines to avoid uncomfortable questions.

"Describe attackers."

"Two initially. Dark clothing, gloves. One tall, maybe six feet. The other shorter, stockier build. The tall one used a taser on me."

"Say anything else?"

"Just that they needed Dr. Foster to come with them. Nothing about ransom or demands or what they wanted."

Frank continued studying David's face. The man was holding something back—question was whether it was embarrassment, guilt, or something more dangerous. People lied for many reasons, but witnesses to kidnappings usually wanted to help unless they had something to hide.

"Before dinner?"

"I'm sorry?"

"Where were you?"

David's confusion seemed genuine, but Frank had learned to distrust emotional responses that appeared too perfectly timed. "At home. Getting ready for the date."

"How long knowing Foster?"

"We'd never met before tonight. Blind date arranged by a mutual friend, Lisa Chen from medical school."

Frank filed that information away. Too many coincidences in kidnapping cases usually meant careful planning rather than bad luck. Professional kidnappers didn't rely on chance encounters—they created opportunities through manipulation and surveillance.

"I want Dr. Foster found safely," said David.

Frank nodded and walked away without further conversation, leaving David standing beside his car in the parking garage's artificial light. But he didn't go far. From the stairwell, Frank had a clear view of David's BMW through the reinforced glass windows.

He waited.

Seven minutes later, David made a phone call from his car. Brief conversation, maybe thirty seconds. Animated gestures visible through the windshield despite the distance. Then he drove away, but not toward his home address listed in the police report.

Frank followed at a distance, using traffic and natural camouflage to avoid detection. The Imperial's bulk made stealth difficult, but Frank understood how to use space between the cars to remain invisible to casual observation.

David drove to a pay phone outside a convenience store in Fell's Point and made another call. Longer this time, nearly five minutes. More animated gestures, obvious stress in his body language. Someone was receiving information that caused significant anxiety.

When David finished and drove away, Frank approached the pay phone, deposited a quarter, and dialed star-69. The automated voice provided the last number called.

Frank dialed it.

"You've reached Whitfield Capital. Please leave a message and someone will return your call during normal business hours."

Frank hung up and climbed back into the Imperial. He studied the file Culper had given him. He had recognized the name Whitfield. The file identified Marcus Whitfield as a venture capitalist with a substantial investment in Daou Therapeutics.

Frank dialed Culper's secure number on his cell phone.

"What do you need?" Culper answered.

"David Carpenter. Background check."

"Hold on." Frank could hear Culper typing on his computer, accessing databases that contained information civilians never saw. "Carpenter, David Michael. Age thirty-four. Johns Hopkins Medical School. Cardiac surgeon at Baltimore General."

"Financial status?"

More typing. "That's interesting. Three months ago, Carpenter was questioned about injuries he incurred. The injuries weren't life threatening but were painful. His file suggests he may have had a run-in with a loan shark or a heavy-handed debt collector."

"Financial trouble?" Frank said.

"Seems that way. Maybe gambling." Culper's keyboard clicked steadily. "Credit reports show mounting debt. Medical school loans, personal credit cards maxed out. His condo in mortgaged to the hilt."

Frank studied Carpenter's photograph from the police file. Expensive suit, confident smile, the appearance of success masking deeper problems.

"His medical practice is profitable, but he's leveraged beyond his income capacity."

Frank made notes in his phone. Desperate people made convenient tools for those willing to exploit their vulnerabilities.

"Whitfield Capital," Frank said.

"Why Whitfield?"

"Carpenter called Whitfield."

"Interesting."

Culper's typing became more intensive. "Marcus Whitfield, founder and CEO of Whitfield Capital. Major investor in biotech companies, including Daou Therapeutics."

"Connection to Carpenter?"

"Not showing direct financial ties, but..." Culper paused. "Whitfield Capital has shell companies that provide personal loans to high-net-worth individuals. Medical professionals, specifically."

Frank felt pieces clicking into place. "He owes Whitfield."

"Or someone connected to Whitfield. The debt structure suggests professional money lending rather than traditional banks."

Frank hung up without saying anything more. He started the Imperial's engine, but sat for a moment to consider his next move.

David Carpenter thought he was clever but was clearly panicking. He was an amateur playing in a professional's game. He would provide the information Frank needed, voluntarily or otherwise. The only question was how much pain would be required to encourage his cooperation.

Dr. Foster's life depended on extracting truth from someone who preferred comfortable lies. Frank intended to make lying significantly more uncomfortable than honesty.

Frank threw the Imperial in drive and drove away.

Frank parked the Imperial and waited until David returned to his Federal Hill condominium building near the harbor. The converted warehouse offered multiple entry points and minimal security—perfect for what Frank needed to accomplish without creating unnecessary complications.

He parked the Imperial three blocks away and approached on foot through shadows that seemed to pool around his massive frame. David's condo was on the third floor, corner unit with large windows facing the Inner Harbor. Light glowed behind closed blinds, suggesting someone home and unprepared for visitors.

Frank entered through the building's service entrance using lock picks to gain access. The security system was basic consumer-grade equipment, easily bypassed with wire cutters and electrical tape applied to circuits that weren't designed to resist professional penetration.

The elevator carried him silently to the third floor. Carpeted hallways muffled his footsteps as he approached David's door. Television noise from adjacent units provided audio cover for any minor disturbances that might alert neighbors to unusual activity.

David's lock required more sophisticated tools. Frank used a tension wrench and rake picks to manipulate the pin tumblers while listening for the subtle clicks that indicated proper alignment. Locks were just metal puzzles. Patience always solved puzzles if you understood the underlying principles.

The condo was expensive and sterile. Modern furniture arranged for maximum visual impact rather than comfort. Stainless steel kitchen appliances that looked unused. Harbor views through floor-to-ceiling windows. The kind of place that impressed dates and visiting colleagues but revealed nothing about the person who lived there.

Frank found David in the bathroom, standing under a rainfall shower head. Steam filled the space like fog, creating artificial weather inside climate-controlled luxury.

Frank waited silently in the bedroom doorway.

When David emerged with a towel around his waist, water still dripping from his hair, Frank was leaning against the dresser like a piece of furniture that had been there all along.

"Quiet," Frank said.

David froze, hand reaching instinctively for something to cover himself more completely. His brain processed the impossibility of Frank's presence—doors locked, security system armed, no sounds of forced entry. "What do you want?"

"Truth."

"I told you everything I know about Dr. Foster's abduction."

Frank shook his head slowly. "Get dressed."

"I'm not going anywhere with you."

Frank drew one of the Redhawks and held it casually at his side. Not pointing it at David, but making its presence unmistakably clear. The revolver's mass was intimidating.

"Get dressed."

David moved to his walk-in closet with careful, controlled movements. No sudden gestures that might be misinterpreted as aggression. His hands shook slightly as he selected jeans and a sweater, the tremor revealing fear that adrenaline couldn't completely suppress.

"Where are we going?"

Frank declined to answer.

"Look, I don't know what you think I'm hiding, but I told you everything about the abduction."

Frank remained silent while David dressed. Words were weapons that should be conserved for maximum impact. Silence created pressure.

"My patients need me. I have surgery scheduled Monday morning."

Frank said nothing.

David finished dressing and turned to face Frank. The cardiac surgeon was trying to project calm authority, but sweat beaded on his forehead despite the condo's air conditioning. Fear had a scent that Frank recognized from countless interrogations.

"This is kidnapping. You're committing a federal crime."

Frank still said nothing.

Frank gestured toward the door with his free hand. David walked ahead of him, moving slowly, looking for opportunities to escape or call for help that wouldn't come. The building's hallways remained empty, other residents asleep or occupied with their own Friday night activities.

In the elevator, David tried again. "Whatever you want to know, I'll tell you here. You don't need to take me anywhere."

Frank pressed the button for the parking garage without responding. Conversation would come later, in a place designed for extracting information rather than maintaining comfortable deceptions.

"I swear to you, I'm telling the truth about Dr. Foster's abduction. I want her found safely."

The elevator doors opened onto the garage's concrete tomb. Frank guided David toward the exit with a hand on his shoulder, feeling tension in muscles that expected violence but couldn't prepare for what was coming.

"Please," David said as they reached Frank's car. "I'm a doctor. I save lives for a living."

Frank opened the Imperial's trunk, revealing plastic zip ties, duct tape, and other restraint equipment.

"So do I," Frank said.

David looked at the restraint equipment and understood that his comfortable world of medical practice and suburban safety was ending. Whatever Frank intended, it would happen in a place where David's professional status and social connections meant nothing.

Frank secured David in the trunk with zip ties and duct tape, positioning him for transport while ensuring adequate air circulation. Professional abduction required attention to details that separated successful operations from newspaper headlines about accidental deaths.

The Imperial moved through Baltimore's empty streets like a mechanical predator.

David had made choices that connected him to Dr. Foster's abduction. Frank intended to understand those choices and extract information that might save her life.

The abandoned meat processing plant sat in Baltimore's industrial district like a concrete monument to economic decay. Broken windows stared blindly at surrounding warehouses while weeds pushed through cracked asphalt where delivery trucks had once loaded beef destined for suburban tables.

Frank had chosen the location because sound didn't carry through the thick concrete walls and visitors were unlikely. The building's isolation made it perfect for conversations that couldn't happen in civilized settings.

Parking the Imperial at the loading dock, Frank opened the trunk and pulled David out. David was wide-eyed when he saw the abandoned plant. It looked like something out a horror film.

Frank set David in a chair and secured him with more zip ties, positioning him beneath an overhead chain hoist system that had once moved cattle carcasses through the slaughter process. Ancient motors and pulleys waited silently for commands that would never come from their original operators.

Frank removed the duct tape over David's mouth, then removed his KA-BAR fighting knife from its sheath and began sharpening it on a whetstone. The steel sang against stone in the cavernous space, each stroke ringing like a meditation bell in the industrial cathedral that had once processed life into packaged meat.

"This is insane," David said, testing his restraints with careful movements that revealed his growing understanding of the situation. "You can't do this to me. I have constitutional rights."

Frank continued working the blade, checking its edge with professional attention. Seven inches of high-carbon steel that had drawn blood in a dozen countries where constitutional rights meant nothing to people who understood that survival required practical solutions to immediate problems.

"I want a lawyer. I want to call my attorney right now."

Frank said nothing as he stood and walked to the manual chain hoist, testing the ancient mechanism. He pulled the chain hand over hand, steel links clanking through their tracks like mechanical ghosts haunting the industrial space where thousands of animals had died according to schedule. David lifted off the ground and hung in the air, swaying slowly back and forth.

"You can't torture information out of me. Whatever you think I know, this isn't how civilized people get answers."

Frank returned to his knife, stroking the blade against the whetstone with meditative rhythm. The sound echoed off concrete walls that had witnessed decades of professional slaughter conducted with efficiency.

"I'm a cardiac surgeon. I save lives every day. Children who need heart operations. Mothers with coronary disease. You're threatening to torture someone who dedicates his life to helping people."

Frank tested the knife's sharpness by shaving a thin curl from a piece of scrap wood. The blade passed through fiber like it was made of air, cutting cleanly without resistance. Satisfied with the edge, he approached David's chair.

"I told you everything I know about Dr. Foster's abduction. The phone calls, the men who took her, the white van. Every detail I remember."

Frank cut David's shirt away with the blade moving close enough to feel cold against skin but never quite touching. Cotton fell away in strips, revealing the chest and arms of someone who spent more time in operating rooms than gyms.

"Please," David whispered. "I'm telling the truth."

The chair swayed slightly, metal creaking under human weight. David looked down at the stained floor below.

"Jesus Christ," David gasped. "Put me down."

Frank kept sharpening his knife, letting the sound fill the space between them. Steel against stone. Ancient rhythms that preceded violence.

"Okay!" David shouted, voice echoing off concrete walls designed to contain sounds that society preferred not to hear. "Okay, there's more. I wasn't completely honest with the police."

Frank looked up from his blade but said nothing.

"I was paid to make sure she left the restaurant at a specific time and witness the abduction. They wanted to control the narrative."

"Who?" Frank asked.

"I don't know names. Contact through intermediaries, payments in cash. I needed the money," David said, while avoiding eye contact. "I have debts. They offered one hundred and fifty thousand dollars for one evening's work."

"You're lying," said Frank as he placed the knife's blade against David's bare chest.

"He's kill me if I tell you his name."

"I'll kill you if you don't."

"Okay, okay. It was Whitfield. Marcus Whitfield."

"Why?"

"I don't know. I just did what he asked. I had no choice. I owe him money. A lot of money."

Frank grunted. With a flash of the blade, he cut the plastic ties restraining David. He fell to the hard concrete floor with a whimper.

Frank holstered the knife and headed toward the exit, leaving David on the floor.

"What happens now?" David called after him.

Frank paused at the doorway and looked back at the cardiac surgeon laying on the stained floor.

"Confess to police."

"And if I don't?"

"I cut off your fingers."

"Okay. No need for that. I'll tell the police what I know. But what happens if Whitfield's men come after me for talking?"

"Run," said Frank, then left.

Frank sat in the Imperial outside the abandoned meat processing plant and dialed Culper's secure number.

"Status?" Culper answered.

"Carpenter talked."

"And?"

"Whitfield hired him."

"Marcus Whitfield of Whitfield Capital?"

"Yes."

Culper was quiet for a moment, processing the implications. "How much did Whitfield pay him?"

"One fifty. Cash."

"For what exactly?"

Frank started the Imperial and pulled away from the industrial district. "Witness. Control the narrative."

"So Whitfield orchestrated the entire abduction?"

"Yes."

"Why?"

"I don't know."

"He has a huge amount invested in the therapy. Why would he want to endanger his investment with the disappearance of Foster? Especially right before their IPO."

"Stupid is as stupid does."

"No. It's not that easy. There's something we're not seeing."

"Yes."

Frank drove through Baltimore's empty streets while Culper digested the information.

"Frank, if Marcus Whitfield's behind Foster's abduction, this isn't foreign espionage. It's a domestic conspiracy of some sort."

"Motive?"

"You got me. But if we are going after Whitfield we're going to need strong evidence that he is involved. His attorneys will tie our prosecutors up in knots."

"I'll find evidence."

Frank ended the call and drove toward Daou Therapeutics.

Tracking

Frank arrived at Daou Therapeutics at two AM when the building stood empty except for night security. Downtown Baltimore slept around the glass tower while inside, fluorescent lights created islands of illumination in an ocean of darkness.

The parking garage was nearly deserted. Frank's footsteps echoed off concrete walls as he approached the security desk in the main lobby. Behind bulletproof glass, a heavyset man in his fifties read a paperback novel while nursing coffee from a thermos.

Frank tapped on the glass.

Kevin Mitchell looked up, startled by the massive figure standing in front of him and said, "Building's closed, sir. If you have business here, you'll need to come back during regular hours."

"Foster's abduction. Delivery attempt."

Mitchell set down his book—a detective novel, ironic under the circumstances—and straightened in his chair. "Of course. Terrible thing about Dr. Foster. She's good people, always treated security staff with respect."

"The delivery."

Mitchell opened a logbook and flipped back several pages. Handwritten entries in careful script, the kind of documentation that old-school security guards maintained out of professional pride.

"Courier showed up around eight-thirty, said he had genetic lab equipment for Dr. Foster's special project. High-priority delivery that couldn't wait until Monday."

"Describe him."

"White male, maybe early thirties. Professional appearance, proper uniform, official-looking paperwork. But something felt wrong about the whole situation."

"What?"

"Timing, mainly. We don't get equipment deliveries at night unless there's advance notice and special authorization from department heads. This guy just showed up expecting us to accept a delivery worth hundreds of thousands of dollars."

"And?"

"I called Dr. Foster to verify. Company policy for any unusual delivery requests." Mitchell turned the logbook around so Frank could see the entry. "She said she hadn't authorized anything and told me to turn them away."

"Delivery company?"

Mitchell reached into a desk drawer and pulled out a clipboard with delivery forms. "Made him sign our visitor log even though I wasn't accepting the shipment. Standard security protocol for anyone who enters the building."

Frank examined the signature and delivery slip. "Johnson Medical Equipment Sales and Rental" with a local address and phone number written in block letters that suggested deliberate anonymity.

"You verify?"

"Called the company Saturday morning after I heard about Dr. Foster's abduction on the news. Phone number's disconnected, address turns out to be a vacant lot in East Baltimore."

Frank photographed the delivery slip with his phone. "The courier?"

"He seemed surprised when I called Dr. Foster. Like he expected her to authorize the delivery without question. And he kept asking where I should redirect the shipment if she wasn't accepting it here."

"You said?"

"Nothing. Told him to contact Dr. Foster directly during business hours if he wanted to arrange proper delivery through official channels."

Frank studied the visitor log, noting the time stamps and signature.

"His reaction?"

"Disappointed, maybe a little angry. But he left without making trouble. Professional about it."

Frank looked up from the paperwork. "Security footage?"

Mitchell led him to the security office behind the main desk. Banks of monitors displayed feeds from cameras throughout the building and parking areas. The night guard accessed archived recordings and fast-forwarded to Friday evening's delivery attempt.

Frank watched the courier on screen. Average height and build, nothing distinctive about his appearance.

"Copy?"

"Sure. Just be a minute."

Mitchell burned the video files onto a disc while Frank continued reviewing the recordings frame by frame looking for any clue that would help him locate Dr. Foster.

"Here you go," Mitchell said, handing Frank the disc. "Hope this helps find Dr. Foster."

Frank pocketed the disc and headed toward the lobby doors.

"Mr. Kane," Mitchell called as Frank reached the exit. "Do you think she's still alive?"

Frank paused with his hand on the door. Outside, Baltimore's downtown core stretched dark and empty in all directions. Office buildings stood like glass monuments to commerce while their human occupants slept safely in suburban homes. Only security guards, janitors, and predators moved through the urban landscape after midnight.

"I hope."

Frank climbed into the Imperial and drove off. He pulled in front of a vacant lot where weeds pushed through cracked asphalt and parked. It would be dawn soon. He considered going back to his hotel for a couple of hours sleep. It wasn't worth the effort. Instead, he lowered the driver's seat and closed his eyes. Like most veteran soldiers, Frank could sleep anywhere at any time. His back would be sore when he woke, but he didn't care. A little back pain was nothing compared to the pain from his old wounds. Just one more thing to ignore. He was asleep two minutes later.

Frank slept. The car's bulk blocked most streetlight, creating shadows dark enough for rest between missions that never seemed to end.

A tap on the driver's window woke him. Frank opened his eyes and saw a flashlight beam cutting through the darkness and shining in his eyes. Behind it stood a security guard in a uniform that suggested private patrol rather than municipal police.

Frank rolled down the window halfway.

"You can't sleep here," the guard said. He was young, maybe twenty-five, with the kind of aggressive posture that came from wearing a badge without understanding its limitations.

Frank said nothing.

"This is private property. You need to move along."

Frank looked around the empty street. No buildings, no businesses, no reason for security patrols except to hassle people who had nowhere else to go.

"I said move along." The guard tapped his baton against the window frame. "Get out of the car. I want to see some ID."

Frank opened the door slowly and unfolded his massive frame from the Imperial's interior. Six feet seven inches, four hundred pounds of muscle and bone that cast a shadow over the guard like an eclipse.

The guard's eyes widened. His hand tightened on the baton as he realized he'd made a serious miscalculation about who he was dealing with.

Fear made him stupid.

"Put your hands on the hood of your car," demanded the guard.

"No," said Frank after looking around for security camera and witnesses. There were none.

"Fine. Have it your way, Lurch."

The guard swung his baton at Frank's head.

Frank caught the weapon mid-swing and drove his other fist into the guard's solar plexus. The man folded around the impact and dropped to the cracked asphalt, gasping for air that wouldn't come. He passed out.

Frank snapped the baton over his knee and tossed the pieces beside the unconscious guard. He climbed back into the Imperial and drove away, leaving the man beside his patrol car in the vacant lot where nobody would find him until daylight.

Some people learned respect through education. Others required more direct instruction.

Frank drove through the warehouse district as morning shift workers arrived. Truck drivers, dock workers, warehouse supervisors beginning another day of honest labor.

The warehouse sat among similar structures near the port, indistinguishable from dozens of others housing auto parts distributors, import companies, and storage facilities.

Frank found Johnson Medical Equipment Sales and Rental in an industrial park. The building was legitimate—trucks in the loading dock, employees moving equipment in and out of a warehouse, the organized chaos of a functioning business.

The receptionist directed him to the shipping department where a supervisor named Martinez reviewed delivery records on a computer terminal surrounded by invoices and shipping manifests.

"Dr. Foster's order," Martinez said, pulling up the file. "High-end genetic analysis equipment. We've done business with her before. Always shipped to Daou Therapeutics."

"Friday night," Frank said.

"Right. Got a call around seven PM. Woman said the delivery address had changed. Emergency relocation."

Frank studied the shipping records. The equipment had been expensive, specialized, the kind of gear that required advance ordering and careful handling.

"Verify caller?"

Martinez shifted uncomfortably. "She knew the order details. Equipment specifications, delivery schedules, billing information. Sounded legitimate."

"New address?"

"Industrial warehouse in East Baltimore. Temporary research facility while one of the labs at Daou was being renovated."

Frank looked up from the paperwork. Martinez was nervous now, understanding that his company had been manipulated into participating in something that required investigation.

"Who took call?"

"Tommy Barnes. Night shift shipping clerk. He'll have the redirected address."

Martinez led Frank to a cluttered desk where Barnes sat updating delivery schedules. The clerk was young, maybe early twenties, with the eager efficiency of someone trying to impress supervisors.

"Tommy, this is Frank Kane. He needs to ask about Foster's delivery."

Barnes looked up from his computer. "The address change? Woman called around seven. Said Dr. Foster needed the equipment delivered to a temporary lab."

"Address," Frank said.

Barnes pulled up the delivery record. "2247 Industrial Boulevard. Chesapeake Research Solutions."

Frank memorized the address and left the shipping office. Someone had used Foster's previous ordering history to redirect expensive research gear to a new location.

The trail was getting warmer.

Frank sat in the Imperial outside Johnson Medical reviewing the warehouse address he'd obtained from the shipping clerk. He dialed Culper's secure number.

"Update," Culper answered.

"Equipment redirected. Warehouse address."

"What equipment?"

"Foster's order. Genetic lab gear. Someone called Friday night. Changed delivery location."

Culper was quiet for a moment, considering. "I don't see how equipment delivery connects to Foster's abduction, but it's worth checking out. What's the address?"

"Chesapeake Research Solutions. Industrial Boulevard."

"Okay. I'll pull up the company's business records and see what I can find."

"Going in."

"Wait for backup, Frank. It could be a trap. I can have a tactical team there in two hours."

"No."

Frank started the Imperial's engine. The warehouse might contain Foster or evidence of where she was being held. Two hours could mean the difference between rescue and recovery of a body.

"Frank, if this is connected to Whitfield and he has professional security, you could be walking into an ambush."

"Won't matter."

"At least do reconnaissance first. Don't go in blind."

Frank ended the call and drove toward the industrial district. Culper meant well, but backup teams required coordination, authorization, time that Foster didn't have.

Foster had been missing for over twenty-four hours. Every minute of delay decreased her chances of survival. Professional kidnappers didn't keep victims alive longer than necessary once they'd extracted the information they needed.

The warehouse was either empty or occupied by people who had answers about Foster's location. Frank would find out which within the hour.

After parking the Imperial two blocks away, Frank approached Chesapeake Research Solutions on foot through the maze of shipping containers and industrial equipment that cluttered the port district. Morning fog rolled in from the harbor, providing natural concealment as he moved toward the building's loading dock area.

The main overhead doors were closed, but a personnel entrance showed signs of recent use—fresh scuff marks on concrete steps, disturbed dust patterns around the doorframe. Frank tested the handle and found it locked. He pulled out his lock picks and went to work. After a moment, the lock clicked open.

He drew both Redhawks and opened the door slowly, letting his eyes adjust to the interior lighting. The entrance led to a corridor lined with office spaces containing basic furniture but no personal belongings. The offices were unoccupied.

Frank moved through the corridor toward the main warehouse space, listening for voices, footsteps, machinery, anything that might indicate activity. The building hummed with the sound of operating equipment, but so far he hadn't seen anybody.

He reached the end of the corridor and peered through a window into the warehouse proper. What he saw stopped him cold.

The warehouse had been converted into a sophisticated genetics laboratory. Stainless steel equipment worth millions of dollars, computer workstations running complex analysis software, DNA sequencing machines, climate-controlled storage units containing samples and compounds.

As he surveyed the lab, he saw something that surprised him even more... Dr. Sarah Foster examining a chimpanzee on a steel table while a video camera documented everything. But there were no guards around her. She didn't seem to be under watch of any kind.

Frank entered the lab space with weapons ready, scanning for immediate threats while processing what he was seeing. Foster wore a hazmat suit with a respirator, completely focused on the dying animal before her.

The chimpanzee looked ancient. Gray fur, wrinkled skin, hands that trembled with what appeared to be severe arthritis. But something was wrong with the picture. The animal's eyes were young, alert, terrified.

Foster spoke into the camera as she examined the dying primate.

"Subject Seven shows complete cellular breakdown consistent with accelerated aging protocols. Organ failure progressing on schedule. Time from initial exposure to terminal symptoms: four hours, seventeen minutes."

The chimpanzee's breathing became labored, then stopped entirely. Its body went limp on the steel table as Foster documented the exact time of death.

She looked up and saw Frank approaching with weapons drawn. Her face showed complete shock.

"You shouldn't be in here. Who are you? What do you want?"

"You weren't abducted," Frank said, realizing.

"Are you with the police? FBI?"

"No. Rescue you."

"Well, as you can see that's not necessary. You need to leave now."

"No. Not without you."

Foster backed away from the examination table, fear replacing surprise in her expression. She slammed her palm against a red emergency button mounted on the wall. Sirens wailed throughout the building as emergency lights bathed everything in hellish red.

"You're with them?" said Frank.

"I'm not going with you. You should leave before security arrives."

"No."

She sprinted through a doorway, ran deeper into the laboratory, disappearing behind equipment racks and chemical storage units. Frank pursued, but his mind churned with confusion. Nothing about this matched what he'd expected to find.

The sound of boots on concrete announced incoming security personnel. Three men in tactical gear and wearing full-face respirators burst through the main laboratory entrance, automatic weapons raised. They moved with professional coordination, spreading out to establish overlapping fields of fire.

Seeing an intruder, they opened fire immediately at Frank, muzzle flashes strobing in the laboratory's fluorescent lighting. Bullets sparked off steel equipment and shattered glass containers as Frank dove behind a DNA analyzer.

Frank rolled left and came up firing. The first Redhawk fired once, its .44 magnum round taking the nearest gunman's head apart in a spray of blood and bone fragments that painted nearby computer monitors red. The massive bullet's impact threw the body backward into a centrifuge unit with enough force to crack the steel housing.

The second man turned toward Frank's muzzle flash, raising his weapon. Frank's second shot caught him center mass, the heavy round punching through body armor and dropping him instantly. Blood pooled on the polished floor and flowed beneath equipment.

The third man had taken cover behind a laboratory bench filled with delicate instruments. He opened fire with an automatic rifle, bullets sparking off steel equipment and shattering glass containers filled with chemical compounds.

Frank rolled behind a different workstation as rounds chewed through the space where he'd been standing. Chemical smells filled the air as damaged containers leaked their contents, creating toxic clouds.

Frank coughed heavily. His mouth filled with saliva

More security personnel arrived through side entrances. Frank counted at least six additional shooters moving through the equipment maze. Professional killers rather than rent-a-cops.

They concentrated their fire on Frank's last known position, forcing him to move constantly through the maze of expensive machinery. Bullets sparked off steel surfaces and shattered monitoring equipment worth hundreds of thousands of dollars.

Frank emerged from cover and fired both Redhawks simultaneously at two men flanking his position. The massive rounds tore through laboratory equipment and human targets with equal efficiency.

Frank reloaded behind an industrial centrifuge while automatic weapons fire chewed through everything around him. He had no idea where Foster had gone, but he had to find her. He had to know the truth.

One of the remaining gunmen spun as Frank's .44 magnum round caught his shoulder, his finger locked on the trigger of his automatic rifle as he fell. The dying man's weapon sprayed bullets wildly across the laboratory, sparks flying as rounds struck steel surfaces, shattered lab windows, and pitted concrete walls. One burst caught a pressurized acetylene tank.

Seeing the gas spraying from the hole in the tank, Frank ran toward an industrial autoclave chamber, yanking open the heavy steel door to reveal trays of sterilized glassware and surgical instruments. He pulled the trays out and dropped them onto the floor. The metal instruments clattered, and the glassware shattered as he climbed into the stainless steel chamber and reached for the door just as the tank exploded with a roar that shook the entire structure. The reinforced chamber, built to withstand extreme pressure and temperature, absorbed the explosion's fury while flames erupted from ruptured gas lines outside, spreading to chemical storage areas where volatile compounds ignited in secondary explosions that chain-reacted through the laboratory.

The remaining gunmen screamed as the fireball engulfed them, their tactical gear melting against their bodies as they burned alive in the inferno. Sections of the roof collapsed, raining burning debris onto expensive equipment that dissolved into molten metal.

Frank emerged from the autoclave chamber as the building groaned and began collapsing. Foster had vanished into the smoke and chaos, along with any evidence of what she had been working on in the secret laboratory.

Refusing to leave without Dr. Foster, Frank moved through the burning wreckage, calling her name. Smoke filled his lungs as flames consumed equipment worth millions of dollars. Ceiling panels crashed around him, but he continued searching through the maze of twisted metal and shattered glass.

He found her near the back exit, pinned beneath a fallen steel beam and concrete debris. Blood pooled around her head where jagged metal had torn through scalp and bone. Her breathing was shallow, labored.

Frank grabbed the beam and tried to lift it. The steel was too heavy even for him, twisted at angles that made leverage impossible. Foster's legs were crushed beneath tons of wreckage that would require machinery to move.

"I'll get help," Frank said.

Foster's eyes opened, focusing on him with effort. Blood frothed at the corners of her mouth. "You're too late," she whispered. "The Wraith is already here."

"What's 'The Wraith'?"

But her eyes had gone still. Whatever 'The Wraith' was would continue without explanation, leaving Frank with a dead scientist and questions that burned hotter than the flames consuming the laboratory around him.

Frank left her body beneath the steel beam and escaped the collapsing building. Outside, sirens wailed as emergency responders arrived to fight fires that would burn for hours.

Deadend

Cole Brennan moved through the world like smoke given human form. Average height, brown hair, forgettable features that witnesses struggled to describe afterward. The kind of face that blended into crowds and disappeared from memory the moment he left a room. Professional invisibility that made him perfect for work that required no witnesses.

The fire trucks departed, leaving smoke and ash where the warehouse had stood twelve hours before. Brennan arrived in a Baltimore Fire Department vehicle stolen from a maintenance yard, complete with turnout gear and official identification that would pass casual inspection.

He parked among the emergency vehicles still processing the scene. Investigators moved through debris fields like archaeologists excavating recent violence. Steam rose from concrete where water had mixed with chemicals that burned at temperatures exceeding normal combustion.

Brennan walked past yellow tape wearing gear that made him invisible among legitimate responders. Helmet, reflective stripes, radio chatter that suggested official business rather than evidence recovery. Professional camouflage that relied on human assumptions about authority.

The warehouse floor was ankle-deep in twisted metal and melted plastic. Laboratory equipment worth millions had become abstract sculptures. But explosions were imperfect tools. Materials sometimes survived in unexpected locations.

Brennan found the cryogenic chamber beneath a collapsed section of reinforced ceiling. Steel beams had protected it from the worst heat, creating a pocket where science had survived the violence intended to destroy it.

The chamber's exterior showed scorch marks and impact damage, but internal systems still hummed with electrical life. LED displays showed stable temperatures below freezing. Whatever lay inside had been preserved through catastrophe.

Brennan opened the chamber with tools hidden in his equipment bag. Inside, a label marked 'The Wraith' identified twelve glass vials nested in receptacles that had protected them from shock and heat. Clear liquid that looked like water but carried death in molecular form.

The Wraith. Foster's creation that could accelerate cellular breakdown beyond natural limits. Invisible assassination tool that killed through apparent natural causes.

Each vial contained enough compound to age thousands of people to death. Applied correctly, the weapon could eliminate entire populations while leaving investigators with nothing but elderly corpses to examine.

Brennan transferred the vials to a portable cryogenic unit designed for medical transport. The device looked like standard emergency equipment, indistinguishable from dozens of similar units used by paramedics and hospital staff. He closed the dented chamber and left it among the building ruins as he returned to his vehicle.

The safe house occupied three floors of a converted tobacco warehouse in Southeast Baltimore. Brick walls thick enough to stop bullets. Windows that hadn't seen cleaning since the Clinton administration. The kind of place where conversations stayed private.

Frank sat at a steel table in what had once been a curing room. The air still held traces of old smoke and industrial chemicals. Dr. Foster's body lay on a gurney against the far wall, covered by a green military blanket.

He'd been staring at that blanket for two hours.

Culper entered carrying coffee in paper cups and a manila folder thick enough to choke a horse.

"Foster's research," Culper said, setting coffee and folder on the table. Steam rose from the cups like incense.

Frank didn't touch his coffee. Still looking at the blanket.

Frank picked up his coffee. It tasted like burnt motor oil but he drank it anyway.

"How do you know she wasn't abducted?" Culper asked.

"Not guarded. Not watched."

"So, she was working on something uncoerced?"

"Yes."

"Why would she do that?"

"Don't know."

"Before she died, she said 'You're too late. The Wraith is already here', right?"

"Yes."

"What's 'The Wraith'?"

"Don't know."

"Something she was working on?"

"Probably."

"Her research was about helping people live longer. How can that be a bad thing?"

"Don't know. Unless…"

"Yes?"

"Maybe something else."

"Like what?"

"Chimpanzee."

"The one that died in the lab?"

"Yes. Old age."

"So, the longevity therapy didn't work on it. That happens in research. I don't see how—"

"Maybe not."

"Maybe not what?"

"Maybe didn't fail."

"The longevity therapy?"

"Yes. Something else."

"The Wraith?"

Frank nodded.

Culper considered for a moment, then… "You think she killed the chimpanzee with old age?"

"Maybe."

"Why?"

"Don't know. New therapy."

"Aging something to death is hardly a therapy," said Culper. Then he stopped as if something occurred to him. "But The Wraith could be a weapon."

"Weapon?" said Frank trying to follow Culper's line of thought.

"Think about it. It's the perfect covert weapon. The target dies of old age. Undetectable."

"Assassination?"

"Why not?"

"Why make it?"

"Obviously she or her sponsors wanted to kill someone."

"Who?"

"An enemy?"

"What enemy?"

"Someone attacking her life's work?"

"Longevity?"

"Sure. Why not? She was passionate about it."

"Who?"

"That's a much tougher question. There's a long list of people that oppose longevity research. Religious groups. Financial interests. Politicians. Foreign governments."

"She had partners."

"Somebody was backing her. Lab equipment isn't cheap. How sure are we that the formula and all the samples of The Wraith were destroyed? Foster was cautious and paranoid. She must have made copies."

Frank grunted, displeased at the thought, then said, "Where?"

"Daou Therapeutics? Her home? A safety deposit box at a bank? Copies of the formula for The Wraith could be anywhere."

"Her sponsor."

"That makes the most sense. Now we just need to figure out who that is."

"FBI surveillance. Why?" said Frank.

"You think they might know something?"

"Maybe."

"I doubt they'll be much help."

"Blackmail."

"You want to blackmail the FBI?"

Frank nodded once.

"This should be interesting," said Culper, cautiously.

The J. Edgar Hoover Building squatted on Pennsylvania Avenue like a concrete fortress designed to intimidate rather than inspire. Frank and Culper showed their credentials at three separate checkpoints before reaching Director Harrison's office on the seventh floor.

Harrison's secretary looked up from her computer with the expression of someone who had learned to recognize dangerous men regardless of their official credentials. "The Director is in a meeting—"

"Not anymore," Culper said, walking past her desk toward the mahogany door marked with federal seals.

Harrison was reviewing case files when they entered without knocking. The FBI Director looked up with barely controlled irritation that transformed into wariness when he saw Frank's massive frame filling the doorway.

"Gentlemen. I wasn't expecting you."

Frank closed the door behind them with deliberate finality. The sound echoed in the spacious office lined with law enforcement awards and photographs of Harrison with presidents who had required his services.

"Foster's dead," Culper said.

Harrison set down his pen. Twenty-eight years of federal law enforcement had taught him to recognize when conversations would become unpleasant.

"I wasn't aware. How?"

"She was conducting research at a covert facility when the building was demolished by an explosion."

"A covert facility? What kind of research?"

"You first. Why was the FBI conducting surveillance on Daou Therapeutics?"

"You know I can't discuss ongoing—"

"Save it, Harrison. I'm not in the mood and neither is Frank."

Harrison turned to Frank, "I assume you're Frank?"

Frank grunted.

"Fine. The President requested we keep an eye on the scientists that made the longevity breakthrough."

"Why?"

"I suppose he was concerned something might happen and he wanted them protected. I guess he was right."

"So, why stop?"

"Bradley was being his usual pain in the ass self. My budget is tight enough as it is. I don't need it cut."

"So, Dr. Foster died to save your precious budget?"

"You said she was conducting some kind of research at a covert facility. That seems a bit strange. She had a state-of-the-art lab at Daou."

"We think she was developing a weapon codenamed 'The Wraith'."

"A weapon?"

"Some kind of drug that rapidly ages people."

"That's even more strange. Why would she do that?"

"We're guessing she wanted to kill someone without anyone noticing."

"Wouldn't be easier to just push someone in front of a bus or subway?"

"Probably. But maybe it wasn't just one person."

"Do you think that's possible? A weapon of mass destruction that kills people by aging them?"

"I don't know what's possible. But I think we should find out. Don't you?"

"Bradley has tied my hands for the moment. I'm guessing that's why the White House called you."

"Good guess. You need to look beyond politics and budgets, Harrison. This could be a real threat to the nation."

"You said the lab was demolished in an explosion and Dr. Foster was killed. The weapon and the research that made it was destroyed, wasn't it?"

"We assume so, but Foster must have had a financial backer. The person is still out there."

"Any idea who that might be?"

"If I had to guess… I'd say Marcus Whitfield."

"That's a pretty bold guess."

"He's invested over 700 million in Daou's longevity research. He has the most to lose if the IPO doesn't go through."

"And who could stop the IPO from going through?"

"That's a good question."

"Maybe you should ask Marcus Whitfield?"

"You're not going to help us, are you?"

"Let's be realistic, Culper. I have access to far more resources than you. But those resources come with strings attached. Political strings. Budget strings. Oversight strings. You don't have the same problem, do you?"

"No. I don't."

"Then let's see how far you can run with the ball. If you hit a roadblock you can't get past, the FBI will step in and save the day. We're good at that."

"Letting others do the hard lifting?"

"Yes. You handle one crisis at a time. We handle hundreds."

"Time wasted. We're done," said Frank heading for the door.

"I hope you're right, Harrison," said Culper following Frank to the door. "If not, a lot of people are going to die badly."

"Welcome to my world," said Harrison.

Frank and Culper stood in the Hoover Building's shadow. Pedestrians flowed around them like water around stones. The federal fortress loomed above while they planned their next moves.

"Time to divide and conquer," Culper said. "You go back to Baltimore. Interview Foster's associates at Daou. See what you can dig up."

Frank checked his watch. "Whitfield?"

"I'll pay him a visit in his Manhattan office."

"I'll drive you."

"No. I'll take the train. You need to get back to Baltimore. We need to figure out what's happening before the trail goes cold."

A taxi pulled up to the curb. Culper opened the door and paused.

"Frank. Foster's research team is scared. They lost their leader and don't know who killed her or why. Handle them carefully."

Frank nodded.

The taxi pulled away toward midtown Manhattan where money bought protection from questions that billionaires preferred not to answer.

The elevator rose forty stories through steel and glass toward money that moved markets and toppled governments. Culper watched floor numbers climb while calculating the conversation ahead. Whitfield Capital commanded Manhattan like a fortress built from leveraged buyouts and human ambition.

The reception area smelled of leather and power. Original Picassos hung beside windows that framed Central Park like a painting worth more than small nations. The receptionist's smile never wavered as she announced his arrival.

Marcus Whitfield stood behind a desk that could land aircraft. Expensive suit, perfect posture, eyes that calculated profit margins while shaking hands. The kind of man who viewed human suffering as market inefficiency.

"I was wondering when you'd call," Whitfield said without turning from the windows. "Kosovo was a long time ago."

"Not long enough."

"Thirty-seven Swiss bank accounts. The Zukić arms deal. My father's art collection that disappeared after Sarajevo." Whitfield faced him now. "You still have those files, don't you?"

Culper remained standing while Whitfield settled behind his fortress desk. Power games played with furniture and elevation. Corporate warfare conducted through positioning and silence.

"Just like you still have documentation about certain CIA operations that were never officially authorized."

"Mutually assured destruction. How civilized." Whitfield poured whiskey from crystal that sang when touched. "But you didn't come here to reminisce about war crimes."

"Dr. Foster's research."

"Brilliant woman. Revolutionary work. Longevity therapy could extend human life by decades."

"The warehouse lab."

Whitfield's hand paused over the bottle. Fraction of a second too long. Professional tell that separated lies from truth in men who killed with spreadsheets.

"I funded her research, yes. Seven hundred million over three years."

"Why the secret facility?"

"Foster requested additional laboratory space. Said the work required absolute privacy." Whitfield's fingers drummed against crystal. "Confidentiality is standard in biotech research. Competitors steal formulas worth billions."

"You didn't know what she was developing?"

"Something to do with longevity therapy I imagine. Extension of healthy human lifespan. The greatest medical breakthrough in history."

Culper studied the man's micro-expressions. Eye movement patterns that revealed deception beneath practiced sincerity. Whitfield was holding back information about Foster's true work.

"The warehouse was equipped for weapons research."

Whitfield set down his glass with ceramic finality. The whiskey remained untouched. Props in a performance that required dignity rather than honesty.

"I provided funding. Foster provided expertise. Our agreement didn't require detailed oversight of her methodologies."

"Seven hundred million without oversight?"

"Venture capital operates on trust. I trusted Foster's scientific reputation." Whitfield's eyes hardened. "Besides, her work was about to make me a very rich man… once again. Her little secret was something I could easily afford. I wasn't concerned."

Culper walked to the windows overlooking Central Park. Below them, people lived ordinary lives while above them, men made decisions that determined who lived and who died.

"Foster developed an aging weapon codenamed 'The Wraith'. Accelerated cellular breakdown. Designed to kill through apparent natural causes."

Whitfield's breathing changed rhythm. Deeper, more controlled. The physical response of someone calculating how much truth he could afford to reveal.

"That's impossible. Foster's research focused on extending life, not ending it."

"Same science, different application. Instead of repairing cellular damage, accelerate it."

Whitfield stood and moved toward a wall safe hidden behind a Rothko that governments had tried to purchase. His hands shook slightly as he worked the combination.

"Here." Whitfield removed a manila folder thick enough to choke democracy. "Every communication between Foster and my organization. Financial records, research reports, progress updates. You can have a look at whatever you want, but the files stay here."

Culper reviewed documents that reduced human mortality to investment opportunities. Quarterly projections based on extending human life indefinitely. Profit margins calculated from the defeat of death itself.

"She never mentioned weapons applications?"

"Never. Our conversations focused entirely on therapeutic benefits."

Culper found correspondence dated three weeks before Foster's kidnapping. Her final reports to Whitfield about research that could transform humanity's relationship with aging.

"This says she was concerned about UN restrictions."

"The ethics committee vote. If they banned longevity research, our entire investment would become worthless overnight."

"Seven hundred million?"

"Plus projected revenues in the trillions. We're talking about the end of human mortality as a business model."

Culper studied financial projections that treated death as market failure. Actuarial tables that assumed people would live for centuries instead of decades. Economic models that required complete restructuring of human civilization.

"Foster's final communication mentions preserving the research."

"She was worried politicians would destroy everything before the therapy could benefit humanity."

"So you authorized the warehouse facility?"

Whitfield walked back to his desk. His movements had lost their corporate confidence. Fear was beginning to show through expensive tailoring.

"I authorized funding for whatever Foster believed was necessary to protect our research."

"Without knowing what she was really developing?"

"Venture capital requires faith in brilliant people doing impossible things."

Culper closed the folder and prepared to leave. Outside the windows, Manhattan continued its relentless commerce while inside this office, money had enabled weapons that could age people to death.

"Foster's dead. The warehouse is destroyed. Your investment is worthless."

"Then we've all lost something important."

"You more than others."

"It's a setback, I admit. But Foster had already completed the initial research and development. Longevity therapy will go forward even without her. I am sure that's what she would have wanted."

Culper paused at the door. Forty floors below, eight million people went about their business, unaware that someone had tried to weaponize time itself.

"You must have an idea of who Foster feared most. The organization that was most likely to stop Longevity."

"It's a long list and Sarah kept her own counsel. Our relationship was not based on sharing beyond what was necessary."

"You'll give me a call if something occurs to you?"

"Of course. Do you have a card or something?"

"I think you know how to get ahold of me."

"I suppose I do. Good seeing you again, Culper. I enjoy our visits."

"I don't."

The office door closed as Culper left. He walked to the elevator then descended through steel and glass toward street level where normal people conducted normal business with normal lifespans.

As Culper left the elevator, he brushed past Brennan, wearing a custom-tailored suit as he entered the elevator.

A few minutes later, Brennan entered the executive floor without announcement, moving through the reception area and entering Whitfield's office. The receptionist knew better than to try and stop him.

Whitfield didn't look up from his financial reports. "How many vials?"

"Twelve. The cryogenic system was intact. The liquid nitrogen protected the vials from the fire." Brennan settled into Italian leather. No invitation needed between men who understood violence as commerce.

"Viable?"

"Full potency."

Whitfield set down his Mont Blanc with movements that suggested satisfaction rather than surprise. Men like him planned for contingencies that others couldn't imagine.

"The Wraith needs field testing before full deployment."

"Shouldn't be a problem. Target?"

"Loose ends require attention."

"The abduction witness?"

Whitfield nodded. David Carpenter had served his purpose in the Foster operation. Now he represented liability that venture capital couldn't tolerate.

"Carpenter is too young to die of natural aging. Dispose of the body afterwards. I don't want any evidence that can be traced back to us.

Brennan stood and moved toward the door. His footsteps made no sound on Persian carpets worth more than houses. Professional movement that left no traces except in the memories of people who would soon be too dead to remember.

"Consider it done. I'll report back with the results."

The door closed and the human smoke was gone.

Frank entered the Daou Therapeutics building through corridors that felt like a morgue. Scientists moved with the hollow-eyed exhaustion of people processing trauma they couldn't understand. Conversations happened in whispers. Laboratory equipment sat idle while researchers stared at computer screens without seeing data.

The building's atmosphere had transformed from celebration to wake. Foster's empty office remained sealed behind yellow tape that reminded everyone their mentor wasn't coming back. Security guards watched entrances with nervous attention that suggested threats could come from anywhere.

Chen's laboratory felt isolated from the grief that permeated other floors. She had thrown herself into her work with the desperate focus of someone avoiding emotions too large to process. As Frank entered, the young scientist looked up from her computer screen with eyes red from crying.

"It's hard to believe that Dr. Foster is dead," she said without preamble.

Frank nodded.

Chen set down her stylus. Her hands shook as she tried to maintain professional composure that kept cracking like ice under pressure.

"She was brilliant. Dedicated. The longevity therapy was her life's work. With her gone I don't know who will lead us. Who could possibly replace her?"

Frank studied the lab equipment. Glass and steel. Everything clean and ordered except for the grief that made Chen's voice unsteady.

"I revered her," Chen continued. "I followed her from MIT. She believed in me when other professors said I was too young for serious research."

Frank grunted like he was listening, encouraging her to go on.

Chen's composure broke entirely. Tears fell onto laboratory notes that documented cellular regeneration in careful handwriting.

"Two days before she disappeared. Foster wanted me to work on a side project at another facility. She was very secretive about the project. She didn't want others to know she was working on something outside the company."

Frank waited.

"She said it was vital. That our longevity therapy might be suppressed before people could see what it accomplished. The side project would ensure our research survived political interference."

"You helped?"

"No. I didn't. I turned her down. My visa status. I couldn't risk getting involved in something unauthorized. Foster understood but she was disappointed."

Frank gave another grunt like it was supposed to mean something. Reassurance.

"She said the work was essential. That someone was trying to destroy everything we'd built. But she wouldn't explain the details of what she was working on. Dr. Foster died believing I'd abandoned her when she needed help most."

Chen turned to face Frank. Her eyes held the particular guilt that came from surviving those who hadn't.

"I can't believe I did that. Dr. Foster was my mentor. She was worried about something, but I was too concerned about my own safety to help her."

Frank grunted understanding.

"What if my help could have prevented her death? What if the side project was protection against whoever killed her?"

"Accident. Not your fault."

Chen wiped her eyes with laboratory tissue that left lint on her cheeks. The gesture made her look younger than her twenty-eight years.

"Foster mentioned foreign interest in our research. Companies that wanted to steal or destroy what we'd created before it reached market."

"Which companies?"

"She didn't say. But she was concerned about industrial espionage. Said someone with significant resources was targeting our laboratory."

Frank memorized Chen's account while studying her body language. Fear mixed with genuine grief. No deception that he could detect.

"Her research?" Frank asked.

Chen hesitated. Her eyes moved toward laboratory computers that stored terabytes of genetic data.

"I'm sure it's safe. Foster was paranoid about backup systems. Multiple encryption protocols. She probably hid research files somewhere off the main network."

"Where?"

"I don't know. She handled data security personally after the espionage concerns began."

Frank headed toward the laboratory exit. Chen followed with the desperate energy of someone seeking absolution for choices that couldn't be changed.

"Mr. Kane. If Foster's death was connected to the side project she wanted my help with, then my refusal might have contributed to whatever happened."

Frank paused at the door. "Survivors' guilt."

"What?"

"Won't help."

Chen nodded slowly. The simple truth cutting through complicated emotions that transformed hindsight into self-torture.

Frank left her standing among equipment that documented humanity's attempt to defeat aging. Outside, Baltimore continued its ancient rhythm while inside the laboratory, a young scientist learned that some regrets couldn't be undone through scientific method.

The investigation would continue elsewhere. But Chen's account had provided another piece of the puzzle that was slowly revealing Foster's final days and the forces that had led to her death.

Foster's rowhouse sat in Federal Hill like a brick monument to academic achievement. Three stories of Baltimore architecture where a murdered scientist had tried to save the world from mortality.

Frank picked the front door lock in darkness. The mechanism yielded to patient manipulation, pins falling into alignment with soft clicks that spoke of quality craftsmanship from an era when locks were built to last.

Inside, the house reflected Foster's personality. Books lined every wall from floor to ceiling. Scientific journals stacked on tables beside coffee cups that would never be washed. The organized chaos of someone who lived for research rather than domestic order.

Frank moved through rooms that told stories about a woman who had dedicated her life to extending human existence. Medical textbooks in multiple languages. Genetic research papers annotated in precise handwriting. Photographs of laboratory equipment and cellular structures that revealed the beauty hidden in microscopic worlds.

The living room coffee table held newspaper clippings arranged like evidence in a criminal case. Foster had been collecting articles about opposition to longevity research.

Religious protests outside biotech companies. Insurance executives worried about actuarial tables. Politicians calculating Social Security bankruptcy.

Frank studied the headlines. "LONGEVITY THERAPY THREATENS RETIREMENT SYSTEMS." "RELIGIOUS LEADERS CALL RESEARCH BLASPHEMOUS." "UN COMMITTEE TO VOTE ON GENETIC RESTRICTIONS."

Each article represented potential enemies. People who profited from human mortality or believed it served divine purpose. Foster had been documenting threats from multiple directions. It was like a giant wave ready to crash on her life's work as it finally came to fruition.

Frank climbed narrow stairs that creaked under his weight. Each step protested the burden of someone who had grown too large for normal residential architecture.

The second floor bedroom had been converted into a home laboratory. Computer workstations surrounded by equipment worth more than most people's annual salaries. Microscopes and centrifuges and analysis machines that transformed living tissue into digital data.

Frank found the laptop Chen had mentioned. A desktop system with no network connections, designed for processing sensitive information without risk of electronic surveillance or data theft.

The computer was password protected. Foster's final work locked behind encryption that would require Culper's expertise to crack. Frank photographed the system's serial numbers and technical specifications, then texted them to Culper.

On the desk beside the laptop, a yellow notepad held Foster's handwriting. Most pages were blank except for laboratory calculations and appointment reminders. But the top sheet contained a single word written in heavy ink.

"Degeneration."

Frank tore off the page and pocketed it.

He continued searching through drawers filled with research documentation. Laboratory protocols. Genetic modification procedures. Technical specifications for equipment that could extend human life.

In the bedroom closet, Frank found a hidden safe behind hanging clothes. The combination lock was high-quality, but Frank's training included safecracking techniques learned in places where state secrets were protected by mechanical rather than electronic security. A few minutes later, the safe opened.

Inside the safe: backup hard drives labeled with dates and project codes. Foster had been maintaining multiple copies of her research, protecting it against theft or destruction. But the drives were encrypted with the same military-grade security as her laptop.

Frank gathered the drives and laptop for Culper to examine. Foster's house contained answers, but they remained locked behind digital barriers that required specialized skills to penetrate.

As he prepared to leave, Frank noticed something else on Foster's desk. A printed email from an address he didn't recognize. The message was brief: "Your research is being monitored. Take precautions immediately."

No signature. No return address. But someone had been warning Foster about surveillance operations that had ultimately led to her death.

Foster's house told the story of a scientist who had understood the dangers surrounding her work but hadn't been able to protect herself from enemies who viewed human mortality as a business opportunity.

Frank locked Foster's house and disappeared into the night.

Brennan parked the Honda across from Baltimore General Hospital at shift change. Medical personnel streamed through revolving doors, white coats mixing with scrubs in patterns that created perfect camouflage for someone who understood institutional rhythms.

He opened the cryogenic case and removed one vial. Clear liquid that looked like saline but carried death in molecular form. The pipette extracted a single drop of The Wraith onto his latex glove's palm.

Invisible. Odorless. Undetectable until symptoms began twelve hours later.

Carpenter emerged from the cardiac surgery wing carrying coffee and exhaustion. His expensive suit couldn't disguise the strain of eighteen-hour shifts spent cutting into human hearts.

Brennan intercepted him at the parking garage elevator. "Dr. Carpenter?"

"Yes?"

"Mark Morrison from Franklin Medical Supply. Your office called about equipment delivery." Brennan shook Carpenter's hand exposing him to The Wraith. Brief contact that transferred microscopic death through skin absorption.

"I didn't order anything."

"Must be a scheduling error. Sorry to bother you."

Carpenter stepped into the elevator without another thought. The Wraith was already spreading through his bloodstream, beginning cellular breakdown that would accelerate beyond natural limits.

Brennan drove away knowing the doctor wouldn't see the sunrise.

The first symptoms of The Wraith appeared during Carpenter's post-surgery shower. Gray streaks threading through his hair like spilled paint. Lines deepening around his eyes with each breath.

By midnight, Carpenter looked seventy. By two AM, he resembled something ancient. His class ring clattered to the bathroom floor as his fingers withered to bone and spots.

Death came quietly. Cellular collapse that resembled natural aging compressed into hours instead of decades.

Brennan returned at dawn wearing a maintenance uniform that made him invisible to security cameras. He used stolen key cards to access Carpenter's building through service entrances designed for people nobody noticed.

The porcelain bathtub filled with hydrochloric acid that dissolved organic tissue on contact. Carpenter's aged corpse disappeared molecule by molecule, leaving nothing for investigators to examine. Bones, teeth, DNA evidence—all reduced to chemical soup that would drain into municipal systems.

By noon, Dr. David Carpenter had never existed. No body, no evidence, no trace that he had lived or died or been murdered by invisible weapons that aged people to death.

The Wraith had claimed its first test victim. The formula worked perfectly in field conditions, leaving investigators with nothing but an empty condo and questions that had no answers.

The restaurant occupied a converted rowhouse in Federal Hill. Exposed brick walls and mismatched furniture that suggested authenticity rather than budget constraints. The lunch crowd had thinned to a few stragglers nursing coffee and avoiding responsibility.

Frank sat across from Culper at a corner table, methodically consuming his third hamburger while Culper picked at a Caesar salad like he was performing surgery.

"Jesus Christ, Frank," Culper said, watching in fascination. "I've seen you eat more food in twenty minutes than most people consume in three days."

Frank grunted and took another bite. The hamburger disappeared with efficiency. No wasted motion. No conversation during consumption.

"Seriously. What's your daily caloric intake? Four thousand? Five?"

Frank gestured at his massive frame with a French fry. "Takes fuel."

The waitress approached their table with the weary expression of someone who'd learned not to question customer requests, no matter how unusual. Frank's appetite had become legendary during their brief residence.

"You could feed a small village."

Frank signaled the waitress for another hamburger. She nodded without surprise and headed toward the kitchen where the cook had started preparing Frank's meals in advance.

"Same as before?" she asked when she returned.

Frank nodded.

Culper shook his head and returned to his notes. His appetite was normal compared to Frank's requirements. Fighting men needed protein, but Frank's consumption suggested a metabolic process that operated beyond normal parameters.

Frank handed Culper Foster's laptop and the hard drives. "Foster's."

"I'll get my contact at NSA to break the password, then we can have a look at the data," said Culper.

"As I see it, there are three things we need to find out. First, who was Foster's partner. Second, who did Foster want to eliminate," said Culper. "And finally, how can we be sure that Foster's research was destroyed and no copies exist that could be used to recreate her aging weapon."

Frank grunted in agreement.

"My money is still on Whitfield being her partner and knowing what she was creating in that lab. He has the most to win or lose from the longevity therapy. The only problem is proving it. He's slippery."

"I could ask," said Frank.

"You could and knowing your methods I have no doubt we'd get our answer, but he'd probably have you thrown in jail and his confession wouldn't be admissible in court. We may need another way to deal with him, but I want to be dead sure before we go that route. Whitfield has powerful friends, especially in Washington. We don't want to stir that hornet's nest if it can be helped."

Frank grunted his displeasure and said, "Politics."

"I agree. But it is what is. Let's put a pin in Whitfield for the moment. I think we've got the right man we just need the right solution."

"Targets?"

"It's a long list. Religious groups. The idea of scientists playing God is always a crowd pleaser and they'll be backed by conservatives in Congress. I'm just not sure how big of a real threat they are at actually stopping longevity research and therapy. Protests, yes. But getting legislation passed, not really their bailiwick. More of a thorn than a dagger. At least that's the way Foster would have seen it."

Frank grunted and nodded.

"Politicians are probably a bigger threat when it comes to legislation. But I'm not sure where they really stand on issues. I think powerbrokers in Washington are taking a wait and see attitude when it comes to longevity. The populists will want to gauge which way the wind is blowing before taking a stand. They all know it's a threat to Social Security and Medicare, but that may not be enough to get them to act. I don't think Dr. Foster will have identified them as a real threat… yet."

Frank grunted in agreement.

"Now, the United Nations is a different story. I think their ethics committee is taking a hard look at longevity. They might act. And if they get something passed in the General Assembly it could block the research worldwide. That's a big threat."

"Vote coming."

"In the ethics committee, yes. But getting a vote in the General Assembly is a different ball of wax. Those folks can't agree on anything. And even if they do, I would bet dollars to donuts that the US will use its veto power to squash it. Still, the UN is a real threat and a big one. A resolution against longevity could gain momentum and be difficult to stop."

"Medical companies?" said Frank.

"Another big player with a lot to lose. Longevity therapy could wipe out their entire business model. No need for an oncology clinic if cancer is cured. Same with geriatrics. Entire profit centers could disappear. Just the news of longevity human trials beginning has sent their stocks tumbling. Their board directors would sleep a lot better is longevity disappeared. Foster would have seen the entire medical industry as a threat with deep pockets."

"Environmental groups," said Frank.

"A threat for sure. Longevity would put a huge strain on earth's resources. Climate change would be in deep trouble if more people live longer. But I think they sort of fall in the same category as religious groups – big bark, little bite. Getting legislation passed based on longevity would not be an easy task even with all their money. If the people want it the odds of stopping it grow dim."

"And foreign interests?"

"That's the wild card. Some will try and stop it just to keep America from gaining a strategic advantage. Others will try and stop it based on their current populations. China and India come to mind. Overpopulation might once again explode in those countries and so will all the problems that come with too many people refusing to die. It wouldn't take much and it could cause massive destabilization."

"So, which one?"

"I have no idea. Every group we just discussed is a potential threat, some more than others. How we can zero in on Foster's target group is beyond me at the moment. Do you have any ideas?"

Frank considered then said, "Maybe not a problem."

"You mean if Foster research was destroyed and there are no copies?"

Frank grunted regretting that he even mentioned it.

"At least we have some idea where to look now. I say we keep putting one foot in front of the other and see what we come up with."

Frank nodded, then finished the last of six of his onion rings in one massive bite.

"I suppose choking is not a big concern of yours?" said Culper.

Bandaid

Marcus Whitfield's penthouse office overlooked Central Park from fifty-two stories above Manhattan's relentless energy. Autumn trees spread like a russet carpet between glass towers where lesser mortals conducted their business in the shadows of true power.

Brennan sat on the designer sofa, face showing nothing that might reveal his thoughts.

"The glove approach won't work for high-profile targets," Whitfield said, setting down his crystal tumbler. "Too visible. Someone will notice a man wearing rubber gloves during handshakes."

Brennan nodded once. The assassin understood missions that required subtle deployment methods. Professional invisibility that relied on appearing completely normal.

"You'll need something more discreet," Brennan said.

"Can you develop an alternative?"

"Yes."

Brennan left through the private elevator, taking the service exit to avoid security cameras that documented visitors to Whitfield's residential fortress. The streets below buzzed with afternoon traffic.

Brennan stopped at a CVS pharmacy six blocks from Whitfield's building. He purchased a box of standard adhesive, cloth-style bandages and paid cash to avoid creating digital records. The kind of medical supplies that attracted no attention from cashiers who processed hundreds of similar transactions daily.

His hotel room was spartan. Single bed, basic furniture, no personal belongings that could identify him if discovered. Professional accommodations for someone who lived temporarily in multiple cities under various identities.

Brennan cleared the small desk and arranged his materials. The bandages, a micropipette, a vial of The Wraith that resembled ordinary saline solution. Tools that transformed healing into killing through careful application of scientific knowledge.

He selected one bandage and placed it adhesive-side down on the metal surface. Using the micropipette, Brennan deposited a single drop of The Wraith on the bandage's outer fabric. Clear liquid that looked like water but carried death in molecular form.

The compound dried within minutes, creating an invisible coating that would transfer through skin contact. Perfect camouflage for assassination through routine human interaction.

Brennan examined his work under a magnifying glass. The dried compound was completely undetectable, leaving no visible residue on the fabric surface. Someone could shake hands normally while delivering microscopic amounts of The Wraith through palm contact.

The television studio lights burned white-hot against Senator Bradley's face. Makeup couldn't hide the exhaustion in his eyes or the tension in his jaw. The reporter sat across from him like a predator sensing weakness, ready to exploit any moment of vulnerability for the sake of compelling television.

Bradley had agreed to the interview against his staff's advice. Public statements about ongoing investigations violated protocols, but the murder of Dr. Foster demanded political response. Someone needed to speak for the dead scientist.

"Senator Bradley, what can you tell us about Dr. Sarah Foster's death?"

Bradley leaned forward in his chair, hands gripping the armrests until his knuckles went pale. The studio felt smaller than it looked on television. Cramped space designed to create intimacy between interviewer and subject.

"A brilliant American scientist was murdered. Someone doesn't want longevity research to succeed."

The camera's red light blinked steadily. Live broadcast to millions of viewers who thought politics was theater rather than warfare conducted through legislation and bureaucracy.

"Are you suggesting this was politically motivated?"

"I'm stating facts." Bradley's voice rose despite his attempts to maintain senatorial composure. "Dr. Foster dedicated her life to saving others. Someone killed her for that dedication."

The reporter's pen scratched against paper. Taking notes that would become follow-up questions designed to generate controversy rather than illumination.

"What about reports of federal surveillance at Daou Therapeutics?"

Bradley's eyes flashed. The question he'd been expecting and dreading. Official denials would sound like cover-ups. Admissions would compromise ongoing operations.

"No comment on classified operations. But I promise you this—whoever murdered Dr. Foster will face the full weight of American justice."

"Some critics suggest the surveillance was inappropriate federal overreach—"

"Some critics can go to hell." Bradley stood abruptly, microphone falling from his lapel to clatter against the floor. "This interview is over."

The camera kept rolling as Bradley ripped off his remaining equipment and stormed from the studio. His aide followed, speaking rapidly into her phone while trying to manage the political fallout from an outburst that would dominate news cycles.

In the control room, the producer smiled. Television valued emotional truth over diplomatic answers. Bradley's anger would generate more viewer engagement than carefully crafted talking points.

The Senator's rage would be replayed on every network, analyzed by talking heads who had never faced decisions about life and death. Political theater for audiences who thought government was entertainment.

Whitfield watched a financial news broadcast. Senator Bradley's face filled three different screens mounted on the mahogany wall. Bradley's angry departure played in slow motion while financial analysts debated the political implications of his outburst.

Whitfield muted the audio and swiveled his chair toward his guest - Brennan, his face showing nothing that might reveal his thoughts.

"Problem?" Brennan asked.

Whitfield set down his crystal tumbler. Macallan 25, neat. The whiskey cost more per bottle than minimum wage workers earned in a week, but wealth was meaningless without the power to protect it.

"The senator's becoming vocal about his investigation. How is your delivery method developing?"

"Done. Completely undetectable."

"Good." Whitfield's fingers drummed against the glass.

"Field test?"

Whitfield nodded once, then glanced at Bradley on the three screens.

"Understood," said Brennan. "Timeline?"

"Tonight. Before he can schedule those hearings he keeps threatening."

Whitfield had spent the morning reviewing intelligence reports about Bradley's congressional activities. Committee investigations, subpoena powers, oversight authority that could expose operations that required secrecy to succeed.

"Agreed," said Brennan as he stood and moved toward the elevator.

"It shall be done."

After the elevator doors closed, Whitfield went back to watching the financial news.

Senator Bradley emerged from the Hart Senate Office Building into crisp October air that carried the scent of autumn leaves and urban exhaust. Reporters waited beyond the security perimeter like vultures circling fresh carrion, their cameras ready to document whatever news he might provide.

His chief of staff walked beside him, reviewing tomorrow's schedule on a tablet computer. Committee meetings, floor votes, constituent services that defined the rhythm of democratic government.

A young man in a navy suit approached from the visitor area. Clean-shaven, professional appearance, congressional ID badge visible on his lapel. The kind of earnest staffer who populated Capitol Hill like worker ants serving democracy.

"Senator Bradley?"

Bradley paused on the marble steps. Security protocols required caution around unknown individuals, but the man's credentials appeared legitimate, and his manner suggested routine business.

"Yes?"

"John Lewis, legislative assistant to Senator Morrison. He asked me to thank you personally for your support on the agriculture appropriation."

Bradley smiled for the first time that day. Morrison was an old friend from his early years in the House, someone he could trust in an increasingly hostile political environment.

"Tell Jim he owes me dinner at the Old Ebbitt Grill."

Brennan extended his hand with practiced sincerity. Political handshakes were currency in Washington, exchanged thousands of times daily as legislators built coalitions and maintained relationships.

"I'll make sure he gets that message, sir."

Their palms met in routine greeting. Bradley felt nothing unusual—just a firm handshake from a polite young staffer delivering thanks from a colleague. Brennan's grip lasted exactly three seconds, no longer than normal courtesy required.

The Wraith had been applied to Brennan's palm in microscopic amounts. Invisible liquid that penetrated skin contact and began spreading through Bradley's bloodstream within seconds.

"Pleasure meeting you, Senator."

Brennan melted back into the crowd of staffers and tourists moving through the building complex. His appearance was already forgotten, his face lost among hundreds of similar young men in similar suits conducting similar business.

Bradley continued toward his car, discussing Medicare funding with his chief of staff while the invisible death spread through his circulatory system. Each heartbeat carried the weapon closer to cellular targets throughout his body.

The first symptoms appeared during the drive home. Bradley rubbed his eyes, feeling suddenly tired despite having slept eight hours the previous night. When he pulled his hand away from his eyes, fine lines had appeared around his knuckles like cracks in old leather.

"Senator?" His driver glanced in the rearview mirror with professional concern. "You feeling alright?"

Bradley studied his reflection in the window. Gray streaks threaded through his brown hair like spilled paint, appearing even as he watched. The lines around his eyes had deepened into permanent creases.

"Must be the stress," he said, but his voice carried uncertainty that hadn't been there an hour before.

The driver had transported politicians for fifteen years. He'd seen the toll that public service took on human bodies. But he'd never witnessed aging that happened in real time.

By the time they reached Bradley's McLean estate, the Senator's watch hung loose on his wrist. Liver spots dotted the back of his hands like dark islands on pale skin. His expensive suit seemed designed for a larger man.

"Sir, we should call a doctor."

Bradley tried to respond, but his voice crackled like old parchment. He stumbled up the front steps, each movement more labored than the last, his body betraying him with increasing speed.

His wife gasped when she saw him.

The transformation was accelerating beyond natural limits. Hair white as winter snow. Skin like tissue paper stretched over bones that seemed to be shrinking. Hands spotted and gnarled with arthritis that had appeared in minutes.

The driver and his wife helped the senator inside and set him down in his study.

Margaret Bradley stayed by her husband's side, while the drive called for an ambulance.

"Bill?" She touched his face. The skin felt papery, stretched tight over bones that seemed smaller than they had been that morning. "What's happening to you?"

His eyes opened. Clouded with cataracts that had formed while she watched. The man who had kissed her goodbye six hours earlier looked like his own grandfather.

"Can't," he whispered. His voice belonged to someone she didn't recognize.

Margaret took his hand. His wedding ring hung loose on fingers spotted with liver marks that mapped decades of aging compressed into hours. She interlaced their fingers the way they had on their first date thirty-five years ago.

"I'm here. I'm not leaving."

Bradley's breathing became shallow. Irregular. His grip weakened until she was holding dead weight that had once lifted her off her feet when he proposed.

"The doctors are coming," she said.

But Bradley's eyes had already gone still.

Margaret held his hand for twenty minutes after his heart stopped. She stroked skin that continued changing even in death. The weapon couldn't be paused by mortality.

When the paramedics finally arrived, they found her sitting beside the chair, tears falling onto hands that showed the first brown spots of aging. Her hair had whisps of gray.

"Ma'am, we need you to step back."

Margaret looked up with eyes that held confusion she couldn't name. Lines had appeared around her mouth while she grieved. Fine wrinkles that belonged to someone older.

She released her husband's hand and stood on legs that felt unsteady.

Outside, the driver who had brought Bradley home sat behind the wheel of the black sedan. His hands shook as he tried to light a cigarette. Gray had invaded his temples during the twenty-minute wait. He studied his reflection in the rearview mirror and saw his father's face staring back.

The cigarette fell from fingers that had grown spotted and thin.

The Wraith had found its next hosts through the simple act of love and service.

Senator Bradley was dead. Nobody questioned the diagnosis. Senators died of heart attacks with predictable regularity. The pressure of public office claimed victims who appeared healthy until their bodies surrendered to demands that exceeded human limitations.

The Wraith had done its work perfectly. Bradley's death would be recorded as natural causes. Stress-induced cardiac arrest brought on by the pressures of congressional oversight.

No autopsy would search for genetic modification compounds. No investigation would look for assassins who killed with handshakes rather than bullets. The perfect weapon had claimed its victim while leaving investigators with nothing but an elderly corpse to examine.

Michael Santos worked late reviewing financial reports that predicted immortality measured in market capitalization. The stress of recent events creased his face and caused him to drink more than usual. He rose to refill the scotch in his crystal tumbler when he noticed his office door opening. He always locked it when his secretary left so he couldn't be disturbed.

The imposing silhouette of Frank filled the door frame.

"Jesus Christ," said Santos. "Who the hell are you?"

"Frank Kane," rasped Frank.

"I've never heard of you."

"Good."

"Look, this is a restricted area. You need to leave now or I'll call security."

"Sarah Foster."

"What about her? Are you a journalist? Police?"

Frank said nothing, letting his silence work its magic. A few moments later, Santos's composure cracked. Anger and grief exploded.

"That traitor was working on another project behind my back. Sarah violated her employment contract. Forty million in stock options. Gone. I don't know why she risked everything for some secret project. It was like I didn't pay her enough. She was well compensated."

"About accident?" said Frank, steering the conversation.

"I'm not so sure it was an accident. God knows there are plenty of people that want to stop our research. Sarah was the team leader. It was her project. Many of longevity's critics would benefit from her death."

"Who?"

"It's a long list. Religious groups believed we were playing God. Politicians worried about economic collapse. Insurance companies, the medical establishment, environmental activists." Santos's voice carried the exhaustion of someone who had spent years fighting battles on multiple fronts.

"Biggest threat?"

"I suppose the U.N."

"Why?"

"If the U.N. passes a resolution banning our therapy it's worldwide. We would have no market in which to sell our product. The IPO would be canceled. Funding would dry up. It would over. Humanity would lose the greatest discovery in history. The greatest opportunity to become immortal."

"When?"

"Well, the Ethics Committee will hold a vote at the end of this week. If all twelve members of the committee vote for a resolution, it could be presented to the General Assembly by the end of the month. Right before our IPO. That would be a disaster."

Frank grunted, then left Santos alone with his scotch and spreadsheets.

Frank sat in the Imperial in Daou Therapeutics' parking garage. Santos's revelation about the UN committee had confirmed what he'd suspected since finding Foster's body in the warehouse debris.

He pulled out his secure phone and dialed Culper's number.

"Kane."

"What did Santos tell you?"

Frank watched security cameras track his position while calculating how much truth Santos had revealed versus how much fear had motivated his cooperation.

"UN. Biggest threat."

"The Ethics Committee?"

"Worldwide ban. Twelve votes."

Culper was quiet for a moment, processing implications that extended beyond corporate profits into global policy. "You think that was Foster's target?"

"Yes."

"The Wraith samples from the warehouse. How sure are you they were all destroyed?"

Frank considered the question. Explosions were imperfect weapons.

"Not sure."

"If Foster's partner retrieved even one viable sample, they could continue with the assassination."

Frank started the Imperial's engine. The sound echoed off concrete walls like mechanical thunder in an underground cavern.

"When committee votes?"

"Monday morning. Three days."

Frank backed out of the parking space, heading toward the garage exit. "Going to UN."

"What's your plan?"

"Find assassin."

"In a city of eight million people? Frank, you don't even know what he looks like."

"Always a way."

"Alright. I'm heading to Washington to update the Chief of Staff and find out what kind of strings he can pull within the UN. We'll need all the help we can get to stop this thing before it's too late."

Frank hung up as the Imperial emerged from the garage into Baltimore's empty streets. Above him, Santos's office lights still glowed while the rest of the building slept in corporate darkness. Frank drove toward Manhattan. It was going to be a long night.

Culper's Georgetown townhouse felt like a command center at two in the morning. He had a meeting in the morning with Wilson, the White House Chief of Staff, and he wanted to be well prepared. Intelligence reports covered every surface of his study—photographs of committee members, financial records, surveillance footage from the UN building. Coffee had gone cold hours ago, but sleep seemed impossible when twelve lives hung in the balance.

His secure phone rang with the distinctive tone reserved for priority contacts. Dr. Patricia Hendricks from NSA's Cryptographic Division. She wouldn't call at this hour unless the news was significant.

"Culper."

"I cracked both the laptop and the hard drives," Hendricks said without preface. "You need to see this immediately."

Culper checked his watch. The NSA facility was forty minutes away through empty D.C. streets. "How bad?"

"Worse than we thought. Foster documented everything. The weapon, the targets, the deployment method. And there's video."

"What kind of video?"

"Field testing. She recorded The Wraith's effects on laboratory animals. It's frightening to say the least."

Culper felt his blood go cold. Video documentation meant Foster had perfected the aging weapon. The scope of her research went far beyond theoretical development.

"I'll be there in forty minutes."

The line went dead. Culper gathered his intelligence files and headed for his car. Georgetown's quiet streets stretched empty under streetlights that cast pools of yellow illumination through autumn darkness.

The NSA building squatted beside the Potomac like a fortress designed to protect America's most sensitive secrets. Even at three in the morning, guards checked credentials with the thoroughness of people who understood that national security operated around the clock.

Dr. Hendricks met Culper at the secure entrance. She was a small woman whose appearance belied her reputation as one of the government's most skilled cryptographers. Twenty years of breaking codes and penetrating digital defenses had taught her to recognize when information could reshape the world.

They entered a secure briefing room where multiple screens displayed recovered files. Foster's life work revealed through methods that bordered on technological magic.

"The Wraith works by introducing modified genetic material that hijacks cellular repair mechanisms," Hendricks explained. "Instead of maintaining or reversing aging damage, the modified cells accelerate deterioration exponentially."

Culper studied molecular diagrams that reduced human mortality to mathematical equations. Science stripped of moral considerations and applied to strategic objectives.

"Delivery method?"

Hendricks opened a video file. "Dermal contact. The compound absorbs through skin and spreads via bloodstream within minutes."

Culper watched Foster demonstrate the weapon on a laboratory chimpanzee. Single drop of clear liquid applied to the animal's skin. Within an hour, the primate showed visible aging. Within three hours, it was dead from what appeared to be natural causes.

The transformation was horrifying in its efficiency. Life accelerated beyond sustainable limits. Death disguised as natural aging. The perfect assassination tool for a world where people died of old age every day.

"Invisible, odorless, colorless," Hendricks continued. "Could be applied to any surface that contacts human skin."

"Such as?"

"Doorknobs, handshakes, documents, clothing. Anything the target touches… and it can be passed on."

"What do you mean?"

"Once exposed, the victim can pass The Wraith on to others. Anyone that comes in physical contact with the victim. The Wraith is like an automated factory once it enters the bloodstream. It reproduces itself flooding the body with the compound."

"Jesus."

"Yeah. Nightmare stuff."

Hendricks pulled up molecular diagrams showing how the aging compound penetrated dermal layers and entered bloodstream.

"Lethal dosage?" asked Culper.

"Microscopic amounts. Single drop contains enough active compound to kill multiple people if properly distributed. But here is what I don't get... If all twelve ethics committee members die of old age nobody is going to believe it was a natural occurrence," Hendricks said.

"No. Investigators will probably assume it's some kind of virus, but it will take time to figure it out and that's what Foster wanted—time to introduce longevity therapy to the world."

Culper studied molecular diagrams on adjacent screens. Complex chemical formulas that reduced human mortality to mathematical equations.

"Time frame between exposure and death?"

"Varies with dosage and individual physiology. Minimum one hour for symptoms to appear, maximum five hours for complete cellular breakdown."

Culper read Foster's notes. Detailed observations about the ethics committee schedule, security arrangements, optimal timing for maximum casualties.

"She wasn't a victim," Culper said.

"No. She was the architect. Foster designed The Wraith specifically to eliminate opposition to longevity research."

Hendricks opened Foster's analysis of deployment scenarios. She had considered multiple delivery methods and concluded that diplomatic handshakes offered the most efficient means of exposing all twelve targets.

"Handshake deployment during opening ceremonies would expose all committee members simultaneously. Symptoms begin one hour later. Deaths occur a few hours later appearing to be stress-related health failures."

"While the assassin disappears and the committee vote is canceled."

Culper gathered the printed research files. Evidence of scientific brilliance perverted to murderous purpose. "Foster designed The Wraith to kill through apparent natural causes."

"And someone else has it now," Hendricks added.

Culper headed toward the exit. "Then we better find them before Monday morning."

Somewhere in Manhattan, an assassin was preparing to deploy The Wraith against twelve diplomats whose only crime was trying to regulate humanity's future.

Time was running out faster than anyone had anticipated.

Roosevelt Drive

The United Nations building rose like a glass and steel monument to international cooperation beside Manhattan's East River. Over six thousand diplomats, office staff, maintenance workers, executives, and security guards worked inside the four buildings within the eighteen-acre compound. Frank sat in the Imperial across Roosevelt Drive, studying the structure through binoculars while reviewing intelligence files about the ethics committee.

The afternoon sun reflected off windows in patterns that hurt to observe directly. Architectural mathematics designed to inspire awe rather than provide practical function.

Twelve diplomats from twelve countries. Meeting in three days to vote on restrictions that could ban longevity research worldwide. Each delegate represented different national interests, religious perspectives, economic concerns about extended human life.

Frank adjusted the binoculars and studied security arrangements. Multiple checkpoints, metal detectors, x-ray machines, armed guards. Standard diplomatic protection designed for conventional weapons and explosives.

But they were prepared for threats that announced themselves. Guns and bombs created noise and evidence. The Wraith would kill silently, leaving bodies that appeared to have died from natural causes.

Wearing a visitor's badge, Frank followed the tour group through UN public areas, listening to the guide's rehearsed presentation about international cooperation while scanning for security vulnerabilities and access points.

The guide was young, enthusiastic, practiced in the art of making bureaucracy seem inspiring. "The United Nations was established in 1945," she explained as they walked through the General Assembly Hall. "Fifty-one nations came together to prevent future wars and promote human rights."

Frank studied visitor screening procedures. Which areas required additional clearance. Which could be accessed with basic credentials. The tour route was carefully controlled, designed to impress while keeping civilians away from operational areas.

The General Assembly Hall stretched before them like an amphitheater designed for the performance of diplomacy. Rows of seats where representatives gathered to debate issues that affected billions of people. The setting suggested dignity and purpose.

"This building also houses the Security Council, where fifteen member nations address threats to international peace," the guide continued.

A young boy raised his hand. "Do they ever fight about stuff?"

The guide smiled with practiced patience. "Sometimes representatives disagree, but they use diplomatic discussion rather than conflict to resolve differences."

Frank thought about Foster dying beneath steel beams, crushed while creating weapons that would age people to death. The explosion had killed her before she could see what her research would become. No diplomacy. Just direct action.

The tour moved through conference rooms and committee chambers equipped with sophisticated translation equipment and security monitoring. Frank noted camera positions, guard stations, emergency exits. Information that might prove useful if diplomatic solutions failed.

He memorized the building's geometry. Corridors that connected different sections. Stairwells that provided vertical access. Service areas where maintenance personnel moved without constant observation.

"The Ethics Committee meets in Conference Room 4," the guide mentioned as they passed a restricted corridor. "Where international delegates discuss moral implications of emerging technologies."

Frank memorized the location and continued with the tour, but his attention focused on building layout and access patterns. The committee meeting would be held in a secure area requiring special credentials.

Metal detectors and x-ray machines protected against conventional weapons. But they couldn't detect genetic compounds that resembled ordinary liquids. The Wraith could pass through security as easily as bottled water.

"Questions?" the guide asked as they reached the public tour endpoint.

An elderly woman raised her hand. "How do you become a diplomat?"

"Most representatives are appointed by their governments based on expertise in international law, economics, or specific policy areas."

Frank said nothing. Questions drew attention he couldn't afford.

The group began dispersing toward the gift shop and exit. Frank lingered near a water fountain, then slipped away from the tour route when the guide's attention focused on other visitors.

He walked purposefully toward a men's restroom near the restricted corridor, moving like someone with routine business rather than tourist curiosity. Inside, he waited until the corridor emptied of foot traffic.

Frank emerged and approached the restricted area. Electronic card reader beside a door marked "Authorized Personnel Only." He tested the handle without triggering alarms. Locked, as expected.

He continued down the corridor until voices approached from around a corner. Frank ducked into an alcove and listened as two security guards discussed shift changes and lunch schedules.

"Committee room's sealed until Monday. Extra protocols for the ethics vote."

"Pain in the ass. Three checkpoints just to deliver coffee."

The guards passed without noticing Frank pressed against the alcove wall.

Frank waited until their footsteps faded, then retraced his path toward public areas. A maintenance worker emerged from a service door, propping it open while he retrieved equipment from a cart.

Frank noted the door's location and the worker's casual attitude toward security protocols. Service areas often had fewer monitoring systems than diplomatic spaces.

He returned to the main corridor and rejoined tourists heading toward the exit. The reconnaissance was complete without triggering security responses or generating incident reports.

Outside, Frank walked past the building's perimeter while memorizing guard positions and camera coverage. The Wraith would target this place within days. Somewhere inside, twelve diplomats would gather to vote on humanity's future while invisible death waited in handshakes that appeared completely normal.

Frank had seen the battlefield and identified the vulnerabilities. The real work would begin when biology became warfare and diplomatic protocol became assassination method.

Frank exited the UN complex and walked east toward the river, studying the surrounding structures with tactical awareness that came from years of selecting sniper positions and observation posts.

The neighborhood offered multiple vantage points. Office buildings with rooftop access. Apartment complexes with clear sight lines. Construction sites where scaffolding provided elevated platforms.

Frank identified a twelve-story office building two blocks north that would offer optimal visual coverage of the UN's main entrance and security perimeter. Good angles, minimal obstructions, easy escape routes through the building's interior.

He was calculating access methods when sunlight flashed from the building's rooftop. A brief reflection that could have been window glass or metal fixtures. But the flash repeated twice in rapid succession.

Optics. Someone was using binoculars or a rifle scope to observe the same target Frank had been studying.

Frank crossed First Avenue and entered the office building's lobby. Corporate directory listed accounting firms, law offices, consulting companies. Nothing that would explain rooftop surveillance during weekend hours.

The elevator required keycard access after business hours. Frank took the emergency stairwell, climbing twelve flights while listening for sounds of occupancy above. His aged joints protested the exertion, but determination drove him beyond physical limitations.

The rooftop access door was propped open with a small wedge of wood. Fresh scratches around the lock mechanism suggested recent forced entry by someone with professional skills.

Frank stepped onto the gravel roof surface and immediately saw the observation position. Disturbed gravel where someone had been lying prone.

He examined the position's sight lines. Perfect view of the UN building's main entrance, side exits, and security checkpoints. Whoever had been here could monitor all vehicle and pedestrian traffic.

But the observer was gone. Vanished between Frank's identification of the reflection and his arrival on the rooftop. Either exceptional operational awareness or pure luck in timing.

Frank studied the surrounding buildings for alternative observation posts. Windows in adjacent structures that might conceal watchers with similar objectives. Rooftops that offered comparable sight lines.

Too many possibilities. The UN building attracted surveillance from multiple directions by parties with different motivations. Foreign intelligence services, law enforcement agencies, security contractors, terrorist organizations.

Frank memorized the rooftop layout and evidence patterns, then descended through the building's interior. The stairwell remained empty, but the observer could have used elevator access or alternative escape routes.

Outside, Frank walked the surrounding blocks while watching for anyone who might be conducting counter-surveillance against his own activities. Professional watchers often worked in teams with overlapping coverage.

He found nothing. Whoever had been on the rooftop possessed skills comparable to his own. The kind of operational discipline that came from training similar to Frank's background in covert operations.

Brennan watched from his van parked two blocks away as Frank emerged from the office building and began his systematic search of the surrounding area. The man moved like a hunter tracking prey through urban terrain.

Time to change tactics. Direct surveillance was compromised. The mission would require a different approach.

Frank returned to the Imperial and drove away from the area. The Wraith would target the UN building soon, and someone else was conducting reconnaissance for purposes he couldn't determine.

Enemy or ally, the observer represented another variable in an operation that already involved too many unknowns. Frank would have to assume hostile intent until proven otherwise.

The mission was becoming more complicated than anticipated.

The Chief of Staff's office felt smaller during Culper's second visit in less than a week. James Wilson looked up from budget reports with the expression of someone who had hoped the previous crisis was resolved.

"I thought the Foster case was closed," Wilson said without preamble.

Culper set a thick folder on the mahogany desk. "It's more complicated than we initially assessed."

Wilson closed his budget files and gave Culper his full attention. The afternoon light through bulletproof windows cast long shadows across portraits of former presidents who had faced their own impossible decisions.

"How complicated?"

"Dr. Foster wasn't abducted. She was working voluntarily on an accelerated aging weapon codenamed The Wraith designed to kill the UN Ethics Committee members."

Wilson's expression hardened. Twenty years in Washington had taught him to recognize when situations moved beyond normal crisis management into territory that could end careers.

"You're telling me an American scientist was planning to assassinate foreign diplomats?"

"She was part of a conspiracy funded by a venture capitalist who had seven hundred million invested in longevity research. If the UN bans the research, his investment becomes worthless."

Culper opened the folder and spread intelligence reports across Wilson's desk. Financial records, corporate documents, communications between Foster and her handlers.

"Marcus Whitfield of Whitfield Capital. He funded a secret laboratory where Foster developed The Wraith."

Wilson studied the financial documents. Numbers that told stories about money flowing through shell companies toward objectives that couldn't be discussed in boardrooms.

"Foster's dead. Killed when the laboratory was destroyed. So, the threat is eliminated."

"Unknown. Someone else may have the weapon. Foster's research assistant mentions she was recruited for a separate project she declined to join. There could be others."

Wilson walked to his secure computer and pulled up intelligence files on the UN Ethics Committee. Biographical data on twelve diplomats who believed they were participating in routine international governance.

"Timeline?"

"Committee votes Monday morning. Seventy-two hours."

"Evidence of ongoing threat?"

Culper handed Wilson surveillance photographs from the UN building reconnaissance. "Professional surveillance of the target location. Someone's conducting operational planning."

Wilson examined the photos while calculating political implications that extended beyond the immediate crisis. American scientists conspiring to murder foreign diplomats would create diplomatic disasters lasting decades.

"What do you need?"

"Federal support for enhanced security at the UN. Background checks on everyone with access to Monday's session. Coordinated response if the attack proceeds."

Wilson shook his head before Culper finished speaking. "Absolutely impossible."

"Twelve people will die."

"And if we flood the UN with federal agents based on speculation about weapons that may not exist, we create an international incident that destroys American credibility."

Wilson returned to his desk and activated his secure phone. He briefed the Secretary of State on the possible plot to kill diplomats through a biotech weapon. The Secretary of State brought more officials on the call and informed them what was happening and asked what could be done to protect the diplomats. The State

Department officials confirmed Wilson's worst fears about diplomatic constraints. After reassuring everyone that they would receive updates as the investigation progressed, Wilson ended the call.

"It's like I said. Any American security presence beyond normal protocols would trigger formal protests from Russia, China, and at least four European allies."

"Then people die because of politics," said Culper.

"People die because we can't militarize international institutions based on theories about biological weapons developed by dead scientists. Our UN ambassador will inform the UN security of the threat and offer assistance, but he assures me they will turn it down. America the most powerful nation on earth, but it's not the most trusted member of the UN. Many of the members feel we overreach whenever possible. We live in a violent world. They've grown used to it and prefer a cautious approach."

Culper gathered his intelligence files with growing frustration. Democracy required consensus, but consensus was impossible when enemies used democratic institutions against themselves.

"What about unofficial support? One operative conducting security assessment?"

Wilson considered the request while reviewing diplomatic communications that painted American motives in increasingly suspicious terms.

"The UN building is international territory. We have no jurisdiction, no legal authority, no diplomatic justification for operations inside the complex. We can make a request, but I'm not hopeful that it will be well received."

"So, we do nothing."

"We do what we can within legal and diplomatic constraints. Alert our allies through appropriate channels. Coordinate with UN security through established protocols."

"Which gives the assassin advance warning and time to adapt his methods."

Wilson understood the paradox. Protecting democracy required methods that democracy couldn't officially acknowledge. But acknowledging those methods destroyed the principles they were meant to protect.

"There's another consideration," Wilson continued. "If American scientists were planning to murder UN delegates, exposing the plot creates questions about our own involvement."

Culper felt pieces clicking into place. Political calculations that reduced human lives to acceptable losses in service of larger strategic objectives.

"You're more concerned about the scandal than the murders."

"I'm concerned about American leadership in international institutions. If our allies believe we sponsor assassination attempts against UN committees, our influence disappears permanently."

Wilson returned to his budget reports, signaling that the conversation was ending without resolution. Crisis management sometimes required accepting unacceptable outcomes.

"Your recommendation?" said Wilson without looking up.

"Monitor the situation. Document what intelligence we can gather. Respond appropriately if events warrant intervention."

"Very well."

Culper stood to leave, understanding that he would receive no federal support for preventing mass murder that might embarrass American foreign policy.

"And if the committee members die?"

"Then we express appropriate concern and cooperate fully with whatever investigation follows."

The West Wing continued its eternal political rhythm while Culper walked toward his car. Somewhere in Manhattan, an assassin prepared to murder twelve diplomats with weapons that would make their deaths appear natural.

The Wraith would claim its victims because preventing their murders was diplomatically inconvenient for people who measured human lives against political advantages.

Frank would have to stop the assassin alone, without official support or federal resources. Just one man against an invisible weapon that killed through time itself.

The mission had become impossibly difficult. But impossible missions were why Frank existed.

Culper's phone buzzed with an encrypted message while he drove through Washington's empty pre-dawn streets. Wilson informed him that Senator Bradley was found dead at his McLean residence. Apparent heart failure. Age-related complications.

"You were right. The threat is real."

"Well, this is one of those times I wish I wasn't right. But this maybe an opportunity. I'll get back with you once I know more."

The call ended. Culper pulled over and dialed the secure number for Capitol Police Chief Samuel Morrison. They had worked together during the anthrax investigations, back when biological weapons seemed like abstract threats rather than immediate realities.

"Sam, it's Culper. I need access to Senate security footage from yesterday."

"Jesus, Culper. It's one in the morning. What's this about?"

"Bradley's death. I think he was murdered."

Morrison was quiet for a moment. Career law enforcement officers learned to recognize when routine deaths became something more dangerous.

"Meet me at the Hart Building in twenty minutes. Service entrance."

The Senate security monitoring station occupied a windowless room in the building's basement. Banks of screens showed feeds from hundreds of cameras positioned throughout the complex. Digital archives that documented every public moment in the corridors of American democracy.

Morrison led Culper through security checkpoints with the efficiency of someone who understood that some investigations couldn't wait for proper authorization.

"What exactly are we looking for?" Morrison asked as they descended toward the monitoring station.

"Contact with an unknown individual. Probably sometime yesterday afternoon. Three or four hours from Bradley's death."

"You think someone poisoned Bradley?"

"Something like that."

The monitoring station buzzed with overnight activity. Technicians maintained surveillance systems that never slept, recording everything that happened in areas where national security intersected with political ambition.

Duty Officer Maria Santos looked up from her workstation as Morrison and Culper entered. She had been monitoring Senate security for eight years.

"Chief, what do you need?"

"Senator Bradley's movements yesterday. Complete timeline from the moment he entered the building."

Santos pulled up digital logs that tracked every congressional movement through electronic keycard access. "Bradley arrived at 8:47 AM. Meetings in his office until 4:42 PM, then departed through the main entrance."

Culper calculated backwards from the medical examiner's estimated time of death. Bradley had died around 8:47 PM, approximately four hours after leaving the Capitol. If The Wraith required exposure time to take effect, the weapon had been deployed during his final hours in the building.

"Security footage from 3:00 to 5:00 PM. Focus on areas around Bradley's office and the main exit routes."

Santos accessed archived recordings with the practiced efficiency of someone who had searched thousands of hours of surveillance footage. Multiple screens displayed different camera angles covering the same timeframe.

"There," Culper said, pointing to monitor three.

The timestamp read 4:42 PM. Senator Bradley emerged from the Hart Building into October afternoon sunlight, walking beside his chief of staff while reviewing documents on a tablet computer. Normal departure routine for a busy legislator.

A young man in a navy suit approached from the visitor area. Clean-shaven, professional appearance, congressional ID badge visible on his lapel. The kind of earnest staffer who populated Capitol Hill like worker ants serving democracy.

"Zoom in on the contact," Culper said.

Santos enhanced the image as the stranger intercepted Bradley on the marble steps. Professional handshake, brief exchange of words, polite departure. The entire interaction lasted less than thirty seconds.

But Culper noticed something that triggered his operational instincts. The stranger's grip positioning, the precise timing of contact, the way he moved away immediately after completing the handshake.

"Professional deployment. Get in, get out," Culper murmured.

"What?" Morrison asked.

"Nothing. Can you enhance the stranger's face?"

Santos isolated the clearest frame and applied digital enhancement filters. The stranger's features became sharper, more defined. Average height, brown hair, early thirties. Forgettable except for the eyes that held cold calculation disguised as polite attention.

"Run this through federal databases," Culper said. "FBI, CIA, NSA facial recognition systems."

"That'll take hours."

"Then you should get started."

Santos began the database searches while Culper studied the enhanced photograph. Professional assassin using diplomatic cover to access high-value targets.

Culper's phone was already ringing as he called Frank's secure number.

"Kane."

"Found him. The assassin who killed Bradley."

"Where?"

"Sending you his photograph now. Professional operative, probably hired by Whitfield."

Culper transmitted the enhanced security footage frame to Frank's phone. Clear image of the man who had aged Senator Bradley to death through a handshake that delivered an invisible biological weapon.

"Got him," said Frank studying the face on his phone.

The hunt had acquired a face.

Culper found the UN Security Director in his office on the fifteenth floor of the Secretariat Building. Pierre Dubois was a career diplomat from France who had spent twenty years managing security for international institutions that attracted threats from every corner of the globe.

"Director Dubois, thank you for seeing me on short notice."

Dubois gestured to a chair across from his desk. Behind him, windows overlooked the East River where morning traffic moved toward Brooklyn. "Your message mentioned an imminent threat to tomorrow's Ethics Committee session."

"We have credible intelligence that an assassin is attempting to infiltrate the complex to disrupt the Ethics Committee vote. Former military, explosives training, armed with an unconventional weapon."

Dubois leaned back in his chair. His expression showed the practiced skepticism of someone who had fielded hundreds of threat assessments from agencies that saw dangers everywhere.

"Mr. Culper, we receive similar warnings weekly. Every major vote attracts extremists who believe violence serves their cause better than diplomacy."

"This is different. The weapon is biological. Undetectable by conventional screening."

"Biological weapons." Dubois made notes on his tablet. "From which nation-state actor?"

"Private contractor. American venture capitalist funding the operation."

Dubois stopped writing. "You're telling me that American business interests are planning to assassinate UN delegates on international territory?"

Culper felt the conversation shifting into diplomatic territory that could destroy American credibility for decades. "The individual actors are operating without government sanction."

"But using weapons developed with American research funding?"

"The research was conducted by private companies."

"Companies that receive federal grants and tax incentives from the American government." Dubois set down his tablet. "Mr. Culper, if this attack succeeds, how does it appear to the international community?"

Culper understood the implications. Twelve foreign diplomats murdered on UN territory by weapons developed through American-funded research would create a diplomatic crisis that could take decades to resolve.

"We're trying to prevent the attack."

"With how many agents? Operating under what legal authority? Do you have UN authorization for security operations on international territory? I think not."

"We have two operatives conducting threat assessment."

"Two men against a biological weapon that your own government helped create." Dubois walked to his window overlooking the East River. "The optics are problematic, Mr. Culper."

Culper was beginning to understand Wilson's reluctance to involve federal agencies in UN security operations. Any American presence would be viewed as evidence of government complicity in the attack.

"What would you recommend?"

"Officially? Cancel the Ethic Committee's session. Postpone the vote until we can guarantee delegate safety."

"That achieves the assassin's objectives without him firing a shot."

"Better than achieving his objectives by murdering twelve diplomats." Dubois returned to his desk. "Unofficially?"

"Yes."

"What else can you do?"

"Enhanced patrols throughout the complex. Additional screening of maintenance personnel. Heightened surveillance of service areas."

"That might be enough."

"Might. But if your assassin succeeds despite our precautions, the UN will demand explanations that your government cannot provide without admitting complicity."

Culper stood to leave. "Then we better make sure he doesn't succeed."

"Indeed. Because the alternative is a diplomatic catastrophe that makes the attack itself seem minor by comparison."

After Culper left, Dubois activated his secure communications system and began coordinating enhanced security protocols. Additional guards for service tunnels. Background checks on all maintenance personnel. Surveillance teams monitoring conference room access.

The precautions might stop one assassin, but they couldn't address the larger question of what happened when American research created weapons that threatened international institutions.

Some problems were too large for security solutions.

Just before sunrise, Frank parked the Imperial across the street from the UN complex. Culper had not arrived yet, but it wouldn't be long. Frank hadn't slept much in the last week. He could feel the tiredness in his muscles. He needed fuel. He entered a donut shop, ordered a dozen donuts and two large coffees.

Outside, he set the box of donuts on the roof of the Imperial and went to work stuffing them in his mouth and washing them down with coffee. Five minutes later, the box was empty along with the two coffee cups. Culper pulled up behind the Imperial and parked. He climbed out and said, "I don't suppose any of that is for me?"

Frank shook his head, then downed the last sip of coffee.

"You really need to learn some manners, Kane."

Frank grunted.

"So, you take the employee entrance. I'll watch the main entrance."

Frank nodded.

"No guns or knives. If he goes inside before we can stop him, we'll need to get past the metal detectors to follow him. I doubt he'll be armed except for The Wraith."

Frank grumbled his displeasure, then removed the holster holding the twin Redhawks and slid it under the front seat of the Imperial. He slipped off the sheath housing his KA-BAR and placed under the passenger seat along with the Colt Cobra from his jacket pocket.

The United Nations complex was like any other large organization in New York. The office staff and maintenance crew arrived early. The diplomats and executives arrived later.

Frank positioned himself near the employee entrance where service trucks unloaded supplies and maintenance workers badged through security turnstiles. The morning air carried exhaust fumes and the distant sound of traffic crossing the Queensboro Bridge.

He studied each face against the photograph burned into his memory. Brown hair, average height, early thirties. Features that would blend into any crowd of government workers or diplomatic staff.

The first wave arrived at six-thirty. Custodial crews, food service workers, security guards beginning their shifts. Frank watched them pass through metal detectors and x-ray machines designed to catch conventional weapons but useless against invisible compounds that killed through touch.

Frank spotted the white maintenance van pulling up to the loading dock. The driver stepped out carrying a clipboard and wearing coveralls that looked freshly pressed. Something about his movements triggered Frank's instincts.

The man's profile matched the Senate security footage. Same bone structure. Same controlled efficiency that marked professional killers trying to appear ordinary.

Frank pulled out his phone and dialed Culper.

"Found him."

"Where?"

"Loading dock. White van. Driver matches photo."

Frank began moving toward the vehicle, staying behind concrete barriers that provided cover. The assassin was checking items on his clipboard with the practiced boredom of legitimate maintenance personnel.

"Approaching target," Frank said into his phone.

Brennan looked up from his clipboard. Their eyes met across fifty yards of concrete and steel barriers. Recognition flashed between them like electricity.

Brennan dropped the clipboard and sprinted for the van's driver door. Frank broke into a run, boots pounding against concrete as he closed the distance. The van's engine roared to life.

Frank reached the driver's door as Brennan threw the transmission into gear. He grabbed the handle and yanked, but Brennan floored the accelerator. The van lurched forward, dragging Frank for twenty feet before he lost his grip and rolled across asphalt.

The van careened through the loading area, clipping a security bollard and scraping paint along concrete barriers. Brennan gunned it toward First Avenue where morning traffic provided cover for escape.

Frank got to his feet and ran after the van. His aged legs protested, joints stiff, but determination drove him beyond physical limitations. The van reached the street and turned north, tires screaming against wet pavement.

Frank sprinted back to the Imperial. Culper was running from the main entrance, but Frank didn't wait. He fired up the massive engine and peeled out into traffic, eighteen feet of Detroit steel joining the morning commute with predatory urgency.

The van was three blocks ahead, weaving between delivery trucks and city buses. Frank floored the Imperial's accelerator, using the car's mass to push smaller vehicles aside. Horns blared. Pedestrians scattered.

Brennan turned east onto 47th Street, threading between parked cars and construction barriers. Frank followed, the Imperial's wide frame scraping against a taxi as he made the turn. Sparks flew from metal against metal.

The chase moved through Midtown Manhattan like mechanized violence interrupting the morning routine. Brennan drove with desperation while Frank pursued with methodical fury, gaining ground despite the van's maneuverability advantage.

Brennan jumped the curb at Park Avenue, driving down the sidewalk while pedestrians dove into doorways and pressed against building walls. Frank followed onto the sidewalk, the Imperial's bulk crushing newspaper stands and vendor carts in showers of debris.

The van turned into an alley too narrow for normal traffic. Brennan scraped both sides of his vehicle against brick walls, leaving white paint streaks on buildings that had stood for decades. Frank entered the alley and immediately understood the problem.

The Imperial was too wide. Steel screamed against masonry as Frank forced the massive car between walls designed for pedestrians, not vehicles. Brick dust rained from overhead fire escapes. Windows shattered from the pressure.

Brennan emerged from the alley's far end and turned south toward the financial district. Frank was trapped in a brick canyon that grew narrower with each yard. The Imperial's doors buckled inward. The roof scraped against fire escapes that showered sparks into the car's interior. The windshield shattered.

Frank kept pushing forward until physics won. The Imperial wedged solid between brick walls, engine still running but unable to move in any direction. Steam rose from the crushed radiator. Oil leaked from the punctured oil pan.

Through the shattered windshield, Frank watched Brennan's van disappear into the maze of downtown streets.

Frank climbed through the Imperial's shattered windshield and called Culper.

"Lost him."

"Status?"

Frank looked at his destroyed car wedged between buildings like a steel cork in a brick bottle. His brother Richard wouldn't be happy.

"Taking taxi," said Frank and ended the call.

Resolve

Brennan returned to his hotel room and stripped off the delivery coveralls that had become compromised. Professional surveillance required adaptability, the ability to transform appearance when one identity became burned.

He opened a case containing theatrical makeup, prosthetic pieces, and hair dye. Brennan darkened his hair and applied latex to alter his nose shape. Colored contacts changed his eye color from brown to blue. The transformation took forty minutes but created a face that bore little resemblance to the Senate security footage.

Over the makeup he pulled on maintenance coveralls, work boots, and a laminated badge identifying him as an electronic technician. He opened an electronic testing equipment case and slipped one of the vials of The Wraith in between tools and compact spools of wire. It was invisible to the untrained eye. The disguise would provide access to service areas while making him invisible to security personnel who ignored working-class uniforms.

Brennan studied building schematics spread across the hotel room's desk. The UN complex consisted of multiple structures connected by underground service tunnels designed for utilities and emergency access. Maintenance workers moved through these passages without triggering security protocols.

He memorized the tunnel layouts, entry points, and camera positions. The main building could be accessed through the General Assembly building's basement level, avoiding the scrutiny that surface entrances attracted.

Frank and Culper maintained their watch outside the UN complex as morning traffic thickened along First Avenue. Office workers streamed toward buildings where they would spend their day unaware that an invisible weapon threatened international diplomacy.

Culper's phone rang. He answered while keeping his eyes on the main entrance where delegates were beginning to arrive for preparatory meetings.

"We've got him," the FBI contact said. "Cole Brennan. Former military, discharged for psychiatric issues. Last known address in Miami."

"Background?"

"Special Forces, demolitions expert, three tours in Afghanistan. Civilian employment with private security contractors. No arrests, but multiple red flags for unstable behavior."

Culper ended the call and turned to Frank. "Cole Brennan. Ex-military, explosives training."

Frank grunted acknowledgment. The name meant nothing, but the profile explained the professional surveillance skills and operational discipline he had encountered on the rooftop.

"Dangerous."

"Very."

They continued their vigil as diplomatic vehicles arrived carrying representatives from various nations. Black sedans with tinted windows deposited delegates who believed the committee session would proceed according to normal protocols.

Two blocks away, Brennan parked his van near the General Assembly building. He badged through security using stolen maintenance credentials, his altered face and coveralls making him invisible to guards who processed dozens of similar workers each day.

He used the stairwell to get to the basement level. The basement corridors hummed with mechanical noise from HVAC systems, water pumps, and electrical panels. Brennan followed the service tunnels toward the main building, moving through infrastructure spaces where cameras were sparse and security presence minimal.

He carried the electronic equipment briefcase containing The Wraith vial.

Frank's phone buzzed with a text from Culper: *Maintenance worker just entered General Assembly building. Different face but matches height/build.*

Frank scanned the area but saw no sign of Brennan on the surface. Underground approach meant the assassin was already inside the complex, moving through spaces designed for invisibility.

"No visual," Frank replied.

The hunt had moved inside where metal detectors and security cameras created the illusion of protection against threats that killed through biological warfare rather than conventional weapons.

Time was running out. Somewhere beneath their feet, an assassin was positioning The Wraith for deployment against twelve diplomats whose deaths would reshape the future of human mortality.

Brennan approached Conference Room A carrying a maintenance toolkit and clipboard that identified him as an audio technician responding to equipment failures. The prosthetic nose and darkened hair made him unrecognizable from the Senate security footage that had compromised his original appearance.

A security guard stood outside the conference room doors, checking credentials of staff members preparing for the Ethics Committee session. Translation equipment hummed behind the sealed entrance where twelve nations would decide the future of longevity research.

"Work order for translator headset repair," Brennan said, showing his clipboard to the guard.

The guard studied the paperwork with professional attention. "No maintenance orders this close to session start. Committee meets in thirty-five minutes."

"Equipment failure on Station Seven. French delegation headset cutting in and out." Brennan shrugged with practiced indifference. "Not my problem if you want to reject the work order."

"What's the alternative?"

"Diplomat can share headphones with someone else. Probably the German representative since they're seated adjacent." Brennan made a notation on his clipboard. "I'll mark it as security refusal."

The guard hesitated. International diplomacy required flawless communication between delegates who spoke different languages. Technical failures during important votes created diplomatic incidents that careers couldn't survive.

"Hold on." The guard activated his radio. "Control, this is Station Alpha. Audio technician requesting access for headset repair."

Static crackled through the response. "Negative on maintenance access. Committee session starts in thirty-five minutes."

"French delegation equipment failure. Technician says the alternative is shared headphones."

Longer pause. "The diplomats can't share headphones. That's not how the system works. How long for repairs?"

The guard looked at Brennan questioningly.

"Five minutes. Just need to clean the contacts and test the circuits."

"Five minutes maximum," the guard radioed. "Full escort required."

"Understood. Send him in."

The guard opened the conference room doors and followed Brennan inside. Translators sat at their stations testing audio levels while support staff arranged documents and water glasses for the arriving delegates.

Brennan moved to Station Seven where the French translation equipment waited. He opened his toolkit and removed cleaning supplies and testing equipment that provided perfect cover for his real purpose.

The guard positioned himself near the door where he could observe Brennan's work while maintaining visual contact with other personnel in the room.

Brennan unscrewed the headphone housing and applied a single drop of The Wraith to the earpiece where it would contact the translator's skin. Clear liquid that dried instantly, leaving no visible trace of the weapon that would kill through accelerated cellular breakdown.

"Contact cleaning," Brennan explained as he worked. "Body moisture can cause intermittent connections."

The guard ignored him.

The biological weapon would transfer from the French delegate to the other delegates through normal interaction. Shared documents, handshakes, proximity during breaks would spread The Wraith to other committee members within the first hour of the session.

Brennan didn't need to kill all twelve delegates. Six deaths would postpone the vote indefinitely while replacement diplomats were briefed on issues they hadn't spent months studying. The longevity research ban would fail through bureaucratic delay rather than democratic process.

"Testing circuits now," Brennan said, putting on the uncontaminated side of the headphones to his ear briefly before removing them and packing his equipment.

The guard watched without suspicion as Brennan completed routine maintenance that appeared identical to legitimate repair work. He slipped the vial of The Wraith into his front pocket.

"Fixed?" said the guard.

"Good as new. Should last another decade."

Brennan packed his toolkit and headed for the exit. Behind him, translators continued their preparations while The Wraith waited invisibly on equipment that would soon spread death throughout the most important diplomatic session of the decade.

His work was complete. Within hours, the Ethics Committee would experience mysterious health failures that appeared to be stress-related medical emergencies. The vote would be postponed. Longevity research would continue unrestricted.

The perfect crime was ready for its perfect victims.

Frank and Culper stood across from the Secretariat Building as the volume of diplomatic vehicles arriving tapered off. Black sedans with diplomatic plates deposited delegates who moved through security checkpoints with the confidence of people who believed international law protected them from violence.

"Thirty minutes until the vote," Culper said, checking his watch against the morning sun that cast long shadows across the plaza.

Frank scanned the building's facade through binoculars. Windows reflected light that made observation difficult, but he could see movement on the sixth floor where Conference Room A waited for twelve diplomats who would decide humanity's future.

"No Brennan," Frank said.

They had maintained surveillance for six hours without spotting the assassin despite knowing his name, appearance, and general objectives. Professional invisibility that suggested Brennan had already penetrated the building's security perimeter.

Culper's phone buzzed with updates from Director Dubois. Enhanced patrols had found nothing suspicious in service areas or maintenance tunnels. Background checks on staff revealed no obvious infiltrators. Security cameras showed normal activity patterns.

"He's inside. I know it," Culper said.

Frank lowered his binoculars. The diplomatic vehicles had stopped arriving. Delegates were taking their seats in Conference Room A where The Wraith waited in forms they couldn't detect or defend against.

"How?"

"I don't know. Disguise. False credentials. Alternate access route. Maybe a combination. It's hard to say, but I believe he's already inside." Culper studied the building's multiple entrances that had been designed for international accessibility rather than security. "Brennan's had days to plan this operation. Search the buildings again. We have to find him."

The call ended.

Frank watched emergency vehicles positioned around the building's perimeter. Ambulances and hazmat teams that would respond to medical emergencies no one expected. The authorities were preparing for biological warfare without understanding what they were facing.

"Still time," Frank said.

"For what? We don't know where he is or how he's deploying the weapon," said Culper, the stress clearly showing in the tone of his voice. "We screwed up, Frank."

"No. I find him."

Frank bolted toward the Secretariat Building's main entrance.

"Don't do it, Frank. The guards will shoot you," yelled Culper alarmed.

Security guards at the metal detectors looked up as four hundred pounds of muscle and determination approached at full sprint.

"Stop! Credentials!" The lead guard raised his hand while reaching for his baton.

The lead guard swung his baton in a practiced arc that caught Frank across the ribs. The impact would have dropped most men, but Frank absorbed it. He elbowed the guard's face as he passed, breaking his nose. Blood flowed. The guard folded in pain. Frank kept going.

Frank pushed diplomats in line out of the way and crashed through the metal detector without slowing. Alarms shrieked.

Another guard drew his baton and pivoted, aiming for Frank's head. Frank caught the baton mid-swing and ripped it from the guard's hands, before backhanding the man into one of the metal detector panels.

Another guard drew his pistol with textbook speed. Frank dove left as the shot's crack echoed through the marble entrance hall, the bullet sparking off the metal detector's frame. Frank rolled behind a security checkpoint and disappeared. The guard aimed his pistol where Frank had been and moved closer until he could see over the security checkpoint. No Frank.

Frank's massive hand appeared and closed around the guard's wrist, applying pressure until fingers opened involuntarily. The pistol clattered to polished marble as Frank lifted the disarmed guard and threw him into still another guard closing on Frank's position. Both guards landed on their backs on the marble floor knocking the wind out of them.

The guard monitoring the x-ray screen rose from his chair and charged Frank from behind. He attempted a takedown, going low for Frank's legs. His tackle did little to move Frank's massive frame. He floundered but refused to release the giant's legs. Frank's elbow found the back of his neck, dropping him instantly.

Three more guards from the perimeter rushed toward the disturbance, moving in a coordinated pattern that spoke of serious training. But their tactics assumed normal-sized opponents who followed predictable patterns. Frank's bulk and speed created variables their preparation hadn't covered.

Frank grabbed the dropped pistol as the guards reached him. The first guard swung a telescoping baton that Frank caught barehanded, using the extended weapon to pull its wielder off balance. A knee to the solar plexus sent the guard crumbling to the floor.

Recognizing that conventional tactics weren't working against someone who moved like a force of nature, the remaining two other guards reached for their pistols. Frank charged and plowed into them as their weapons cleared their holsters. Dropped pistols and guards slid across the polished floor.

Hearing rapidly approaching boots from inside the building, Frank aimed the captured pistol. Two guards appeared from around the corner. They saw Frank with the pistol already aimed at them and they saw the other security guards sprawled on the ground groaning. The two guards froze, neither reaching for their sidearms.

Frank motioned with the pistol for them to raise their hands away from their weapons. They complied.

"Conference Room A," said Frank, then disappeared through a doorway marked, 'Emergency Exit.'

The elevator door opened. Responding to the alarm, Dubois exited the elevator just as Culper entered the entrance doorway. Dubois was shocked to see his men scattered across the floor. He looked to Culper and said, "The assassin did this?"

"No," said Culper shaking his head. "This is Frank's work."

"Who the hell is Frank?!"

Culper smiled weakly knowing he was about to catch a barrage of verbal flak.

Marie Roussel adjusted the translation equipment at Station Seven. The French delegation would be arriving shortly and everything needed to function perfectly. International diplomacy collapsed when people couldn't understand each other.

She lifted the headphones that the maintenance technician had just repaired. The earpieces felt clean and looked properly serviced. No visible moisture or debris that might cause audio problems during the crucial vote.

Marie pressed the left earpiece to her ear and activated the test signal. Clear audio. No static or interference that might disrupt translation during heated debates about humanity's future.

The Wraith absorbed through her skin within seconds. Invisible liquid that had dried to microscopic residue on the foam padding. She felt nothing as the compound entered her bloodstream and began its work. She had no idea that death was stalking her.

Frank charged up the emergency stairwell three steps at a time, the pistol feeling light in his hand.

Pain from the baton strike radiated through his ribs, but Frank ignored it. Twelve diplomats were entering a room where invisible death waited to age them decades in hours. He had one weapon and minutes to find an assassin in a building designed to protect international diplomacy.

Sixth floor. Conference Room A. Frank burst through the stairwell door and saw Brennan, disguised exiting the committee chamber wearing maintenance coveralls and carrying a toolkit that had provided perfect camouflage.

Recognition flashed between them across fifty feet of diplomatic corridor. Brennan hurled his toolkit into the guard by the door and ran toward the opposite stairwell, but Frank's bulk gave him surprising speed when adrenaline overrode arthritic limitations.

Brennan reached into his coveralls and pulled out the glass vial filled with clear liquid. He uncapped The Wraith and hurled it at Frank like a grenade designed to age rather than explode.

Glass slammed against Frank's chest. Clear liquid splashed across his shirt and exposed skin, immediately beginning the cellular breakdown that would steal decades from his life in the coming hours.

Frank felt the burning sensation as The Wraith penetrated his skin and entered his bloodstream. But pain was information, nothing more. He continued charging toward Brennan with the relentless determination that had carried him through wars in countries that no longer existed.

Brennan tried to dodge, but Frank's reach caught him, dragging both men to the floor in a tangle of limbs and spreading the biological weapon. The Wraith contaminated everything it touched, condemning both combatants to accelerated aging that would begin within the hour.

They rolled across the corridor, each trying to gain advantage while invisible death soaked into their skin. "You idiot! You've killed us both," said Brennan.

Brennan grabbed Frank's pistol. Metal scraped against marble as he tried to bring the weapon to bear while one of Frank's massive hands closed around his throat and the other grabbed Brennan's hand holding the pistol.

Frank's grip remained strong despite the biological weapon spreading through his bloodstream. The Wraith would claim him eventually, but not before he stopped the assassin.

The two guards from the security checkpoint in the lobby burst through the stairwell doorway. They drew their pistols and took aim at the two men wrestling on the floor down the corridor. They couldn't determine who they should shoot.

Brennan broke free of Frank's grip and kicked him in the chest, sending him backward into a decorative pillar. The pistol in Brennan's hand rose toward Frank's head.

Frank rolled left as two shots echoed through diplomatic corridors. Marble chips exploded from the pillar where Frank's head had been, raining debris onto floor. The two guards took aim at Brennan and shouted, "Drop your weapon!"

Brennan scrambled to his feet and ran toward the emergency exit, leaving Frank on the corridor floor and the two guards running after him.

One of the guards slipped on the clear liquid puddled on the floor. He tumbled to the ground falling in another small puddle. He touched his pants where the liquid was soaking through, then looked at the edge of the corridor and saw the open vial. The blood drained from his face as fear struck.

Frank pulled himself upright and looked over at the frightened guard.

"Don't move," said Frank seeing that the guard was contaminated.

"This is it, isn't it? What they warned us about?" stuttered the guard.

Frank nodded once and climbed to his feet. He ran to the emergency exit doorway and opened it. He saw the security guard laying on the landing below, bleeding from a gunshot wound to his shoulder. Another shot rang out finishing him off.

Frank looked back at the doorway to the conference room. Somewhere inside The Wraith waited. Chase Brennan or save the diplomats. He knew what he had to do - mission first.

He ran down the corridor to the conference room doorway and entered.

"Excuse me, sir, you can't be in here," a UN staffer approached with diplomatic courtesy that barely concealed alarm at Frank's size.

Frank ignored him, his eyes surveying the room. The Wraith could be anywhere. Too many surfaces. Too many potential contact points. Brennan could have contaminated anything the diplomats would touch during the session. Impossible to find it in time.

Frank shouted pushing his strained voice to its limit, "Everyone out! Don't touch anything!"

The diplomats and staff shared confused looks. "This is international territory," the British representative protested. "You have no authority here."

"Hallway. Now!" shouted Frank in the meanest voice he could muster.

It caught their attention. Everyone began moving into the hallway. Frank pulled his phone from his pocket and dialed the last number.

"Frank, where are you?" said Culper answering.

"Conference Room."

"I'm on my way."

"No. Send Hazmat."

"What happened, Frank?"

"Exposed."

"To The Wraith?"

"Yes. Brennan gone."

"Don't worry about Brennan. I'll handle him. You just wait there until the Hazmat team arrives. We'll get the help you need."

"No," said Frank. "Brennan exits compound. Manhattan dies."

"Frank, if you go after Brennan you'll spread The Wraith."

"Too late. Brennan exposed too."

"Jesus."

"I'll find him."

"What about the diplomats?"

"Okay, I think. Security guard exposed."

"Alright. We'll take care of him."

"Culper…"

"Yes, Frank?"

"Seal the building."

There was a long pause. Culper knew it was a death sentence for Frank, but he also knew he was right.

"I'll call the President."

Frank ended the call. He exited the room and walked over to the guard still on the floor, crying, his self-pity overcoming him.

"Pistol," said Frank reaching out.

The guard nodded and handed Frank his pistol. Frank cautiously entered the emergency stairwell and began the hunt for Brennan.

Stalking A Killer

Brennan reached the basement level as alarm klaxons echoed through concrete corridors. Emergency lighting cast red shadows that turned the service tunnels into something from a fever dream.

He moved through mechanical spaces where HVAC systems droned with industrial rhythm. Steam pipes and electrical conduits created a maze that only maintenance workers understood.

Brennan stopped and examined his hands under the red emergency lighting. Were the lines around his knuckles deeper than before? The skin texture different? He flexed his fingers and studied the creases that might have been aging or might have been fear.

Ten minutes since exposure. Foster's research suggested symptoms began within an hour. His imagination could be creating changes that hadn't happened yet. Or The Wraith could already be rewriting his cellular structure millions of molecules at a time.

He forced the thoughts away. Panic was a luxury he couldn't afford. Escape first. Think later. The aging would happen regardless of his mental state.

Footsteps echoed from the main corridor. Multiple sets. Moving with tactical footfalls rather than panic.

Brennan pressed against a water main and listened. Radio chatter in French. Dubois had deployed his rapid response teams through the tunnel system. Professional hunters who knew these passages better than he did.

Three men emerged from the north tunnel. Body armor. Automatic rifles. Night vision goggles that glowed green in the emergency lighting. They moved in formation. Military training.

Brennan waited until they passed his position. He grabbed a section of loose conduit pipe from the floor. Three feet of steel that could crush bone if applied with sufficient force.

The trailing guard paused to check a side passage. Brennan swung the pipe like a club. Metal connected with the back of the man's helmet. The guard stumbled forward and Brennan grabbed his rifle. Brennan fired a shot into his throat below the chin guard. Dead.

The other two spun toward the gunshot. Brennan put a burst of three rounds into the nearest guard's throat above his body armor. Blood sprayed against concrete walls as the man dropped.

Frank heard the gunfire echoing up through the stairwell. Muffled by concrete and steel but unmistakably automatic weapons. Quick bursts followed by silence that felt worse than the noise.

He descended two steps at a time despite his aging joints. Each footstep sent pain through bones that felt increasingly brittle. The Wraith was working faster than he had expected.

More gunfire below.

Frank gripped the captured pistol tighter. Brennan was killing his way through UN security teams hunting him.

The third guard pivoted from behind a vertical water pipe and opened fire. Muzzle flashes strobed in the confined space as automatic weapons rounds sparked off pipes and concrete walls. Bullets whined through spaces designed for water pressure rather than gunfights.

Brennan rolled behind a steam pipe as rounds chewed through the air where he had been standing. Superheated metal fragments showered the tunnel floor like mechanical rain.

He came up firing controlled bursts. The guard tried to find cover behind electrical panels but Brennan's rounds found his face above the body armor. The man collapsed backward into sparking equipment.

Radio voices crackled from the dead men's equipment. More teams converging on his position. French commands that meant cordons and crossfire and overwhelming force.

Brennan grabbed ammunition and moved deeper into the tunnel system. Behind him emergency lighting revealed three bodies cooling in their own blood while Dubois coordinated the hunt through radio frequencies that carried death in multiple languages.

He reached a junction where four tunnels met like the spokes of a wheel. Boot steps echoed from three directions. They had him surrounded with efficiency that left only one escape route.

The tunnel behind him. Back toward the building where Frank waited.

The emergency stairwell door clicked shut two floors below Frank. Metal against metal in the concrete silence.

Frank stopped on the landing. His breathing echoed off bare walls. The sound came from below but felt close enough to touch.

He gripped the pistol and listened. Nothing. But something had made that door close and footsteps didn't lie even when their owners tried to silence them.

Frank leaned over the railing. Empty stairwell spiraled down through shadows that could hide a man if he pressed against the walls and stayed still. The kind of patience that professional killers learned in places where movement meant death.

Several floors below Brennan pressed his back against concrete and controlled his breathing. The giant was up there. Had to be. That bulk made sounds that carried through steel and stone like earthquake tremors.

Frank pulled back from the railing. His heart hammered against ribs that ached from the baton strike. The Wraith was working through his system but adrenaline still functioned normally.

Brennan tilted his head and looked up through the gap between railings. Nothing visible, but he could feel presence the way hunters felt prey. Something large and dangerous waiting above him.

Brennan started up the stairs. Slow steps that barely whispered against concrete. Each footfall placed carefully to avoid the squeaks and groans that old buildings made when stressed by human weight.

Frank heard him coming. Not the footsteps themselves but the displacement of air that moving bodies created in confined spaces. Pressure changes that spoke to instincts older than language.

Brennan reached the first landing. One floor closer to his target. He paused and listened for movement above. The giant would be waiting. Question was whether he had patience or panic driving his decisions.

Frank took one step down.

His boot touched concrete with sound that carried through the stairwell like a gunshot. The noise bounced off walls and railings until it became impossible to locate but unmistakable in meaning.

Brennan heard it and understood. The giant was moving toward him. Time to choose between confrontation and escape in a space designed for neither.

The exit door opened. Brennan slipped through and let it close behind him with the same controlled sound that had announced his arrival.

Frank heard the door and broke into a run. His boots hammered against concrete as he descended toward the sound. Dozens of steps in seconds that felt like hours.

He reached the landing and yanked open the exit door. Empty corridor stretched in both directions. Brennan had vanished into the maze of diplomatic offices and conference rooms that filled the building like cells in a hive.

Frank stood in the doorway listening for footsteps that never came. The hunter had become the hunted and both men knew it. The chase would continue until one of them stopped breathing or aging claimed them both.

The contaminated security guard pressed his back against the hallway wall. Sweat beaded on his forehead as he watched colleagues approach with concerned expressions.

"Stay back," he said, raising both hands. "Don't come near me."

"What's wrong, Michel?" Another guard moved closer. "You look pale."

"The liquid on the floor. I fell in it. The Americans said it was biological." Michel's voice cracked with fear. "Don't touch me. Don't touch anything."

But the warning came too late. Two maintenance workers had already walked through the clear puddles, their boots tracking invisible death down the corridor toward the elevators. Microscopic residue that would contaminate every surface they touched.

Inside the translator's booth, Marie Roussel felt dizzy as she calibrated the French translation equipment. The sensation started as mild fatigue but intensified with each passing minute. She gripped the desk edge to steady herself.

"Marie, are you alright?" Her supervisor approached with motherly concern.

"Just tired. Long morning." Marie's voice sounded older. Rougher.

The supervisor placed a hand on Marie's shoulder. Skin contact that transferred The Wraith from one woman to another without either realizing what had happened.

"You should sit down. Rest for a moment."

Marie nodded and accepted help to a nearby chair. The supervisor's hands guided her gently, spreading contamination through touch that felt like kindness.

Another translator noticed the commotion and joined them. Three women clustered around equipment that hummed with electronic life while biological death passed between them through gestures of human care.

In the basement tunnels, UN response teams arrived to process the scene where Brennan had killed three guards. Emergency lighting cast red shadows across bodies that had cooled in their own blood.

Team leader Captain Moreau knelt beside the first corpse and checked for a pulse. Standard procedure that required touching and examining wounds for evidence.

"Professional," he reported into his radio. "Three guards down. Automatic weapons. Close range."

Sergeant Levesque found the steel pipe that Brennan had used as a weapon. Three feet of conduit stained with blood and contaminated with invisible death from

Brennan's hands. He picked it up to examine the makeshift club.

"Improvised weapon," Levesque said, turning the pipe in his hands. "Used to disable the first guard before taking his rifle."

The Wraith absorbed through his hands within seconds.

Moreau approached to examine the weapon. Both men handled the contaminated steel while discussing tactical implications of the basement battle. The Wraith spread from metal to fabric to skin through contact that felt routine.

"Bag it for evidence," Moreau ordered.

Levesque sealed the pipe in a plastic container that would preserve The Wraith along with fingerprints and DNA evidence. The weapon would travel to laboratories where forensic specialists would unknowingly expose themselves to biological death disguised as criminal evidence.

Above them, Marie Roussel noticed gray streaks threading through her brown hair. Lines appeared around her eyes with each breath. Her colleagues attributed the changes to stress and poor lighting.

The contamination spread through the building like ripples in a pond. Each touch created new victims. Each surface became a reservoir for invisible death.

The Wraith had found new hosts who would carry it further before they understood what was killing them.

Culper stood outside in the UN plaza watching hazmat teams seal the Secretariat Building with plastic sheeting and duct tape. His secure phone felt heavy as he dialed Wilson's direct line.

"Wilson."

"It's Culper. We have a problem."

"How bad?"

"The biological weapon is loose inside the UN complex. Two men contaminated and one is trying to escape into Manhattan right now."

Wilson was quiet for a long moment. "Contaminated how?"

"The Wraith. Foster's aging weapon. Direct skin contact. Both men will be dead within hours, but they can spread it to anyone they touch before they die."

"Jesus Christ. Casualties?"

"Four UN security guards dead. Twelve diplomats evacuated safely. One security guard and one diplomat's staff member exposed and aging as we speak." Culper watched emergency vehicles position around the building's perimeter. "Wilson, if that assassin reaches street level, he becomes a walking biological bomb in a city of eight million people. The Wraith is one hundred percent lethal and highly contagious."

"What do you need?"

"Military cordon. Right now. No one enters or leaves the complex. Shoot to kill orders for anyone attempting to breach the perimeter."

"Absolutely impossible." Wilson's voice carried the strain of someone calculating political disasters. "We cannot militarize international territory based on theoretical threats."

"This isn't goddamned theoretical!" Culper's voice rose despite his training. "The weapon works. Senator Bradley is dead. Aged to death in four hours from a handshake."

"You're asking me to recommend that the President lay siege the United Nations building. Do you understand the diplomatic catastrophe that creates?"

"Do you understand the biological catastrophe we're trying to prevent? Millions dead, Jim. Millions."

"America cannot be seen as occupying UN territory by military force. Our allies would never trust us again."

"Your allies will be too dead from old age to file complaints if this thing spreads beyond our borders!"

Wilson's breathing became sharp through the encrypted connection. "The political ramifications alone could end this administration. Besieging the UN violates every treaty we've signed since World War Two."

"Then find someone else to make the recommendation because I'm done playing politics while people die!"

"What do you mean?"

"Let me speak to the President directly. I'll take full responsibility for the decision. You keep your hands clean and your job safe."

"I'm not asking for—"

"I know you're not. But I'm volunteering anyway. Let me do this, Jim."

The line went deadly quiet. Wilson was calculating whether plausible deniability was worth the risk of letting Culper bypass normal channels and destroy his career.

"Culper, you're talking about ending your own—"

"I'm talking about saving millions of lives. Put me through."

"Hold on."

Culper waited while Wilson transferred him through White House communications systems. His hands shook with rage at bureaucrats who measured human lives against political convenience.

"Culper, this is the President."

"Mr. President, we need immediate military containment of the UN complex. National Guard units with kill orders to prevent anyone from leaving that building."

"Culper, Jim Wilson briefed me on the situation. You're asking me to commit an act of war."

"I'm asking you to prevent biological warfare against eight million Americans!" Culper's voice echoed off the plaza's concrete. "Every second we waste arguing gives that assassin more time to escape."

"Based on the word of one operative about a weapon that may not exist deployed by an assassin we haven't found."

"Based on a dead senator who aged forty years in four hours!" Culper felt his professional composure cracking. "Based on video evidence of laboratory animals dying from accelerated aging. Based on a biological weapon that's spreading through the UN building while we debate international law!"

The President was quiet while advisors whispered frantically in the background. National security decisions that would be judged by historians who never faced impossible choices with countdown timers.

"Military siege of the United Nations violates international law."

"Letting biological weapons escape into Manhattan violates every law of human survival! Mr. President, in two hours this conversation becomes irrelevant because half of New York will be dying of old age."

"What are you recommending specifically?"

"New York National Guard. Perimeter containment. Shoot anything that moves. No exceptions. No negotiations. No diplomatic immunity."

"Including diplomats?"

"Including everyone breathing inside that building!"

Another pause. Longer this time. The kind of silence that preceded decisions that changed history and destroyed careers.

"You understand what you're asking me to authorize?"

"I understand what happens if you don't authorize it. We must accept responsibility for preventing millions of deaths. History can judge whether that was right or wrong."

"Then God help us all." The President's voice carried the weight of choices that would haunt him regardless of their outcome. "I'll call the governor and activate the National Guard."

The line went dead.

Culper looked up at the Secretariat Building where Frank was hunting an assassin while The Wraith consumed his body. The military cordon would save Manhattan but condemn Frank to die in the building he was trying to protect.

Some victories required sacrifices that made winning feel like losing.

The Wraith spread through the UN building like wildfire through dry timber. What had begun as isolated exposures in Conference Room A and the basement tunnels now consumed entire floors through contact that felt routine until symptoms appeared.

Ambassador Elena Vasquez of Spain sat in the emergency assembly area, her breathing becoming labored as decades of aging compressed into minutes. At fifty-seven, her body offered less resistance to cellular breakdown than younger victims. Gray hair had turned white. Deep lines carved themselves around eyes that held the confusion of someone watching her own mortality accelerate.

"I need a doctor," she whispered to her aide, who had been contaminated while helping her to a chair.

The aide was twenty-six and showing the aging effects more slowly. His face had gained lines around the eyes but his voice remained steady. "Medical teams are coming, Ambassador."

But medical teams couldn't treat biological weapons that attacked time itself. EMTs in hazmat suits moved between victims like angels of mercy who had no miracles to offer.

Three floors up, the German delegation had been evacuated from their preparation room after a maintenance worker tracked contaminated boot prints through their corridor. The delegation head, Minister Klaus Weber, was sixty-two and diabetic. The Wraith found his compromised immune system particularly vulnerable.

Weber aged twenty years in thirty minutes. His hands shook with palsy that had developed spontaneously. His breathing became the labored wheeze of someone whose lungs had forgotten how to process oxygen efficiently.

"Mein Gott," he said, looking at his reflection in a conference room window. The face staring back belonged to someone he didn't recognize. "What is happening to us?"

His translator, a healthy twenty-eight-year-old woman, was aging more slowly but still visibly. Her auburn hair showed streaks of silver. Fine lines appeared around her mouth as she spoke.

"They say it's a biological agent," she said, her voice cracking with fear. "Some kind of weapon."

Weber collapsed into a chair that seemed too large for his shrinking frame. His expensive suit hung loose on shoulders that had lost mass along with years. The Wraith was stealing muscle density along with everything else.

In the General Assembly Hall, Ambassador David Kim of South Korea had been helping evacuate younger staff members when he came into contact with contaminated handrails. At fifty-nine, his body processed the aging compound with brutal efficiency.

Kim's hair whitened completely within an hour. Liver spots appeared on his hands like dark islands on pale skin. His voice became the whisper of someone whose vocal cords had aged beyond reliable function.

He tried to call his wife in Seoul, but his fingers shook too badly to dial the phone. The Wraith was stealing fine motor control. Simple tasks became impossible as nervous systems collapsed under biological assault.

"Help me," he said to a passing EMT, but the words came out as barely audible breath.

The hazmat-suited medic knelt beside him and checked vital signs that showed a man dying of old age in real time. Heart rate irregular. Blood pressure unstable. Organ systems failing as if he were ninety instead of fifty-nine.

Ambassador Vasquez's breathing stopped in the emergency assembly area. Her aide held her hand as she died with the appearance of someone who had lived a full life rather than someone murdered by invisible weapons.

The aide looked at his own hands, which now showed the spots and wrinkles of middle age despite his chronological twenty-six years. He understood that he would follow Ambassador Vasquez into death unless something stopped the biological weapon spreading through his bloodstream.

Around him, other victims aged at different rates depending on health, genetics, and original exposure levels. Some showed minor effects. Others were aging decades in hours. All of them were dying the same death, just at different speeds.

The UN building had become a laboratory where The Wraith demonstrated its effectiveness against human subjects who had never consented to participate in biological warfare experiments. Death disguised as accelerated time claimed victims through apparent natural causes that would fool investigators who had never encountered weapons designed to steal years instead of minutes.

The perfect murder weapon was proving itself through demonstration rather than theory.

Brennan moved through the diplomatic corridor past offices where translators had prepared for sessions that would never happen. Emergency lighting painted everything red while alarms wailed like mechanical grief.

He checked his hands again under the crimson glow. The lines around his knuckles had definitely deepened. Skin texture was changing from smooth to papery. The Wraith was working faster than Foster's research had indicated.

His reflection in a glass door showed gray streaks threading through his hair like spilled ash. Features that had been thirty-five were aging toward fifty with each passing minute. Death by minutes instead of decades.

Two security guards rounded the corner ahead. Their faces registered shock at seeing a maintenance worker carrying automatic weapons in a building designed for diplomacy rather than warfare.

"Drop your weapon!" The lead guard's voice cracked with adrenaline.

Brennan raised the rifle. Time slowed as training overcame aging reflexes. The guards were reaching for their sidearms but body armor made them confident in their invulnerability. Fatal mistake against someone who understood anatomy.

The rifle bucked. Muzzle flashes strobed in the narrow corridor. Brennan's first burst caught the lead guard in the throat above his protective vest. Blood sprayed against embassy nameplates in arterial patterns that painted the walls red.

The second guard cleared his holster, but Brennan was already adjusting his aim. Three rounds center mass into the body armor. The man spun and collapsed into a door marked "Republic of Ghana" in gold letters. His body armor had protected him from being killed, but the velocity of the bullets bruised his sternum and drove the air from his lungs. Brennan approached the guard struggling to breath. The helpless guard looked up at Brennan, his eyes pleading. A short burst in the head from Brennan's rifle ended him.

The rifle's bolt locked open. Empty magazine. Thirty rounds expended in basement tunnels and diplomatic corridors. Brennan ejected the spent magazine and reached for another magazine when footsteps pounded through the stairwell behind him.

Heavy boots. Deliberate pace. Someone large moving with determination like a locomotive.

Frank burst through the emergency door. His massive frame filled the doorway. Gray had invaded his hair too. Lines etched deeper around eyes that held the focused intensity of predators who understood their own mortality.

Brennan dropped the rifle and drew the pistol he had taken during their first encounter. Both men moved with diminished speed. Reflexes that had once been lightning fast now struggled against cellular breakdown that stole coordination along with years.

Brennan raised the pistol toward Frank's torso.

Frank dove left as the first shot exploded in the confined space. The bullet sparked off marble where his chest had been, leaving a crater in stone.

Brennan fired again. And again. Rounds chewed through the air with supersonic cracks that shattered office windows and punched holes in conference room doors. Glass cascaded onto corridors like crystalline rain.

Frank rolled behind a marble pillar and felt fragments sting his face. The column was solid enough to stop pistol rounds but wouldn't provide cover if Brennan flanked his position. Staying behind cover, Frank fired two rounds blindly to pin Brennan down. But Brennan kept coming. Kept firing.

Frank counted Brennan's shots. Five fired. Maybe ten rounds remaining depending on magazine capacity.

Mathematics of violence that determined who lived and who died.

Frank's breathing was labored. Each inhalation seemed to require more effort than the last. The Wraith was attacking his respiratory system along with everything else. Time was measured in heartbeats that were slowing despite adrenaline.

Brennan moved along the opposite wall, using doorways and architectural features for concealment. His footsteps whispered against marble floors with the careful placement of someone who understood that noise meant death.

Frank rolled right and came up shooting. His pistol barked twice in rapid succession. Muzzle flashes illuminated the corridor as bullets sparked off walls where Brennan had been standing.

But the assassin was already moving toward new cover behind a reception desk twenty feet closer to the far stairwell. Wood veneer and office furniture that wouldn't stop determined gunfire but might deflect poorly aimed rounds.

Brennan's reflection was visible in the glass door behind the desk. Distorted image that showed a face aging in real time. Skin that had been smooth was developing creases and spots. Hair that had been brown was fading toward white.

Frank aimed at the reflection and fired. Glass exploded, showering Brennan with fragments that drew blood from cuts that seemed to heal slowly. Blood failing to coagulate. The Wraith was affecting even minor wound recovery.

"You're dying," Brennan called from behind the shattered door. His voice sounded rougher than it had an hour before. Vocal cords aging along with everything else. "Do you really want to spend your last minutes on earth hunting me? It's pointless. I'll be dead soon too. You don't need to do anything."

Frank said nothing. Words were for people who had time to waste.

He studied the corridor's geometry. Brennan was trapped behind inadequate cover with limited ammunition. But the assassin only needed to reach the stairwell to continue his escape toward street level where millions of people waited unknowingly.

Frank heard movement behind the reception area. Brennan was gathering ammunition from the dead guards, stuffing magazines into coveralls that hung looser on a frame that seemed to be shrinking.

Frank moved along his pillar toward a better firing angle. His joints protested each step with pain that felt like grinding bone against bone. Arthritis that had developed in minutes.

A hand appeared around the desk's edge. Then an arm holding the pistol. Brennan was preparing to break cover and make his run for the exit.

Frank took careful aim at the spot where Brennan would appear. Patient as stone despite cellular collapse that was stealing his life.

Brennan broke from cover in a sprint that showed his own physical deterioration. Movement that had been fluid was now choppy. Coordination that had been perfect was failing as The Wraith rewrote his nervous system.

Frank's shot caught empty air as Brennan stumbled and fell forward. The assassin rolled and came up firing from a prone position. Wild shots that sparked off marble and punched through office doors in random patterns.

Frank returned fire but his hands were shaking now. Tremors that made aiming impossible at any distance beyond point-blank range. The Wraith was attacking fine motor control along with everything else.

Brennan reached the stairwell door and turned for a final exchange. Both men fired simultaneously. Frank's round chewed splinters from the door frame. Brennan's bullet whispered past Frank's ear close enough to feel the pressure wave.

Brennan disappeared into the stairwell.

Frank staggered toward the door, but his legs felt increasingly unsteady. Each step required conscious effort as automated systems failed under biological assault. The corridor seemed longer than it had been moments before.

By the time Frank reached the stairwell, Brennan was gone. Only footsteps echoing down toward street level where eight million people conducted their lives unaware that biological death was descending toward them through concrete and steel.

Frank began his pursuit knowing that each step brought him closer to preventing catastrophe and closer to his own cellular collapse. The race between duty and mortality had entered its final phase where winners and losers would be determined by who could function longest while dying.

Brennan reached the ground floor and pushed through the stairwell door into a corridor that had become a hospice. UN employees sat slumped against marble walls, their bodies aging decades in hours. Secretaries who had been twenty-five that morning now resembled their own grandmothers.

EMTs in full hazmat suits moved between victims like spacemen walking through an alien graveyard. Their bulky protective gear made them appear inhuman as they checked pulses and administered IV fluids that couldn't slow cellular breakdown.

A young translator clutched her chest as her heart struggled with the rhythm of someone three times her chronological age. Gray hair hung in wisps around a face mapped with lines that had appeared in minutes rather than years.

"Please," she whispered to a passing EMT. "What's happening to us?"

The medic knelt beside her but couldn't offer comfort that his training hadn't provided. No medical school taught treatments for accelerated aging. No protocol existed for biological weapons that stole time itself.

Brennan walked past the dying without looking directly at their faces. His own reflection in office windows showed the same transformation progressing through his body. Hair white as winter snow. Skin like tissue paper stretched over bones that felt increasingly brittle.

An elderly janitor who had been seventy that morning was already dead. His body curled against a wall where he had sought shelter from something that couldn't be avoided. The Wraith had claimed him first because age provided less resistance to cellular collapse.

But a young security guard who had been exposed at the same time was still conscious. His face showed the confusion of someone who had watched himself age forty years while his watch moved through normal minutes.

Marie Roussel sat in the corridor. Her supervisor held her hand despite understanding the risk. Human compassion that spread contamination through gestures meant to provide comfort.

"I can't feel my legs," Marie said in a voice that had roughened beyond recognition.

"Help is coming," her supervisor lied with the kindness that dying people deserved.

Brennan moved through the human wreckage while calculating his remaining options. The main exits were blocked by guards who had received orders to prevent anyone from leaving. Armed men who were aging as they stood post but still capable of following commands.

Four guards positioned near the entrance. All showing signs of contamination, but their weapons remained steady. Professional discipline that functioned despite biological assault on their nervous systems.

Too many. Even weakened by The Wraith, four guards with automatic weapons could cut him down before he reached the exit. Brennan needed another route to get out of the building.

He turned down a service corridor that led toward loading docks and maintenance areas. The kind of infrastructure that security focused on less heavily.

Behind him, footsteps echoed through the stairwell. Frank was still pursuing with the relentless patience of someone who understood duty better than self-preservation.

The corridor stretched ahead through emergency lighting that painted everything red. Brennan's shadow preceded him like a harbinger of biological death searching for cracks in containment that would allow invisible weapons to escape into a world unprepared for warfare conducted through time itself.

Each step brought him closer to street level and farther from the dying diplomats who had gathered to debate humanity's future. The irony wasn't lost on him. Foster's weapon had solved the longevity debate by demonstrating that extended life was meaningless when death could be accelerated beyond natural limits.

The Wraith had won its argument through demonstration rather than discussion.

Margaret Williams sat at the cafeteria table with her lunch tray untouched, beads of sweat forming on her forehead despite the building's air conditioning. At twenty-four, she had worked as a secretary in the Economic and Social Council for two years, but had never felt this sick during office hours.

"You don't look well," said her friend Janet, leaning closer with concern. "Your face is flushed."

Margaret wiped her forehead with a napkin, but perspiration continued forming faster than she could manage it. Drops fell from her face onto her salad plate, mixing with the vinaigrette in patterns that looked like tears.

"I feel terrible," Margaret said, her voice already sounding rougher than it had that morning. "Dizzy. Hot and cold at the same time."

Susan, another secretary from the Translation Department, reached across the table and touched Margaret's forehead with the back of her hand. "You're burning up."

The contact lasted only seconds, but The Wraith transferred through skin-to-skin touch with microscopic efficiency. Susan pulled her hand away, unknowingly contaminated.

"Here, drink some water," Janet said, picking up Margaret's water glass and bringing it to her lips. Margaret's perspiration had condensed on the glass surface, creating an invisible film that transferred to Janet's fingers.

Margaret tried to stand but swayed dangerously. Both friends immediately moved to support her, their hands touching her arms and shoulders as they steadied her against the table. More transfer points. More contamination spreading through gestures of human kindness.

"We're taking you to the medical office," Susan said firmly. "You're in no condition to work."

Margaret nodded weakly, leaving damp handprints on the table surface where her palms had rested. Her untouched lunch remained behind, the plate and utensils contaminated.

The three women left together, arms linked in mutual support, unaware that compassion had just spread The Wraith to two more victims who would begin showing symptoms within the hour.

Behind them, the contaminated table waited for the next group of employees who would unknowingly expose themselves to invisible death through routine contact with surfaces that appeared completely normal.

The Siege

The National Guard convoy arrived with mechanical thunder that shook windows throughout Midtown Manhattan. Humvees and armored personnel carriers rolled down First Avenue while Apache helicopters circled overhead like mechanical vultures. The New York National Guard had mobilized with speed that impressed even Culper. They had practiced for terrorist operations and knew what was expected.

Colonel Marcus Reed stepped from the lead Humvee wearing full battle dress and the expression of someone who had received orders that made no tactical sense. At fifty-five, he commanded respect through competence rather than politics. Desert Storm veteran who understood urban warfare and international complications.

"You Culper?" Reed's handshake was firm but brief. No time for pleasantries when deploying military force on international territory.

"That's right. Thanks for the rapid response, Colonel."

Reed studied the UN complex through binoculars that revealed windows sealed with plastic sheeting and hazmat teams maintaining perimeter positions. "My orders are to establish containment around the building. No one enters or leaves."

"Correct."

"But I'm not authorized to fire on diplomats or UN personnel attempting to exit." Reed lowered his binoculars. "International law prohibits military action against protected persons on neutral territory."

Culper watched soldiers deploy heavy machine guns that could cut vehicles in half with sustained fire. "Colonel, the people inside that building have been exposed to a biological weapon that kills through skin contact."

"So, I've been briefed. But my rules of engagement specify non-lethal force only."

"Non-lethal force won't stop someone contaminated with The Wraith. They're dying anyway. Nothing left to lose."

Reed's jaw tightened. Thirty years of military service had taught him to follow orders even when they contradicted common sense. "I have clear instructions from the Pentagon. Contain but don't engage with lethal force."

"Then you'll be responsible for eight million deaths when that weapon reaches the subway system."

"I'll be responsible for following lawful orders from my chain of command."

Culper felt his patience evaporating as soldiers established firing positions that wouldn't be used when needed most. "Colonel, let me explain something about biological warfare. The weapon inside that building spreads through touch. One contaminated person reaches Times Square and you've got a pandemic that ages people to death. The Wraith is one hundred percent lethal."

"I understand the stakes."

"Do you? Because your non-lethal rules of engagement just became a suicide pact for Manhattan and even you and your troops."

Reed walked toward his command vehicle where radio operators coordinated the siege through encrypted communications. Culper followed, calculating how much military protocol he could violate before being arrested.

"My orders come from the National Security Council through the Joint Chiefs," Reed said without turning around. "I don't have authority to modify rules of engagement based on field recommendations."

"Then get that authority. Call your superiors and explain that biological containment requires different tactics than conventional warfare."

"I've been on the radio with Pentagon for thirty minutes. They're aware of the situation."

Reed opened the command vehicle's rear door to reveal communication equipment that connected field operations to decision makers who had never faced impossible choices in real time.

"And?"

"Politicians are debating international law while scientists calculate casualty projections." Reed's expression showed the frustration of someone caught between bureaucracy and biology. "No consensus on escalation protocols."

Culper studied the soldiers surrounding the UN complex with weapons they couldn't use against targets they couldn't let escape. Military efficiency rendered useless by diplomatic constraints.

"How long before you get authorization for lethal force?"

"Could be hours. Could be never."

"Colonel, we don't have hours. The Wraith is already spreading inside the building. Every minute of delay gives it more time to find new hosts."

Reed activated his secure radio and spoke directly to his Pentagon contact. Military jargon that reduced human catastrophe to operational parameters and casualty projections.

The response crackled through speakers designed for battlefield communication. Political discussions that prioritized international relations over biological reality.

"Negative on lethal force authorization. Maintain containment only."

Reed set down the radio with movements that suggested someone who understood the gap between military capability and political permission.

"There's your answer."

"Then we need to change the answer." Culper pulled out his encrypted phone. "I'm calling the President directly."

"You can't—"

"Watch me."

The call connected through White House communications systems that bypassed normal military channels. Emergency protocols that allowed field operatives to reach decision makers when democracy required choices that democracy couldn't officially acknowledge.

"Mr. President, the National Guard has rules of engagement that guarantee biological catastrophe."

"Explain."

"They're authorized to contain but not to kill. Anyone leaving that building will be stopped with non-lethal force that won't prevent contamination spread. If the guardsmen even touch one of the victims they will be exposed and once that happens it's game over. We won't be able to contain it. Manhattan dies and maybe the rest of the world with it."

The President was quiet while advisors whispered in the background. Voices that debated international law while biological weapons threatened to escape containment.

"Put Colonel Reed on the line."

Culper handed the phone to Reed, who accepted it with the wariness of someone who understood that career-ending conversations often began with direct presidential contact.

"This is Colonel Reed, sir."

The conversation lasted three minutes. Military language that transformed political guidance into operational orders. Reed's expression showed someone receiving instructions that contradicted everything he had been taught about international engagement.

"Understood, Mr. President. Lethal force authorized."

Reed handed the phone back to Culper and immediately began radioing new orders to his unit commanders. Rules of engagement that prioritized biological containment over diplomatic protocol.

"All stations, this is Command. Weapons free. Anyone attempting to breach the perimeter will be engaged with maximum force. No exceptions. Nobody gets out of the UN complex. Nobody."

Culper felt relief mixed with the knowledge that he had just condemned Frank to die in the building he was trying to protect.

"One more thing, Colonel. Your men cannot touch anyone who comes out of that building. Dead or alive."

Reed nodded grimly. "Hazmat protocols for all personnel. No physical contact with potential contamination sources."

Around them, soldiers adjusted their positions and checked their weapons. Professional killers preparing to execute anyone who emerged from the UN complex carrying invisible death toward eight million people who had no idea their lives depended on military and political decisions made in windowless rooms.

The siege had begun.

The Secretary of State's office in the White House had become a diplomatic war room. Five phone lines rang simultaneously while staff members tried to manage conversations with world leaders who demanded explanations for what appeared to be an American military occupation of international territory.

Secretary Patricia Hammond grabbed the red phone that connected directly to Beijing. "Mr. Premier, I understand your concerns—"

"You understand nothing!" The Chinese Premier's voice crackled through encrypted channels. "American troops surround the United Nations complex. This is an act of war against every nation represented there."

Hammond gestured frantically at her deputy, who was fielding an equally hostile call from the German Chancellor. Three more lines blinked with incoming calls from allied governments that had watched CNN footage of National Guard units establishing firing positions around the UN complex.

"Mr. Premier, there is an immediate biological threat that requires—"

"Biological threat created by American scientists with American funding!" The Premier's voice rose with accusation. "You develop these weapons then deploy them against Chinese diplomats when they oppose your interests."

Hammond felt her stomach drop. Intelligence agencies had briefed world leaders about Foster's research origins. "The weapon was developed by private companies without government authorization—"

"Private companies receiving federal grants and tax incentives. American biological warfare program disguised as medical research."

The line went dead. Beijing had severed diplomatic communication rather than listen to explanations that sounded like justifications for unprovoked aggression.

Hammond's deputy covered his phone and shouted across the room. "Chancellor Brenner says Germany has evidence of American biological weapons development. Threatening war crimes tribunal at The Hague."

"Tell him to please hold off taking any action. The President will call within the hour," Hammond replied while answering the line from London.

"Patricia, what the bloody hell is happening?" The British Prime Minister's voice carried the strain of someone whose closest ally had just committed an incomprehensible act. "The BBC is showing American soldiers pointing weapons at the UN building."

"We're containing a biological weapon that threatens—"

"A biological weapon your own scientists created!" The PM's diplomatic composure cracked. "MI6 has files on Foster's research. American genetic modification programs that violate every treaty we've signed since World War Two."

"The research wasn't authorized for weapons development—"

"Yet it killed a sitting US Senator and now threatens foreign diplomats. Parliament is calling this American biological terrorism against international institutions."

Hammond looked around her office where every staff member was managing multiple crisis conversations simultaneously. The international telephone system couldn't handle the volume of diplomatic protests flooding Washington from capitals around the world.

Two floors below, the President sat in the Oval Office while White House operators tried to manage calls from Supreme Court justices, congressional leaders, and heads of state who believed America had declared biological war on international law.

"Chief Justice is on line one," his secretary announced. "Speaker of the House on line two. Senate Majority Leader on line three. French President on line four demanding war crimes investigation. And line five is the first lady."

The President picked up the Chief Justice's call first. Constitutional crises required immediate attention when democratic institutions questioned executive authority.

"Mr. President, I've received reports of military action against international territory and allegations of biological weapons development without congressional oversight," the Chief Justice said. His voice carried the measured tone of someone who had spent decades interpreting constitutional law. "The Court is prepared to issue emergency injunctions for violations of international law."

"John, we're facing biological warfare that could kill millions of Americans."

"Biological warfare using weapons developed through American research programs. Congress was never briefed on genetic modification projects that violate biological weapons conventions."

The President switched to the Speaker's line without resolving the constitutional questions that could impeach him by nightfall.

"Mr. President," the Speaker's voice was tight with political calculation. "I've got two hundred representatives demanding an emergency session to investigate illegal biological weapons programs. What you've done looks like using American-developed bioweapons against foreign nationals."

"We're preventing biological weapons from reaching American cities."

"Weapons that wouldn't exist without American funding and American scientists! The optics are catastrophic. You've essentially admitted to developing prohibited biological agents."

The President's other lines continued blinking as foreign leaders waited for explanations that couldn't be provided without revealing classified information about weapons that officially didn't exist but were apparently killing people.

His Chief of Staff burst through the office door carrying a tablet that showed international news coverage. "Mr. President, the UN Secretary General is calling for emergency Security Council session. Russia's threatening military response and demanding immediate biological weapons inspections of American facilities."

"Military response?"

"Naval vessels moving toward our East Coast. Putin says American biological weapons development threatens global security. He's calling this a violation of the Biological Weapons Convention."

The secure line from Moscow rang with the distinctive tone reserved for communications between nuclear powers. The President looked at the phone with the understanding that the next conversation could determine whether biological warfare accusations escalated into something far worse.

"This is about to become World War Three over weapons we didn't officially authorize," the Chief of Staff said quietly.

Outside the Oval Office windows, Washington continued its ancient rhythm while inside, democratic institutions struggled to contain a crisis that threatened to destroy the international order America had spent seventy years building through trust that was evaporating with each news cycle.

The President reached for the Moscow line knowing that explaining biological weapons development to Russia's president would either prevent nuclear war or accelerate it beyond any possibility of control.

Some decisions were too large for any single person to make correctly, especially when the world believed you had become the monster you were trying to stop.

The portable incinerator arrived on a military trailer towed by a diesel truck that belched black smoke into Manhattan's evening air. Industrial equipment designed for disaster zones where normal burial became impossible. The kind of machinery that civilized nations preferred not to acknowledge existed.

Culper watched hazmat teams position the steel chamber in the UN plaza where diplomats had once gathered for ceremonial photographs. The incinerator's chimney pointed toward sky that would soon carry human ash across a city that had no idea what was burning.

The temporary morgue had overflowed within three hours. Body bags lined the corridors like industrial sausages filled with diplomatic flesh that had aged beyond recognition. Ambassador Vasquez lay beside Minister Weber and Ambassador Kim in rows that spoke of biological efficiency rather than natural death.

Dr. Patricia Davis, the chief medical examiner, approached Culper wearing full protective gear that made her voice sound mechanical. "We have no choice. Standard burial procedures would contaminate every funeral home and cemetery in the region."

"How many?" Culper asked.

"Thirty-seven confirmed deaths. Another dozen showing terminal symptoms." Davis's face mask fogged with breath that carried professional exhaustion. "The aging compound remains active in deceased tissue. Bodies are still contagious. Incineration is the only way to be sure The Wraith doesn't spread beyond the UN complex."

Culper nodded without speaking.

"We now believe that The Wraith has spread to all the buildings within the complex," said the examiner. "Over six thousand workers and diplomats infected and no cure that we know of. I've never seen anything like it."

"Nobody has." said Culper.

The first body bag disappeared into the incinerator's steel maw. Flames that reached two thousand degrees Fahrenheit consumed human flesh in minutes, reducing international representatives and their staff to ash and superheated gas.

Ambassador Vasquez burned first. The Spanish diplomat who had spent her career building bridges between nations became smoke that drifted over Manhattan. Her life's work in international cooperation ended in flames.

Minister Weber followed. Then Ambassador Kim. Then younger victims whose only crime had been working in a building where invisible weapons spread through touch. Each body added fuel to fires that lit the plaza with orange glow.

"Jesus Christ," Culper whispered, watching smoke rise from the chimney.

The scene felt like failure made visible. He had identified the threat, traced the weapon, coordinated federal response, and still people were dying while their bodies burned like cordwood. Professional competence that produced professional catastrophe.

Davis stood beside him in protective gear that couldn't shield against the weight of decisions that transformed human beings into medical waste. "We're saving lives by doing this."

"Doesn't feel like it."

"Biological containment requires industrial solutions. If we buried these bodies normally, The Wraith would contaminate soil and groundwater. Mourning families would be exposed during funeral services."

Another body bag entered the incinerator. Flames roared with renewed intensity as human tissue provided fuel for processes that sterilized biological weapons through temperatures that destroyed DNA along with everything else.

Culper forced himself to watch each cremation. Professional obligation to witness the cost of operations he had authorized. Leadership required to look directly at consequences that others preferred to ignore.

His secure phone rang with updates from Dubois. Frank was still hunting Brennan through corridors filled with dying diplomats. Two men aging to death while pursuing each other.

"Status?" Culper answered.

"Brennan moving toward service exits. Frank in pursuit. Both showing advanced aging symptoms," said Dubois

"Time estimates?"

"Unknown. The weapon affects individuals differently. Could be hours. Could be minutes."

Culper ended the call and returned his attention to the incinerator that processed diplomatic corpses with industrial efficiency. Each body represented someone's parent, spouse, child reduced to ash because biological weapons had been deployed on international soil.

The failure wasn't tactical or strategic. It was moral. He had been too slow to understand the threat, too constrained by bureaucratic processes, too willing to trust that democratic institutions could respond to enemies who operated outside democratic rules.

But moral failure was a luxury he couldn't afford while Brennan remained alive and Frank was dying in pursuit of someone who carried biological death toward eight million people.

Culper walked toward the command vehicle where Colonel Reed coordinated the siege that kept The Wraith contained. Professional duty required functioning despite personal knowledge that good people were burning because he hadn't been good enough at his job.

The war continued while smoke from diplomatic corpses drifted across Manhattan carrying the ashes of international representatives toward a sky that wouldn't remember their names.

Some victories required accepting that success looked exactly like failure.

Ambassador Jean-Michel Cartier of France stumbled through the UN lobby with the desperate movements of someone whose mind had broken under biological assault. At sixty-three, The Wraith had aged him visibly while fever ravaged what remained of his immune system.

"I can't breathe," he gasped to EMTs who tried to guide him back toward the emergency assembly area. "The walls are crushing me. I have to get out."

The claustrophobia had developed along with other symptoms as The Wraith attacked his nervous system and the mind. Rational thought collapsed under psychological pressure that no diplomatic training had prepared him to handle.

Cartier broke away from the medical personnel and ran toward the main exit. His gait was unsteady, coordination compromised by aging that had stolen decades of motor function, but panic drove him beyond physical limitations.

"Stop him!" an EMT shouted, but hazmat suits made pursuit difficult.

Cartier burst through the building's main entrance into plaza air that felt like freedom. Smoke rose from the portable incinerator where his colleagues had been reduced to ash and superheated gas.

"Where is my driver?" Cartier shouted, looking around wildly at military vehicles and hazmat equipment. "Someone get my car! I have diplomatic immunity!"

National Guard soldiers raised their weapons as the diplomat stumbled toward the perimeter. "Halt! Return to the building immediately!" said a Guardsman sergeant.

"I'm the French Ambassador!" Cartier continued his advance despite automatic rifles trained on his chest. "Where is my driver? I demand my vehicle!"

Culper saw the confrontation developing and sprinted toward the perimeter. "Don't shoot! Let me talk to him!"

"Sir, he's breaching containment," the squad leader radioed to Colonel Reed. "Rules of engagement specify lethal force."

Culper reached the fence line as Cartier approached within fifty yards of civilian streets where eight million people continued their evening routines. "Ambassador Cartier, you need to return to the building. Medical help is coming."

"I won't die in that tomb!" Cartier's voice cracked with fever and desperation. "Someone get my car! Where is my driver? I have a meeting at the consulate!"

"Sir, you've been exposed to a biological agent. Anyone you touch will die the same death you're experiencing."

Cartier continued stumbling toward the perimeter, leaving invisible contamination on everything he touched. Handrails, concrete barriers, metal surfaces that would transfer The Wraith to anyone who came into contact with them.

"Last warning!" the squad leader's voice carried through a bullhorn that echoed off surrounding buildings. "Return to the building or we will fire!"

"You wouldn't dare shoot a French diplomat!" Cartier reached the outer barricade and began climbing over it with hands that shook from palsy and fever. "Someone get my car!"

The squad leader looked to Culper with eyes that held the question every soldier faced when orders conflicted with humanity. "Sir?"

Culper felt the weight of decisions that would haunt him regardless of their outcome. Let Cartier escape and condemn Manhattan to biological warfare. Stop him and murder a dying man whose only crime was seeking his driver.

"Your orders are to prevent containment breach," Culper said quietly. "Carry them out."

Rifle fire erupted. Five soldiers firing simultaneously at center mass. Cartier's body jerked backward, blood spreading across diplomatic credentials that couldn't protect him against biological necessity.

He fell to concrete that would remain contaminated until hazmat teams could sterilize surfaces where The Wraith would survive for hours after its host died.

Culper stared at the corpse of a man who had spent his career building bridges between nations. Ambassador Cartier had been murdered by the same government he had worked to maintain diplomatic relations with for twenty years.

"Jesus Christ," Culper whispered.

The soldiers lowered their weapons with movements that suggested people who understood they had just crossed lines that peaceful nations preferred never to acknowledge existed.

Colonel Reed approached with the expression of someone who had authorized necessary atrocities that would require explanations no honest person could provide.

"Had to be done," Reed said without conviction.

Culper nodded while staring at blood that pooled around the dead ambassador. Victory that felt exactly like moral defeat.

Brennan found the service corridor that led to loading docks where delivery trucks had once brought supplies to feed international diplomacy. Emergency lighting cast everything in red shadows that made the concrete tunnel feel like the interior of a beating heart.

Frank's footsteps echoed behind him. Heavy boots that belonged to someone large moving with determination despite physical limitations that were increasing with each heartbeat.

Brennan's reflection in a fire door window showed a face that had aged thirty years in just a few hours. White hair hung in wisps around features mapped with lines that had appeared like cracks in old leather. His hands shook with palsy that made precise movement impossible.

But he was younger than Frank. The Wraith was aging them both but Brennan's body offered more resistance to cellular breakdown than Frank's damaged frame.

Brennan turned and raised his pistol as Frank emerged from the stairwell. Both men moved with the caution of people whose reflexes had been stolen along with their years.

Frank's massive frame had diminished visibly. Muscle mass converted to age-appropriate proportions. His shirt hung loose on shoulders that seemed to be shrinking while his bones became increasingly brittle.

Brennan fired. The pistol bucked in hands that could no longer absorb recoil properly. His shot sparked off concrete beside Frank's head, showering him with dust that settled like snow.

Frank returned fire. His round chewed through air where Brennan had been standing, but the assassin was already moving despite joints that protested each step with grinding pain.

They exchanged shots while circling each other in the confined space. Muzzle flashes strobed like lightning as bullets sparked off pipes and concrete walls. Neither man could aim with the accuracy that had once made them deadly.

Brennan's pistol locked back. Empty magazine. He pulled the trigger twice more before understanding that ammunition was exhausted.

Frank's weapon jammed on the final round. Brass casing caught in the ejection port with mechanical stubbornness that no amount of force could clear. He threw the useless pistol aside.

Both men stared at each other across fifteen feet of concrete that might as well have been an ocean. No weapons. No backup. Nothing but dying bodies and the will to continue fighting despite biological systems that were failing simultaneously.

Brennan charged first. His movement was clumsy but determined, powered by desperation rather than coordination. Frank met him halfway with the lumbering advance of someone whose joints had aged beyond reliable function.

They collided with impact that would have been devastating when they were younger. Now it felt like watching elderly men attempt violence their bodies could no longer support.

Brennan swung a haymaker that Frank caught on his forearm. Bone struck bone with sounds that suggested fractures waiting to happen. Frank's return punch caught Brennan in the ribs with force that sent him stumbling backward.

They grappled with the clumsy intensity of wrestlers whose muscles had forgotten how to coordinate. Brennan tried to trip Frank, but his balance was too compromised to maintain leverage. Frank attempted a chokehold but his grip strength had diminished beyond effectiveness.

Both men fell to the concrete floor. The impact drove air from lungs that struggled to process oxygen efficiently. They rolled apart and struggled to stand on legs that felt like they belonged to strangers.

Brennan got to his feet first but swayed like a tree in high wind. Frank rose more slowly, using the wall for support while his knees threatened to buckle under weight they had carried easily that morning.

They faced each other again. Breathing hard. Sweating despite the building's cool air. Both understanding that their bodies were failing faster than their determination to continue fighting.

Brennan threw another punch that Frank barely blocked. The impact sent pain through both men's arms. Arthritis that made every contact agony.

Frank grabbed Brennan's jacket and tried to throw him against the concrete wall. But his strength was insufficient and Brennan twisted away, leaving Frank holding empty fabric while the assassin stumbled backward.

They separated again. Each man gasping for air that their aged respiratory systems couldn't process properly. Hearts that beat with irregular rhythms. Muscles that cramped from exertion they could no longer sustain.

"Can't," Brennan wheezed.

Frank nodded understanding. Neither could continue the fight their bodies had started. The Wraith had stolen their ability to inflict meaningful violence on each other.

Brennan turned and walked deeper into the service tunnel, moving with the careful steps of someone whose balance could no longer be trusted. Frank let him go. Pursuit was beyond his remaining capabilities.

Both men understood they were dying. The fight had ended not because either had won but because biological warfare had claimed them both regardless of their determination to continue.

Frank slumped against the concrete wall and listened to Brennan's footsteps fade into distance. Somewhere ahead, the assassin was moving toward exits that might or might not exist. Behind them, thirty-seven people had already died from The Wraith while their bodies burned in industrial flames.

The mission continued despite both hunter and prey becoming victims of the weapon they had fought to control.

The Dying Light

Culper stood beside the command vehicle watching the UN building through Colonel Reed's field binoculars. Most windows showed the red glow of emergency lighting, but the cafeteria on the second floor blazed with normal fluorescent illumination.

Movement caught his attention. A woman in kitchen whites moved between tables, loading dirty dishes onto a cart. The cafeteria dining area stood completely empty - no customers, no other staff - but she continued her work as if nothing had changed.

Culper adjusted the focus. The kitchen worker appeared to be in her early twenties with black hair pulled back in a regulation hairnet. Headphones covered her ears, connected to a small device clipped to her apron. She nodded slightly to whatever music was playing, completely absorbed in her routine.

No visible signs of accelerated aging. No shaking hands or labored breathing that characterized everyone else in the building. She moved with the confident stride of someone whose balance remained reliable, oblivious to the biological catastrophe occurring outside her workspace.

She pushed the dish cart toward what appeared to be the kitchen, moving with the same steady rhythm she probably maintained every day. Her posture was straight. Her coordination normal. The headphones had isolated her from the alarms, the screaming, the chaos that had consumed the rest of the building.

Through the binoculars, Culper watched the woman load plates and glasses that had been used by UN staff throughout the morning - dishes that contaminated employees must have handled, surfaces that should have transferred The Wraith through routine contact. Yet she moved with steady hands, showing no signs of the tremors or careful movements that marked every other person in the building.

"Colonel, take a look at the cafeteria on the second floor," Culper said, handing back the binoculars.

Reed raised them and studied the fluorescent-lit windows. "I see a kitchen worker. So what?"

"Watch her movements. Compare them to everyone else we've seen in that building."

Reed adjusted the focus, observing the woman as she loaded dishes onto a cart with steady efficiency. "She's not showing any symptoms. No tremors, no difficulty moving."

"Exactly. And those dishes she's handling - they were used by UN staff this morning. Contaminated employees who should have transferred The Wraith to every surface they touched."

Reed lowered the binoculars with the expression of someone who had just witnessed something that defied biological logic. "She should be dead or dying like everyone else."

"She might be immune," Culper said, taking the binoculars back to track the woman's movements as she disappeared into the kitchen's interior, still wearing headphones that kept her in a bubble of normalcy.

The implications hit him like electricity. If someone was naturally immune to The Wraith, their blood might contain antibodies that could neutralize the weapon. Medical science had developed treatments from immune survivors of biological agents before.

But the woman had vanished deeper into the kitchen where shadows prevented visual contact. She seemed to have no idea that everyone else in the building was dying while she washed dishes and listened to music.

Culper dialed Frank's number on his secure phone. Three rings before the weak, gravelly voice answered.

"Kane."

"Frank, I need you to get to the cafeteria kitchen. Second floor, northeast corner."

"Why?"

"Found a woman who might be immune. Kitchen worker. Appears unaffected by contamination. Wearing headphones. Doesn't know what's happening."

Silence on the line while Frank processed the information. His breathing sounded labored even through the encrypted connection.

"Moving," Frank said finally.

"Frank, if she's immune, her blood could save everyone still alive in that building. Find her. Protect her. Bring her to the entrance. I'll have a Hazmat team waiting that will take her from there."

"Understood."

The line went dead. Culper returned his attention to the kitchen windows where fluorescent lighting revealed an empty dining hall. The woman had disappeared into sections of the cafeteria complex that weren't visible from his position, probably still listening to music while biological warfare raged around her.

Her immunity might represent salvation for thousands of people or simply a cruel coincidence that offered hope where none existed.

The only way to know was to find her before The Wraith claimed Frank along with everyone else trapped in the building.

Frank slumped against the concrete wall, every muscle screaming for rest that his mission wouldn't allow. His body had become a stranger to him - joints that ground like broken machinery, bones that felt hollow, strength that had abandoned him when he needed it most. The Wraith had stolen decades from his frame, leaving him trapped in flesh that no longer obeyed commands. All he wanted was to close his eyes and let the exhaustion claim him, to surrender to the biological collapse that made each breath an effort and every heartbeat uncertain.

But somewhere beneath the cellular wreckage, the man who had never quit found reserves that biology couldn't steal, drew on determination that ran deeper than DNA.

"Once more…" said Frank slowly rising to his feet. "…into the breech." With the only pitiful strength he could summon, Frank stumbled down the corridor toward the cafeteria and the only hope left for the UN.

Brennan stumbled through the service corridor, his vision blurring as chills wracked his aged frame. Sweat beaded on skin that felt paper-thin while tremors shook hands that could barely maintain their grip on the concrete walls.

A sign appeared through his deteriorating eyesight: "Staff Facilities - Showers/Lockers." The kind of amenities provided for maintenance workers who needed to clean up after shifts in the building's mechanical spaces.

He pushed through the door into a tiled room lined with shower stalls and metal lockers. Industrial fixtures designed for function rather than comfort. Brennan's legs gave out and he collapsed against the nearest wall, sliding down to sit on cold tile.

The chills were getting worse. His body temperature seemed to be fluctuating wildly as The Wraith attacked his regulatory systems. Teeth chattered despite the building's normal climate control.

Brennan crawled toward the shower stalls, using his elbows to drag himself across tile that felt like ice against his skin. Each movement required conscious effort as motor control continued deteriorating.

He reached up and turned the hot water handle with fingers that barely responded to commands. Scalding water erupted from the shower head, filling the small space with steam that rose like artificial fog.

The humid air hit his lungs and something changed. His breathing, which had been shallow and labored, seemed to ease slightly. The crushing weight on his chest lifted just enough to allow deeper inhalation.

Brennan pulled himself under the shower spray, letting hot water cascade over his aged body while steam filled the enclosed space. The humidity felt different from normal air. Thicker. More substantial. His respiratory system responded as if recognizing something it needed.

The tremors began to subside. Not completely, but enough that his hands stopped shaking with constant palsy. His vision cleared slightly, bringing the tiled walls into sharper focus.

He leaned against the shower wall and breathed deeply of the steam-saturated air. Whatever was happening, the humidity was slowing The Wraith's effects on his system. The weapon that had aged him decades in hours seemed to be struggling against the moisture-rich environment.

Brennan had no idea why steam would interfere with biological aging compounds, but he could feel his symptoms stabilizing. Not reversing - the gray hair and lined face remained - but the accelerating deterioration had paused.

For the first time since exposure, he wasn't getting worse.

The shower continued running, filling the room with hot mist that might represent the difference between death in minutes and survival long enough to escape the building that had become his tomb.

Steam rose around him like salvation made visible.

Frank's legs gave out as he reached the cafeteria entrance. Getting to the second floor had felt like climbing Everest with joints that ground against each other like broken machinery. His massive frame, diminished by hours of cellular breakdown, collapsed against the doorway.

The dining area stretched empty before him. Tables and chairs arranged for diplomatic meals that would never be served. Emergency lighting cast red shadows through windows while fluorescent bulbs hummed overhead with institutional indifference.

Frank pulled himself across tile floors using his elbows. Each movement sent pain through bones that felt increasingly hollow. The kitchen lay fifty feet away.

His breathing came in shallow gasps. The Wraith was attacking his respiratory system along with everything else. Heart rate irregular. Vision blurring at the edges. Cellular collapse accelerating beyond his ability to compensate through willpower alone.

The kitchen doors swung open under his weight. Commercial equipment filled the space. Prep tables, walk-in coolers, ranges capable of feeding hundreds of diplomats who would never eat again.

The woman stood with her back to him, loading dishes into an industrial dishwasher. Headphones covered her ears while she worked with the steady rhythm of someone completing familiar tasks. Steam rose from the machine's interior where scalding water and detergent created conditions that could sterilize anything.

Frank crawled toward her across kitchen tiles that felt like arctic ice against his palms. His vision darkened around the edges. Consciousness was becoming optional as biological systems shut down one by one.

The woman reached for the dishwasher's control panel. Frank stretched his arm and managed to grab her ankle just as she pressed the start button.

She screamed and jerked backward, headphones flying as she saw the aged figure sprawled on her kitchen floor. "Who are you? What are you doing here?"

Frank tried to speak but his voice had been reduced to whispered breath. The woman backed against the prep table while the dishwasher began its cycle.

Steam erupted from the machine's vents. Hot, humid air that filled the kitchen with moisture-saturated atmosphere. Frank felt his head grow heavy as strength abandoned him completely.

He lay his cheek against cold tile and wondered who would feed the feral cat living in his lighthouse. The animal had survived everything except abandonment. Frank had failed in his most basic responsibility - returning home to something that depended on him.

The kitchen filled with steam from the industrial dishwasher. Humidity levels rising as hot water created atmospheric conditions that Frank's dying body began to process differently.

His breathing eased. Not completely, but enough that oxygen reached his bloodstream with less effort. The crushing weight on his chest lifted slightly, allowing deeper inhalation of air that felt thicker, more substantial.

Frank pulled himself to a sitting position against the dishwasher housing. Steam continued pouring from the machine's vents, creating a microclimate that his respiratory system seemed to recognize as beneficial.

The tremors in his hands were subsiding. Vision clearing. The accelerating deterioration that had been stealing his life minute by minute seemed to be slowing, pausing, even reversing slightly.

Frank reached for his phone with fingers that responded more reliably than they had in hours. He dialed Culper's number while steam swirled around him like fog.

"Frank, where are you?"

"Humidity," Frank rasped, his voice stronger than it had been since exposure. "Kills Wraith."

"What?"

"Dishwasher steam. Breathing easier. Symptoms stopping."

Culper was quiet while processing implications.

"You're certain?"

Frank studied his hands under the kitchen's fluorescent lighting. The liver spots were fading slightly. Lines around his knuckles seemed less pronounced. The aging process had not only stopped but appeared to be reversing incrementally.

"Certain."

"We need to flood that building with humidity immediately. I'll get back to you."

The line went dead. Frank leaned back against the dishwasher while steam continued rising around him like salvation made visible. The kitchen worker watched from across the room with eyes that held confusion and fear.

But Frank was breathing normally for the first time in hours. The Wraith was dying in conditions that resembled a tropical climate rather than the controlled atmosphere that had allowed it to flourish.

Humidity was the weapon's weakness. Steam was its antidote. And Frank Kane was going to live long enough to feed his cat.

Culper sprinted across the plaza toward the hazmat command station where Dubois coordinated emergency response operations. His boots pounded against concrete while smoke from the portable incinerator drifted overhead like black fog.

"Dubois!" Culper shouted, pushing past EMTs who were loading another body bag into the cremation chamber.

The UN Security Director looked up from his radio communications with the expression of someone managing multiple catastrophes simultaneously. "What is it?"

"I need the building's environmental controls. Where are they located?"

"Environmental controls?" Dubois blinked in confusion. "Why do you need—"

"Where are they?!" Culper's voice carried the urgency.

"Northeast corner of the basement. Near the main electrical distribution panels." Dubois gestured toward the Secretariat Building with movements that suggested someone operating beyond exhaustion. "But the area is contaminated. We lost contact with maintenance personnel hours ago."

"Do you know how the controls work? How to adjust humidity levels?"

Dubois shook his head. "I'm security, not facilities management. The environmental systems are computerized. Requires technical expertise I don't possess."

"Where's the building engineer?"

Dubois pointed toward the sealed building where emergency lighting glowed red through plastic sheeting. "In there. Dying like everyone else."

Culper felt precious seconds slipping away while humidity remained the difference between mass death and potential salvation. "Find me someone who understands those systems. Maintenance supervisor, HVAC technician, anyone with knowledge of environmental controls."

"Most of our technical staff were evacuated or..." Dubois gestured toward the incinerator where human ash rose into Manhattan's evening sky. "We might have personnel records in the emergency command trailer."

"How long?"

"Ten minutes to access files. Maybe longer to locate qualified personnel who aren't already inside the building."

Culper calculated time versus lives while The Wraith continued claiming victims on every floor. Ten minutes could mean dozens more deaths from biological weapons that apparently died in humid conditions.

"Get me those files immediately. Anyone with facilities management experience. HVAC contractors. Building automation specialists. I don't care if they're retired or work for competing companies."

Dubois began coordinating the search through radio communications that connected emergency response teams to databases containing technical expertise.

Culper looked up at the Secretariat Building where Frank was breathing steam from a dishwasher while thousands of other victims aged to death in climate-controlled air that allowed The Wraith to flourish unchallenged.

Somewhere in the basement, environmental controls waited to flood the building with humidity that could neutralize biological weapons through atmospheric modification rather than military force.

The race was between finding technical knowledge and watching everyone inside die from weapons that were vulnerable to something as simple as moist air.

Dubois returned from the command trailer carrying a tablet computer and the expression of someone who had just discovered a potential miracle. "I found the building's environmental control manual online. Manufacturer's website has complete technical documentation."

Culper grabbed the tablet and scrolled through digital pages that reduced atmospheric salvation to engineering specifications. Humidity controls, ventilation systems, steam injection protocols designed for comfort rather than biological warfare.

"Can you operate these systems?" Dubois asked.

"Not remotely. The controls are hardwired to prevent unauthorized access." Culper studied schematics that showed the basement control room. "Someone has to be physically present to override the automated systems."

Culper activated his secure phone and dialed Frank's number. Two rings before the gravelly voice answered, sounding stronger than it had in hours.

"Kane."

"Frank, I have the environmental control manual. You need to reach the basement control room. Northeast corner near the electrical panels."

"How far?"

"Two floors down from your current position. But Frank, the basement is where Brennan killed those security guards. It's heavily contaminated."

Silence while Frank processed the implications of returning to the area where The Wraith had been deployed in lethal concentrations.

"Can you make it?" said Culper.

"Yes."

"Frank, once you reach the controls, you need to activate emergency humidity mode. Maximum steam injection through all air handling units. Every floor, every room, every corridor."

Culper read from the manual while Frank listened to instructions that could save thousands of lives or represent the last conversation between men who understood duty better than survival.

"Emergency override is located on panel C-7. Red switch marked 'Atmospheric Emergency.' Flip it and hold for ten seconds. System will flood the building with steam within minutes."

"Understood."

"Frank, the steam will be scalding hot when it first enters the ventilation system. Find cover until temperatures stabilize."

The line went dead. Culper looked up at the Secretariat Building where emergency lighting glowed through sealed windows. Somewhere inside, Frank was preparing to descend into contaminated areas that could once again mean his death.

The war between biology and technology had entered its final phase.

Frank descended through the stairwell using the walls for support. Each step sent pain through joints and muscles. The dishwasher steam had stabilized his condition but hadn't reversed the aging that made every movement an exercise in endurance.

The basement corridor stretched ahead through emergency lighting that painted everything red. Bodies of UN security guards lay where Brennan had left them, their blood pooled on concrete that would remain contaminated until hazmat teams could sterilize surfaces.

Frank stepped carefully around the corpses, avoiding contact. The control room lay fifty yards ahead where pipes and electrical conduits created a maze of building infrastructure.

His phone buzzed with updates from Culper. More deaths on every floor. Ambassador Martinez of Mexico had died while trying to call his family. Dr. Williams from the Australian delegation had collapsed during evacuation. The Wraith was claiming victims faster than bodies could be processed.

Frank reached the control room door and found it locked. Electronic keypad that required access codes he didn't possess. He drew back his fist and struck the reinforced glass. The surface cracked but held, sending pain through knuckles that had been weakened by accelerated aging.

He hit it again. Harder. The glass spider-webbed but refused to break completely. Frank's third punch finally shattered the barrier, cutting his knuckles on glass fragments that scattered across the floor.

Inside, banks of computer monitors displayed building systems in real-time readouts. Ventilation controls, temperature regulation, humidity levels that showed atmospheric conditions throughout the complex.

Frank activated his phone and dialed Culper's number while studying control panels that looked like aircraft instrumentation.

"Kane. In control room."

"Good. Reset the humidity controls on panel C-4 to maximum steam injection."

Frank followed Culper's instructions resetting the controls.

"Panel C-7. Red switch marked 'Atmospheric Emergency.'"

Frank scanned the equipment until he found the designated panel. Emergency override controls that could flood the building with steam.

"Found it."

"Flip the switch and hold for ten seconds."

Frank reached for the red switch when footsteps echoed in the corridor behind him. Heavy boots moving with purpose rather than the shuffling gait of Wraith victims struggling with aged coordination.

Brennan appeared in the doorway. Steam from the shower had restored enough strength for him to function despite visible aging. Gray hair hung in wisps around features that resembled his grandfather more than himself.

"Can't let you do that," Brennan said, raising a steel pipe he had taken from the maintenance area.

Frank turned to face him. Both men moved with diminished speed, but Brennan had recovered more function through his longer exposure to humid conditions. Youth provided advantages that Frank's experience couldn't completely overcome.

Brennan swung the pipe at Frank's head. Frank caught it with both hands, feeling the impact vibrate through bones that had become increasingly brittle. They struggled for control of the improvised weapon while computer monitors displayed atmospheric readings that determined who lived and who died.

Frank twisted the pipe away and drove his elbow into Brennan's solar plexus. The assassin doubled over but came up swinging a haymaker that caught Frank in the ribs. Pain exploded through his chest as aged bones absorbed impact they could no longer handle.

They grappled among the control panels, each trying to prevent the other from reaching the emergency override. Brennan was faster, but Frank was larger. Mass versus coordination in a space designed for building maintenance rather than hand-to-hand combat.

Brennan grabbed Frank's throat with hands that showed liver spots and prominent veins. Pressure that would have been devastating when applied by a thirty-five-year-old felt manageable against someone whose grip strength had been reduced by biological warfare.

Frank broke the chokehold and slammed Brennan against the control panel. Computer screens cracked under the impact, showering both men with sparks and electronic debris. Warning lights began flashing as building systems registered damage to critical monitoring equipment.

Brennan reached for Frank's eyes with fingers that had been steadied by humid air. Frank caught his wrists and applied leverage that sent the assassin stumbling backward into electrical panels that sparked with dangerous voltage.

The steel pipe lay on the floor between them. Both men lunged for it simultaneously. Frank's reach was longer but Brennan was faster. Their collision sent them rolling across concrete while the weapon skittered beyond immediate grasp.

Brennan grabbed Frank's throat with hands that showed liver spots and prominent veins. Pressure that would have been devastating when applied by a thirty-five-year-old felt manageable against someone whose grip strength had been reduced by biological warfare.

Frank wrapped his own massive hands around Brennan's neck and applied counter-pressure. Both men squeezed with what strength remained in fingers that had been aged beyond reliable function.

Frank's vision began to darken as oxygen flow ceased despite his struggles. His grip on Brennan's throat loosened involuntarily. He clawed at Brennan's hands around his neck but couldn't break the chokehold.

On the verge of losing consciousness, Frank released Brennan's hands entirely and reached up to grab the assassin's face. His massive palms covered Brennan's ears while his fingers found purchase around the skull.

Frank twisted with the last of his strength. Cervical vertebrae snapped with sounds like breaking kindling. Brennan's hands went limp around Frank's throat as his body went slack.

The assassin collapsed forward onto Frank's chest, dead weight that pinned both men to the control room floor. Frank pushed the corpse aside and gasped for air that his damaged respiratory system could barely process.

Brennan stared at the ceiling with eyes that would never age another day.

The control room remained filled with flashing warning lights and damaged equipment. But Panel C-7 was intact. The red switch waited to flood the building with steam that could neutralize The Wraith through atmospheric modification.

Frank reached for the emergency override and flipped the switch. He held it for ten seconds while building systems responded to commands that would transform climate-controlled air into tropical humidity.

Throughout the Secretariat Building, ventilation systems began injecting steam at temperatures that would stabilize into life-saving moisture. Air handling units carried salvation through ducts and vents to every floor where victims waited.

On the fifth floor, Ambassador Torrent felt his breathing ease as humid air filled his lungs. The accelerating deterioration that had been stealing his life slowed, paused, began reversing incrementally.

In the lobby, Marie Roussel looked at her hands and noticed the liver spots fading slightly. Lines around her eyes seemed less pronounced.

Frank leaned against the control panel while steam rose from ventilation grates.

The Wraith was dying. The victims were stabilizing. The building that had become a demonstration of how humidity could defeat invisible enemies through atmospheric rather than military force.

Frank's phone buzzed with calls from Culper demanding status updates, but Frank was too exhausted to answer. He slumped to the floor beside Brennan's corpse and listened to building systems that hummed with life-saving efficiency.

Steam continued rising through ventilation systems like prayers made visible, carrying hope to people who had thought death was inevitable.

Frank emerged from the basement stairwell like a ghost made flesh. His massive frame had withered to proportions that seemed impossible - shoulders narrowed, height diminished, hands spotted with liver marks that mapped decades of accelerated aging. Gray hair hung thin and white around a face carved with lines that had appeared in hours rather than years.

Wearing a hazmat suit and respirator, Culper had entered the building. But nothing had prepared him for seeing Frank transformed from an imposing warrior into someone who resembled his own grandfather.

"Jesus Christ, Frank."

Frank looked up with eyes that held the same determination despite being set in features that belonged to someone thirty years older. His voice was barely a whisper. "Mission complete."

Steam continued rising from ventilation grates throughout the corridor. Around them, UN personnel were showing signs of stabilization as The Wraith died in humid conditions that felt like tropical air rather than institutional climate control.

Justice

Culper helped Frank back to the cafeteria kitchen where steam from the industrial dishwasher created the humid conditions that had saved his life. Frank slumped against the machine's housing, breathing the moisture-rich air that his damaged respiratory system craved.

"Stay here," Culper said. "The humidity is keeping you stable."

Frank nodded without speaking. Each breath came easier in the artificial tropical climate that neutralized whatever residual Wraith compounds might still be attacking his cells.

Culper moved to the far corner of the kitchen and activated his secure phone, dialing the number he had memorized during the Foster investigation.

"This is Lisa Chen."

"Dr. Chen, this is Culper. Frank Kane has been exposed to The Wraith. He doesn't have long to live unless we do something to help him. I need your longevity therapy. Immediately."

"The therapy isn't ready for human patients yet. We're still months, or even years away from completing clinical testing."

Culper watched Frank lean against the dishwasher while steam swirled around him like mechanical fog. "Dr. Chen, without intervention, Frank'll be dead within days."

"I understand the urgency, but the therapy hasn't been tested on humans. There could be serious side effects. Cellular rejection. Genetic instability. We don't know—"

The kitchen's humid air continued rising around Frank like salvation made visible, but Culper understood that atmospheric moisture could only stabilize his condition, not reverse the biological damage that had already been done.

"He's dying anyway. Let Frank be your first Guinea pig."

Chen was quiet for a moment, processing the implications of using experimental medicine on someone who represented the only hope for reversing biological weapons damage.

"Where are you?"

"United Nations building. Manhattan."

"I'll need laboratory equipment. Sterile conditions. Proper medical monitoring during administration."

"How long to prepare?"

"Two hours minimum. The compound has to be mixed fresh and calibrated for the patient's current cellular condition."

Culper calculated time versus Frank's deteriorating condition.

"I'm sending a military helicopter to Daou Therapeutics. Can you have everything ready for transport?"

"Yes. But this is completely experimental. No guarantees the therapy will work or that it won't kill him faster than The Wraith."

"Understood."

Culper ended the call and immediately coordinated military transport through channels that bypassed normal medical protocols. Emergency authorization for experimental treatment of biological weapons exposure.

Ninety minutes later, the helicopter settled onto the UN plaza with rotor wash that scattered ash from the portable incinerator. Dr. Chen emerged carrying a sealed medical case that contained humanity's first attempt at reversing accelerated aging through genetic modification.

She entered the building wearing hazmat protection and found Frank in the cafeteria where humidity levels remained highest. His condition had stabilized, but his appearance was shocking.

"Frank, can you hear me?"

Frank nodded weakly.

"I'm going to try to reverse what The Wraith did to your cellular structure."

Frank nodded again without speaking. Words required energy he needed to conserve.

Chen opened her medical case and removed a syringe filled with clear liquid that looked identical to The Wraith but carried genetic modification designed to restore rather than destroy. Longevity therapy that had never been tested on humans, much less someone whose biology had been artificially accelerated beyond normal limits.

"This may cause severe reactions. Nausea, fever, cellular inflammation. We're essentially asking your body to reverse decades of aging. It'll take time. Probably months before full restoration. Are you okay with that?"

Frank extended his arm. Skin that had been smooth that morning now resembled old leather stretched over bones that showed prominently.

Chen found a vein despite skin that had lost elasticity. The injection took seconds to administer but would require days to determine whether experimental medicine could reverse the damage The Wraith had done.

"How long?" Frank whispered.

"Unknown. The therapy works gradually in laboratory animals. But your case is unprecedented."

Frank closed his eyes and leaned back against the dishwasher that had saved his life through steam rather than science.

The longevity therapy spread through Frank's bloodstream like hope through the mind. Whether it would restore his lost years or kill him remained to be determined. But it was his only chance at being Frank again.

Culper looked on while Chen monitored Frank's vital signs as the drug performed its magic, carrying hope to a man who had sacrificed his future to save millions of people who would never know his name.

Wearing a Sartoria Partenopea suit and Berluti shoes, Richard Kane stood at the mouth of the alley staring at eighteen feet of Detroit steel wedged between brick walls like a mechanical cork in an urban bottle. The Imperial's doors had buckled inward from the pressure. The roof showed scrape marks from fire escapes. The windshield was completely gone.

His sixteen-year-old daughter Grace stood beside him, jaw hanging open.

"How did Uncle Frank get it in there?" she asked.

Richard studied the alley's dimensions. The Imperial was six inches wider than the space between walls.

"I have no idea."

"How are you going to get it out?"

Richard looked up at the brick walls that rose three stories on either side of the trapped vehicle.

"Cut it in half. Have them weld it back together at the shop."

Grace stared at him. "You're going to cut Uncle Frank's car in half?"

"It's the only way. Frank won't let me replace it. Says this one has character."

"Uncle Frank's insane."

"Yes, he is, Gracie. Yes, he is."

It was just past midnight when Frank moved through Whitfield's office reception area in complete silence, his massive frame somehow avoiding every creak in the hardwood floors. The longevity therapy had restored some of his lost years, but his face still carried lines that belonged to someone decades older. Gray hair remained thin and white. Hands showed spots that might fade with time.

The twin Redhawks rested in his shoulder holster beneath his jacket. Frank had entered through the stairwell twenty minutes earlier. It had been a long journey up the stairs to the top floor, but Frank needed to rebuild the muscles in his legs. He would deal with the pain tomorrow.

Whitfield sat at his mahogany desk reviewing financial reports, his back to the office entrance. The venture capitalist often worked late hours, managing investments that spanned multiple time zones.

He rose and moved to his personal bar where he poured three fingers of Macallan 25 into a crystal tumbler, the whiskey catching light from his desk lamp.

With Whitfield's back to him, Frank pulled out a vial of clear liquid and placed one small drop on Whitfield's phone receiver, then pressed himself against the shadows, becoming invisible through absolute stillness. Whitfield loosened his silk tie and returned to his chair. He saw Frank when he stepped forward into the light. "Late night?" said Frank.

His eyes widened as he recognized the predatory stillness that marked a professional killer.

"What the hell do you want?"

"Justice."

"You've come to wrong place," said Whitfield as he picked up the phone receiver and dialed security.

"I think not."

The line was dead. Whitfield pressed the button again. Nothing.

"No matter. The security guards will be checking in soon anyway."

"No. They won't."

Whitfield looked down at the receiver still in his hand, feeling the first tingling sensation where The Wraith penetrated his skin. No visible contamination. Nothing that looked dangerous. Just the beginning of cellular breakdown that would accelerate beyond natural limits.

"What did you do?"

Frank set the vial on the edge of Whitfield's desk.

"What's that?"

"The Wraith."

Whitfield's face went pale as he understood. The biological weapon that had killed Senator Bradley was now spreading through his bloodstream with microscopic efficiency.

"You can't. There's an antidote. Humidity. Steam."

"Yes."

Frank removed one of his Redhawks, then sat in a leather chair across from Whitfield and said, "We'll wait. Together."

"I'll do no such thing," said Whitfield rising to leave.

Frank cocked the Redhawk's trigger, shook his head, then motioned for Whitfield to sit back down. Whitfield complied.

The first gray streaks appeared in Whitfield's brown hair within thirty minutes. Lines deepened around his eyes as he watched his reflection in the office windows. Skin texture changed from smooth to papery while liver spots bloomed on hands that had signed death warrants disguised as investment portfolios.

"This is murder."

Frank grunted acknowledgment.

"I was protecting American economic interests. Longevity research represents strategic advantages that..."

Whitfield's voice was already changing. Rougher. Older. The Wraith was attacking his vocal cords along with everything else.

Frank waited. Justice sometimes required patience rather than violence. Watching rather than acting. Allowing synthetic consequences to proceed without interference.

By two AM, Whitfield resembled someone thirty years older. His expensive suit hung loose on a frame that seemed to be shrinking. His voice had become the whisper of someone whose body was betraying him.

"Please," Whitfield said. "I have money. Connections. I can make this worth your while."

Frank checked his watch. The aging was proceeding faster than it had with Bradley or the UN diplomats. Concentrated doses worked with brutal efficiency that compressed decades into hours.

"My children. They don't deserve to lose their father."

Frank thought about Dr. Foster crushed beneath steel beams. Ambassador Vasquez dying in assembly halls. UN security guards killed for following orders. Whitfield's children would join thousands of others who had lost parents to decisions made in boardrooms by men who treated human lives as acceptable losses.

At three AM, Whitfield's breathing became labored. His heart struggled with rhythms that belonged to someone approaching the end of natural lifespan. Organ systems failing under biological assault that stole time instead of blood. Pain. Lots of pain.

"Why?" Whitfield whispered.

"Justice," Frank said.

Whitfield's eyes closed for the final time at 3:47 AM. His body slumped in the chair with the appearance of someone who had lived a full life rather than someone murdered by invisible weapons that aged people to death.

Frank activated his secure phone and dialed Culper's number.

"Culper."

"Finished."

"Whitfield?"

"Dead."

"How?"

"Wraith."

Culper was quiet while processing the implications of biological weapons being used for execution rather than mass destruction.

"We'll need hazmat teams to clean up the contamination."

"Yes. Send them."

"Frank, this stays between us. Official report will show Whitfield died of natural causes."

Frank understood. Some justice operated outside legal systems.

Thirty minutes later, hazmat teams arrived to process Whitfield's corpse and sterilize surfaces where The Wraith might survive to claim additional victims. The venture capitalist who had funded biological warfare would be cremated like the diplomats he had tried to murder.

The Wraith had claimed its final victim through personal application rather than mass deployment. Invisible justice for crimes that democracy couldn't prosecute through normal channels.

Frank left through the service elevator, carrying the satisfaction of someone who had completed his mission.

The war was over. The weapon was contained. The guilty had been punished.

Riding in a military helicopter that Culper had arranged, Frank flew toward his lighthouse where a feral cat waited for someone who kept promises despite the cost of keeping them.

Author's Biography

Born in 1958, David grew up on a horse ranch in Northern California, breeding and training appaloosas. He has had all his toes broken at least once and survived numerous falls and kicks from ornery colts and fillies. David started writing professionally as a copywriter in his early 20's. At thirty-two, he packed up his family and moved to Malibu, California, to live his dream of writing and directing motion pictures. He has four motion picture screenwriting credits and two directing credits. His movies have been viewed by over fifty million movie-goers worldwide and won a multitude of awards, including the Malibu, Palm Springs, and San Jose Film Festivals. In addition to his twenty-four screenplays, he has written twenty-nine novels. He developed his simplistic writing style after rereading his two favorite books, Ernest Hemingway's *The Old Man and the Sea* and Cormac McCarthy's *No Country For Old Men*. An avid student of world culture, David lived as an expat in both Thailand and Mexico. At fifty-six, he sold all his possessions and became a nomad for four years. He circumnavigated the globe three times and visited fifty-six countries. Known for his detailed descriptions, his stories often include actual experiences and characters from his journeys.

www.ingramcontent.com/pod-product-compliance
Lightning Source LLC
Chambersburg PA
CBHW021041310726
48969CB00006B/1760